CW00455343

Richard Marsh

A Hero of Romance

Richard Marsh

A Hero of Romance

1st Edition | ISBN: 978-3-75244-006-5

Place of Publication: Frankfurt am Main, Germany

Year of Publication: 2020

Outlook Verlag GmbH, Germany.

A HERO OF ROMANCE

BY

RICHARD MARSH

Chapter I

PUNISHMENT AT MECKLEMBURG HOUSE

It was about as miserable an afternoon as one could wish to see. May is the poet's month, but there was nothing of poetry about it then. True, it was early in the month, but February never boasted weather of more unmitigated misery. At half-past two it was so dark in the schoolroom of Mecklemburg House that one could with difficulty see to read. Outside a cold drizzling rain was falling, a shrieking east wind was rattling the windows in their frames, and a sullen haze was hiding the leaden sky. As unsatisfactory a specimen of the English spring as one could very well desire.

To make things better, it was half-holiday. Not that it much mattered to the young gentleman who was seated in the schoolroom; it was no half-holiday to him. A rather tall lad, some fourteen years of age, broad and strongly built. This was Bertie Bailey.

Master Bertie Bailey was kept in; and the outrage this was to his feelings was altogether too deep for words. To keep him in!—no wonder the heavens frowned at such a crime!

Master Bertie Bailey was seated at a desk very much the worse for wear; a long desk, divided into separate compartments, which were intended to accommodate about a dozen boys. He had his arms upon the desk, his face rested on his hands, and he was staring into vacancy with an air of tragic gloom.

At the raised desk which stood in front of him before the window was seated Mr. Till. Mr. Till's general bearing and demeanour was not much more jovial than Master Bertie Bailey's; he was the tyrant usher who had kept the youthful victim in. It was with a certain grim pleasure that Bertie realized that Mr. Till's enjoyment of the keeping-in was perhaps not much more than his own.

Mr. Till had a newspaper in his hand, and had apparently read it through, advertisements and all. He looked over the top of it at Bertie.

"Don't you think you'd better get on with those lines?" he asked.

Bertie had a hundred lines of *Paradise Lost* to copy out. He paid no attention to the inquiry; he did not even give a sign that he was aware he had been spoken to, but continued to sit with his eyes fixed on nothing, with the same air of mysterious gloom.

"How many have you done?" Mr. Till came down to see. There was a torn copy of Milton's poems lying unopened beside Bertie on the desk; in front of him a slate which was quite clean, and no visible signs of a slate pencil. Mr. Till took up the slate and carefully examined it for anything in the shape of lines.

"So you haven't begun?—why haven't you begun?" No answer. "Do you hear me? why haven't you begun?"

Without troubling himself to alter in any way his picturesque posture, Bertie made reply,—

"I haven't got a slate pencil."

"You haven't got a slate pencil? Do you mean to tell me you've sat there for a whole hour without asking for a slate pencil? I'll soon get you one."

Mr. Till went to his desk and produced a piece about as long as his little finger, placing it in front of Bertie. Bertie eyed it from a corner of his eye.

"It isn't long enough."

"Don't tell me; take your arms off the desk and begin those lines at once."

Bertie very leisurely took his arms off the desk, and delicately lifted the piece of slate pencil.

"It wants sharpening," he said. He began to look for his knife, standing up to facilitate the search. He hunted in all his pockets, turning out the contents of each upon the desk; finally, from the labyrinthine depths of some mysterious depository in the lining of his waistcoat, he produced the ghost of an ancient pocket-knife. As though they were fragile treasures of the most priceless kind, he carefully replaced the contents of his pockets. Then, at his ease, he commenced to give an artistic point to his two-inch piece of slate pencil. Mr. Till, who had taken up a position in front of the window with his hands under his coat tails, watched the proceedings with anything but a gratified countenance.

"That will do," he grimly remarked, when Bertie had considerably reduced the original size of his piece of pencil by attempting to produce a point of needlelike fineness. Bertie wiped his knife upon his coat-sleeve, removed the pencil dust with his pocket-handkerchief, and commenced to write. Before he had got half-way through the first line a catastrophe occurred.

"I've broken the point," he observed, looking up at Mr. Till with innocence in his eyes.

"I tell you what it is," said Mr. Till, "if you don't let me have those lines in less than no time I'll double them. Do you think I'm going to stop here all the afternoon?"

"You needn't stop," suggested Bertie, looking at his broken pencil.

"I daresay!" snorted Mr. Till. The last time Bertie had been left alone in the schoolroom on the occasion of his being kept in, he had perpetrated atrocities which had made Mr. Fletcher's hair stand up on end. Mr. Fletcher was the head-master. Orders had been given that whenever Bertie was punished, somebody was to stay in with him. "Now, none of your nonsense; you go on with those lines."

Bertie bent his head with a studious air. A hideous scratching noise arose from the slate. Mr. Till clapped his hands to his ears.

"Stop that noise!"

"If you please, sir, I think this pencil scratches," Bertie said. Considering that he was holding the pencil perpendicularly, the circumstance was not surprising.

"Take my advice, Bailey, and do those lines." Advancing with an inflamed countenance, Mr. Till stood over the offending pupil. Resuming his studious posture Bertie recommenced to write. He wrote two lines, not too quickly, nor by any means too well, but still he wrote them. In the middle of the third line another catastrophe happened.

"Please, sir, I've broken the pencil right in two." It was quite unnecessary for him to say so, the fact was self-evident, though with so small a piece it had required no slight exertion of strength and some dexterous manipulation to accomplish the feat. The answer was a box on the ears.

"What did you do that for?" asked Bertie, rising from his seat, and rubbing the injured portion with his hand.

Now it was distinctly understood that Mecklemburg House Collegiate School was conducted on the principle of no corporal punishment. It was a prominent line in the prospectus. "*Under no circumstances is corporal punishment administered.*" As a rule the principle was consistently carried out to its legitimate conclusion, not with the completest satisfaction to every one concerned. Yet Mr. Fletcher, one of the most longsuffering of men, and by no means the strictest disciplinarian conceivable, had been more than once roused into administering short and sharp justice upon refractory youth. But what was excusable in Mr. Fletcher was not to be dreamed of in the philosophy of anybody else. For an assistant-master to strike a pupil was a crime; and Mr. Till knew it, and Master Bertie Bailey knew it too.

"What did you do that for?" repeated Bertie.

4

Mr. Till was crimson. He was not a hasty tempered man, but to-day Master Bertie Bailey had been a burden greater than he could bear. Yet he had very literally made a false stroke, and Bertie was just the young gentleman to make the most of it.

"If I were to tell Mr. Fletcher, he'd turn you off," said Bertie. "He turned Mr. Knox off for hitting Harry Goddard."

Harry Goddard's only relation was a maiden aunt, and this maiden aunt had peculiar opinions. In her opinion for anybody to lay a punitory hand upon her nephew was to commit an act tantamount to sacrilege. Harry had had a little difference with Emmett minor, and had borne away the blushing honours of a bloody nose and a black eye with considerable *sang-froid*; but when Mr. Knox resented his filling his best hat with half-melted snow by presenting him with two or three smart taps upon a particular portion of his frame, Harry wrote home to his aunt to complain of the indignity he had endured. The result was that the ancient spinster at once removed the outraged youth from the sanguinary precincts of Mecklemburg House, and that Mr. Fletcher dismissed the offending usher.

As Mr. Till stood eyeing his refractory pupil, all this came forcibly to his mind. He knew something more than Bertie did; he knew that when Mr. Fletcher, smarting at the loss of a remunerative pupil, had made short work of his unfortunate assistant, he had also taken advantage of the occasion to call Mr. Till into his magisterial presence, and to then and there inform him, that should he at any time lay his hand upon a pupil, under any provocation of any kind whatever, the result would be that Mr. Knox's case would be taken as a precedent, and he would be instantaneously dismissed.

And now he had struck Bertie, and here was Bertie threatening to inform his employer of what he had done.

"If you don't let me off these lines," said Bertie, pursuing his advantage, "I'll tell Mr. Fletcher as soon as he comes home, you see if I don't."

Mecklemburg House Collegiate School was not a scholastic establishment of any particular eminence; indeed, whatever eminence it possessed was of an unsavoury kind. Nor was the position of its assistant-master at all an enviable one. There was the senior assistant, Mr. Till, and there was the junior, Mr. Shane. Mr. Till received £30 a year, and Mr. Shane, a meek, melancholy youth of about seventeen, received sixteen. Nor could the duties of either of these gentlemen be considered light. But if the pay was small and the work large, the intellectual qualifications required were by no means of an unreasonable kind. Establishments of the Mecklemburg House type are fading fast away. English private schools are improving every day. Mr. Till, conscious of his deficiencies, was only too well aware that if he lost his present situation, another would be hard to find. So, in the face of Bertie's threat, he temporized.

"I didn't mean to hit you! You shouldn't exasperate me!"

Bertie looked him up and down. If ever there was a young gentleman who needed the guidance of a strong hand, Bertie was he. He was not a naturally bad boy,—few boys are,—but he hated work, and he scorned authority. All means were justifiable which enabled him to shirk the one and defy the other. He was just one of those boys who might become bad if he was not brought to realize the difference between good and evil, right and wrong. And it would need sharp discipline to bring him to such knowledge.

He had a supreme contempt for Mr. Till. All the boys had. The only person they despised more was Mr. Shane. It was the natural result of the system pursued at Mecklemburg House that the masters were looked upon by their pupils as quite unworthy their serious attention.

Bertie had had about a dozen impositions inflicted on him even within the last days. He had not done one of them. He never did do them. None of the boys ever did do impositions set them by anybody but Mr. Fletcher. They did not by any means make a point of doing his.

"You will do me fifty lines," Mr. Till would say to half a dozen boys half a dozen times over in the course of a single morning. He spoke to the wind; no one ever did them, no one would have been so much surprised as Mr. Till if they had been done.

On the present occasion Mr. Fletcher had gone to town on business, and Mr. Till had been left in supreme authority. Bailey had signalised the occasion by behaving in a manner so outrageous that, if any semblance of authority was to be kept at all, it was altogether impossible to let him go scot free. As it was a half-holiday, Mr. Till had announced his unalterable resolve that Bertie should copy out a hundred lines of *Paradise Lost*, and that he should not leave the schoolroom till he had written them.

The result so far had not been satisfactory. He had been in the schoolroom considerably over an hour; he had written not quite three lines, and here he was telling Mr. Till that if he did not let him off entirely he would turn the tables on his master, and make matters unpleasant for him. It looked as though Bertie would win the game.

Having taken the tutor's mental measure, he thrust his hands into his trousers pockets, and coolly seated himself upon the desk. Then he made the following observation,—

6

"I tell you what it is, old Till, I don't care a snap for you."

Mr. Till simply glared. He realized, not for the first time, that the pupil was too much for the master. Bertie continued,—

"My father always pays regularly in advance. If I wrote home and told him that you'd hit me, for nothing"—Bertie paused and fixed his stony gaze on Mr. Till—"he'd take me home at once, and then what would Fletcher say?" Bertie paused again, and pointed his thumb over his left shoulder. "He'd say, 'Walk it'!"

This was one way of putting it. Though Mr. Bailey was by no means such a foolish person as his son suggested. He was very much unlike Harry Goddard's maiden aunt. Had Bertie written home any such letter of complaint —which, by the way, he was far too wise to have dreamed of doing—the consequences would in all probability have been the worse for him. The father knew his son too well to be caught with chaff. Unfortunately, Mr. Till did not know this; he had Mr. Knox's fate before his eyes.

"You'd better let me off these lines," pursued the inexorable Bertie; "you'd better, you know."

"You're an impudent young—" But Bertie interrupted him.

"Now don't call me names, or I'll tell Fletcher. He only said the other day that all his pupils were to be treated like young gentlemen."

"Young gentlemen!" snorted Mr. Till with scorn.

"Yes, young gentlemen. And don't you say we're not young gentlemen, because Mecklemburg House Collegiate School is an establishment for young gentlemen." And Bertie grinned. "You'd better let me off these lines, you know."

"You know I never hurt you; you shouldn't exasperate me; you're the most exasperating boy I ever knew; there's absolutely no bearing with your insolence! You'd try the patience of a saint."

"I shouldn't be surprised if I was deaf for a week." He rubbed the injured part reflectively. "I've heard Fletcher say it's dangerous to hit a fellow on the ear. You'd better let me off those lines, you know."

Mr. Till, fidgeting about the room, suddenly burst into eloquence. "I wonder if it's any use appealing to your better nature? They say boys have a better nature, though I never remember to have seen much of it. What pleasure do you find in making my life unbearable? What have I ever done to you that you should try to drive me mad? Are you naturally cruel? My sole aim is for your future welfare! Your sole aim is for my ruin!"

Bertie continued to rub his ear.

"Bailey, if I let you off these lines will you promise to try to give me less cause to punish you?"

"You can't help letting me off them anyhow," said Bertie.

"Can't I? I suppose, young gentleman, you think you're getting the best of me?"

"I know I am," said Bertie.

"Oh, you know you are! Then let me do my best to relieve you of that delusion. Shall I tell you what you are doing? You're doing your best to sow the seeds of a shameful manhood and a wasted life; if you don't take care you'll reap the harvest by-and-by! It isn't only that you're refusing to avail yourself of opportunities of education, you're doing yourself much greater harm than that. You think you're getting the best of me; but shall I tell you what's getting the best of you?—a mean, cruel, cowardly spirit, which will be to you a sterner master than ever I have been. You think yourself brave because you jeer and mock at me, and flout all my commands! Why, my boy, were I better circumstanced, and free to act upon my own discretion, you would tremble in your shoes! The very fact of your permitting yourself to threaten me, on account of punishment which you know was perfectly well deserved, shows what sort of boy you are!"

Bertie's only comment was, "You had better let me off those lines."

"I will let you off the lines!"

Bertie sprang to his feet, and began to put slate and book away with abundance of clatter.

"Stay one moment—leave those things alone! It is not the punishment which degrades a man, Bailey; it is the thing of which he has been guilty. I cannot degrade you; it is yourself you are degrading. Take my advice, turn over a new leaf, learn not to take advantage of a man whose only offence is that he does his best to do you good; don't think yourself brave because you venture to attack where defence is impossible; and, above all, don't pride yourself on taking your pigs to a bad market. You are so foolish as to think yourself clever because you throw away all your best chances, and get absolutely worse than nothing in return. Bailey, get your Bible, and look for a verse which runs something like this, 'Cast your bread upon the waters, and you shall find it after many days.' Now you can go."

And Bertie went; and, being in the safe neighbourhood of the door, he put his fingers to his nose; by which Mr. Till knew, not for the first time, that he had spoken in vain.

Chapter II

TUTOR BAITING

There were twenty-seven boys at Mecklemburg House; and even this small number bade fair to decrease. Last term there had been thirty-three; the term before there had been forty. Within quite recent years considerably over a hundred boys had occupied the draughty dormitories of the great old red-brick house.

But the glory was departing. It is odd how little our fathers and our grandfathers in general knew or cared about the science of education. Boys were pitchforked into schools which had absolutely nothing to recommend them except a flourishing prospectus; schools in which nothing was taught, in which the physique of the lads was neglected, and in which their moral nature was treated as a thing which had no existence. A large number of "schoolmasters" had no more idea of true education than they had of flying. They were speculators pure and simple, and they treated their boys as goods out of which they were to screw as much money as they possibly could, and in the shortest possible space of time.

Mecklemburg House Collegiate School was a case in point. It had been a school ever since the first of the Georges; and it is, perhaps, not too much to say, that out of the large number of boys who had been educated beneath its roof, not one of them had received a wholesome education. Yet it had always been a paying property. More than one of its principals had retired with a comfortable competency. Certainly the number of its pupils had never stood at such a low ebb as at the time of which we tell. Why the number should be so uncomfortably low was a mystery to its present principal, Beauclerk Fletcher. The place had belonged to his father, and his father had always found it bring something more than daily bread. But even daily bread was beginning to fail with Beauclerk Fletcher. Twenty-seven pupils at such a place as Mecklemburg House! and the majority of them upon "reduced terms"! Mr. Fletcher, never the most enterprising of men, was beginning to be overwhelmed beneath an avalanche of debt, and to feel that the fight was beyond his strength.

A great, old, rambling red-brick house, about equi-distant from Cobham, Byfleet, Weybridge—all towns in Surrey—lying in about the middle of the irregular square which those four towns form, the house carried the story of its decaying glories upon its countenance. Those Georgian houses were solid structures, and the mere fabric was in about as good a condition as it had ever been! but in the exterior of the building the change was sadly for the worse. Many of the rooms were unoccupied, panes were broken in the windows, curtains were wanting, the windows looked as though they were seldom or never cleaned. The whole place looked as though it were neglected, which indeed it was. Slates were off the roof, waste water pipes hung loose and rattled in every passing breeze. As to the paved courtyard in front, grass and weeds and moss almost hid the original stones. Mr. Fletcher was only too conscious of the story all this told; but to put things shipshape and neat, and to keep them so, required far more money than he had to spend; so he only groaned at each new evidence of ruin and decay.

The internal arrangements, the domestic economy, the whole system of education, everything in connection with Mecklemburg House was in the same state of decrepitude and age—worn-out traditions rather than living things. And Mr. Fletcher was very far from being the man to breathe life into the dead bones and bid them live. The struggle was beyond his strength.

There is no creature in God's world sharper than the average boy, no one quicker to understand the strength of the hand which holds him. The youngest pupil at Mecklemburg House was perfectly aware that the school was a "duffing" school, that Mr. Fletcher was a "duffing" principal, and that everything about the place was "duffing" altogether. Only let a boy have this opinion about his school, and, so far as any benefit is concerned which he is likely to derive from his sojourn there, he might almost as profitably be transported to the Cannibal Islands.

On the half-holiday on which our story opens, the pupils of Mecklemburg House were disporting themselves in what was called the playroom. Formerly, in its prosperous days, the room had been used as a second schoolroom, the one at present used for that purpose being not nearly large enough to contain the pupils. But those days were gone; at present, so far from being overcrowded, the room looked empty, and could have with ease accommodated twice the whole number of pupils which the school contained. So what was once the schoolroom was called the playroom instead.

"Stupid nonsense! keeping a fellow in because it rains!" said Charles Griffin, looking through the dirty window at the grimy world without.

"It doesn't rain," declared Dick Ellis. "Call this rain! I say, Mr. Shane, can't we go down to the village? I want to get something for this cough of mine; it's frightful." And with some difficulty Dick managed to produce a sepulchral cough from somewhere about the region of his boots.

"Mrs. Fletcher says you are not to go out while it rains," answered Mr. Shane in his mildest possible manner.

"Mrs. Fletcher!" grunted Dick. At Mecklemburg House the grey mare was the better horse. If Mr. Fletcher was not an ideal head-master, Mrs. Fletcher was emphatically head-mistress.

That half-holiday was a pleasant one for Mr. Shane. It was a rule that the boys were never to be left alone. If they were out a master was to go with them, if they were in a master was to supervise. So, as Mr. Till was engaged with the refractory Bertie, Mr. Shane was in charge of the play-room.

In charge, literally, and in terror, too. For it may be maintained without the slightest exaggeration, that he was much more afraid of the boys than the boys of him. On what principle of selection Mr. Fletcher chose his assistant-masters it is difficult to say; but whatever else Mr. Shane was, a disciplinarian he certainly was not. He was the mildest-mannered young man conceivable, awkward, shy, slight, thin, not bad-looking, with a faint, watery smile, which at times gave quite a ghastly appearance to his countenance, and a deprecatory manner which seemed to say that you had only to let him alone to earn his eternal gratitude. But the boys never did let him alone, never. By day and night, awake and sleeping, they did their best to make his life a continual misery.

"If we can't go out," suggests Griffin, "I vote we have a lark with Shane."

Mr. Shane smiled, by no means jovially.

"You mustn't make a noise," he murmured, in that soft, almost effeminate voice of his. "Mrs. Fletcher particularly said you were not to make a noise."

"Right you are. I say, Shane, you stand against the wall, and let's shy things at you." This from Griffin.

"You're not to throw things about," said Mr. Shane.

"Then what are we to do, that's what I want to know? It seems to me we're not to do anything. I never saw such a beastly hole! I say, Shane, let half of us get hold of one of your arms, and the other half of the other, and have a pull at you—tug-of-war, you know. We won't make a noise."

Mr. Shane did not seem to consider the proposal tempting. He was seated in the window, and had a book on his knees which he wanted to read. Not a work of light literature, but a German grammar. It was the dream of his life to prepare himself for matriculation at the London University. This undersized youth was a student born; he had company which never failed him, a company of dreams. He dreamed of a future in which he was a scholar of renown; and in every moment he could steal he strove to bring himself a step nearer to the realization of his dreams.

"Get up, Shane!—what's that old book you've got?" Griffin made a snatch at the grammar. Mr. Shane jealously put it behind his back. Books were in his eyes things too precious to be roughly handled. "Come and have a lark; what an old mope you are!" Griffin caught him by the arm and swung him round into the room; the boy was as tall, and probably as strong as the usher.

The boys were chiefly engaged in doing nothing; nobody ever did do much in that establishment. If a boy had a hobby it was laughed out of him. Literature was at a discount: *Spring-Heeled Jack* and *The Knights of the Road* were the sort of works chiefly in request. There was no school library, none of the boys seemed to have any books of their own. There was neither cricket nor football, no healthy games of any sort. Even in the playground the principal occupation was loafing, with a little occasional bullying thrown in. Mr. Fletcher was too immersed in the troubles of pounds, shillings, and pence to have any time to spare for the amusements of the boys. Mr. Till was not athletic. Mr. Shane still less so. On fine afternoons the boys were packed off with the ushers for a walk, but no more spiritless expeditions could be imagined than the walks at Mecklemburg House. The result was that the youngsters' life was a wearisome monotony, and they were in perpetual mischief for sheer want of anything else to do. And mischief so often took the shape of cruelty.

Charlie Griffin swung Mr. Shane out into the middle of the room, and immediately one boy after another came stealing up to him.

"I say, Shane, let's play roley-poley with you," said Brown major. Some one in the rear threw a hard pellet of brown paper, which struck Mr. Shane smartly on the head. He winced.

"Who threw that?" asked Griffin. "I say, Shane, why don't you whack him? If I were a man I wouldn't let little boys throw things at me; you are a man, aren't you, Shane?" He gave another jerk to the arm which he still held.

"You're not to pull my arm, Griffin; you hurt me. I wonder why you boys can't leave me alone."

"Go along! not really! We're only having a game, Shane; we're not in school, you know. What shall we do with him, you fellows? I vote we tie him in a chair, and stick needles and pins into him; he's sure to like that—he's such a jolly old fellow, Shane is."

"Why don't you let us go out?" asked Ellis.

"You know Mrs. Fletcher said you were not to go."

"Oh, bother Mrs. Fletcher! what's that got to do with it? We won't tell her if you let us go."

Mr. Shane sighed. Had it rested with him he would have been only too glad to let them go. Two or three hours of his own company would have been like a glimpse of paradise. But there was Mrs. Fletcher; she was a lady whose indignation was not to be lightly faced.

"If you won't let us go," said Ellis, "we'll make it hot for you. Do you think we're a lot of babies, to be melted by a drop of rain?"

"You know it's no use asking me. Mrs. Fletcher said you were not to go out if it rained, and it is raining."

"It's not raining," boldly declared Griffin. "Call this rain! why, it's not enough to wet a cat! I never saw such a molly-coddle set-out. I go out when I'm at home if it pours cats and dogs; nobody minds; why should they? Come on, Shane, let's go, there's a trump; we won't sneak, and we'll be back in half a jiff.

"I wish you would let me alone," said Mr. Shane. Somebody snatched his book out of his hand. He turned swiftly to recover it, but the captor was out of reach. "Give me my book!" he cried. "How dare you take my book!"

"Here's a lark! catch hold, Griffin." Mr. Shane, hurrying to recover his treasure, saw it dexterously thrown above his reach into the hands of Charlie Griffin.

"Give me my book, Griffin!" And he made a rush at Griffin.

"Catch, boys!" Griffin threw the book to some one else before Mr. Shane could reach him. It was thrown from one to the other, from end to end of the room, probably not being improved by the way in which it was handled.

The usher stood in the midst of the laughing boys, a picture of helplessness. The grammar had cost him half a crown at a second-hand bookstall. Half a crown represented to him a handsome sum. There were many claims upon his sixteen pounds a year; he had to think once, and twice, and thrice before he spent half a crown upon a book. His books were to him his children. In those dreams of future glory his books were his constant companions, his open sesame, his royal road to fame; with their aid he could do so much, without their aid so little. So now and then he ventured to spend half a crown upon a volume which he wanted.

The grammar, being badly aimed, fell just in front of him. He made a dash at it. Some one gave him a push and he fell sprawling on the floor; but he seized the book with his left hand. Griffin, falling on it tooth and nail, caught hold of it before he could secure it from danger. There was a rush of half a dozen. Every one wanted a finger in the pie. The grammar was clutched by half a dozen hands at once. The back was rent off, leaves pulled out, the book

14

was torn to shreds. Mr. Shane lay on the floor, with the ruins of his grammar in his hands.

Just then Bertie Bailey entered the room, victorious from his contest with Mr. Till. A shout of welcome greeted him.

"Hullo, Bailey! have you done the lines?"

Bertie, a deliberate youth as a rule, took his time to answer. He surveyed the scene, then he put his fingers to his nose, repeating the gesture with which he had retreated from Mr. Till.

"Catch me at it!—think I'm a silly?" Then he put his hands into his pockets, and slouched into the centre of the room. The boys crowded round him.

"Did he let you off?" asked Griffin.

"Of course he let me off; I made him: he knew better than to try to make me do his lines."

Then he told the story; the boys laughed. The way in which the ushers were compelled to stultify themselves was a standing joke at Mecklemburg House. That Mr. Till should have been forced to eat his own words, and to let insubordination go unpunished, was a humorous idea to them.

Mr. Shane still remained upon the floor. He was engaged in gathering together the remnants of his grammar. Perhaps a pot of paste, with patient manipulation, might restore it yet. He would give himself a great deal of labour to avoid the expenditure of another half-crown; perhaps he had not another half-crown to spend.

"What's the row?" asked Bertie, seeing Mr. Shane engaged in gathering up the fragmentary leaves. They told him.

"I'm going out," said Bailey, "and I should like to see anybody stop me. I say, Mr. Shane, I want to go down to the village."

Mr. Shane repeated his stock phrase.

"Mrs. Fletcher said no one was to go out while it rained." He had collected all the remnants of his grammar, and was rising with them in his hand.

"Give me hold!" exclaimed Bertie; and he snatched what was left of the book out of the usher's hands.

"Bailey!" cried Mr. Shane.

"Look here, I want to go down to the village. I suppose I may, mayn't I?"

"Mrs. Fletcher said no one was to go out if it rained," stammered Mr.

Shane.

"If you don't let me go, I'll burn this rubbish!" Bertie flourished the ruined grammar in the tutor's face. Mr. Shane made a dart to recover his property; but Bertie was too quick for him, and sprang aside beyond his reach. It is not improbable that if it had come to a tussle Mr. Shane would have got the worst of it.

"Who's got a match?" asked Bertie. Some one produced half a dozen. "Will you let me go?"

"Don't burn it," said Mr. Shane. "It cost me half a crown; I only bought it last week."

"Then let me go."

"What'll Mrs. Fletcher say?"

"How's she to know unless you tell her? I'll be back before tea. I don't care if it cost you a hundred half-crowns, I'll burn it. Make up your mind. Is it going to cost you half a crown to keep me in?"

Bertie struck a match. Mr. Shane attempted to rush forward to put it out, but some of the boys held him back. His heart went out to his book as though it were a child.

"If I let you go, you promise me to be back within half an hour? I don't know what Mrs. Fletcher will say if she should hear of it;—and don't get wet."

"I'll promise you fast enough. Mrs. Fletcher won't hear of it; and what if she does? She can't eat you. You needn't be afraid of my getting wet."

"I shan't let anybody else go."

"Oh yes, you will! You'll let Griffin and Ellis go; you don't think I'm going all that way alone?"

"And me!" cried Edgar Wheeler. Pretty nearly all the other boys joined him in the cry.

"I am not going to have all you fellows coming with me," announced Bertie. "Wheeler can come; but as for the rest of you, you can stay at home and go to bed—that's the best place for little chaps like you. Now then, Shane, look alive; is it going to cost you half a crown, or isn't it?"

Mr. Shane sighed. If ever there was a case of a round peg in a square hole, Mr. Shane's position at Mecklemburg House was a case in point. The youth, for he was but a youth, was a good youth; he had an earnest, honest, practical belief in God; but surely God never intended him for an assistant-master.

Perhaps in the years to come he might drift into the place which had been prepared for him in the world, but it was difficult to believe that he was in it now. A studious dreamer, who did nothing but dream and study, he would have been no more out of his element in a bear garden than in the extremely difficult and eminently unsatisfactory position which he was supposed—it was veritable supposition—to fill at Mecklemburg House.

"How many of you want to go?"

"There's me,"—Bertie was not the boy to take the bottom seat—"and Griffin, and Ellis, and Wheeler, that's all. Now what is the good of keeping messing about like this?"

"You're sure you won't be more than half an hour?"

"Oh, sure as sticks."

"And what shall I say to Mrs. Fletcher if she finds out? You're sure to lay all the blame on me." Mr. Shane had a prophetic eye.

"Say you thought it didn't rain."

"I don't think it does rain much." Mr. Shane looked out of the window, and salved his conscience with the thought. "Well, if you're quite sure you won't get wet, and you won't be more than half an hour—you—can—go." The latter three words came out, as it were, edgeways and with difficulty from the speaker's mouth, as if even he found the humiliation of his attitude difficult to swallow.

"Come along, boys!—here's your old book!" Bertie flung the grammar into the air, the leaves went flying in all directions, the four boys went clattering out of the room with noise enough for twenty, and Mr. Shane was left to recover his dignity and collect the scattered volume at his leisure.

But Nemesis awaited him. No sooner had the conquering heroes disappeared than an urchin, not more than eight or nine years of age, catching up one of the precious leaves, exclaimed,—

"Let's tear the thing to pieces!" The speaker was little Willie Seymour, Bertie Bailey's cousin. It was his first term at school, but he already bade fair to do credit to the system of education pursued at Mecklemburg House.

"Right you are, youngster," said Fred Philpotts, an elder boy. "It's a burning shame to let them go and keep us in. Let's tear it all to pieces."

And they did. There was a sudden raid upon the scattered leaves; at the mercy of twenty pairs of mischievous hands, they were soon reduced to atoms so minute as to be altogether beyond the hope of any possible recovery. Nothing short of a miracle could make those tiny scraps of printed paper into a book again. And seeing it was so Mr. Shane leaned his head against the window-pane and cried.

Chapter III

AT MOTHER HUFFHAM'S

It was only when Bailey and his friends were away from the house that it occurred to them to consider what it was they had come out for. They slunk across the grass-grown courtyard, keeping as close to the wall as possible, to avoid the lynx-eyes of Mrs. Fletcher. That lady was the only person in Mecklemburg House whose authority was not entirely contemned. Let who would be master, she would be mistress; and she had a way of impressing that fact upon those around her which made it quite impossible for those who came within reach of her influence to avoid respecting.

It was truly miserable weather. Any one but a schoolboy would have been only too happy to have had a roof of any kind to shelter him, but schoolboys are peculiar. It was one of those damp mists which not only penetrate through the thickest clothing, and soak one to the skin, but which render it difficult to see twenty yards in front of one, even in the middle of the day. The day was drawing in; ere long the lamps would be lighted; the world was already enshrouded in funeral gloom. Not a pleasant afternoon to choose for an expedition to nowhere in particular, in quest of nothing at all.

The boys slunk through the sodden mist, hands in their pockets, coat collars turned up about their ears, hats rammed down over their eyes, looking anything but a cheerful company. Griffin asked a question.

"I say, Bailey, where are you going?"

"To the village."

"What are you going to the village for?" This from Ellis.

"For what I am."

After this short specimen of convivial conversation the four trudged on. Alas for their promise to Mr. Shane! The wet was already dripping off their hats, and splashings of mud were ascending up the legs of their trousers to about the middle of their back. In a minute or two Wheeler began again.

"Have you got any money?"

Bertie pulled up short. "Have you?" he asked.

"I've got sevenpence."

"Then lend me half?"

"Lend me a penny? I'll pay you next week; honour bright, I will," said Ellis.

Griffin was more concise. "Lend me twopence?" he asked.

Wheeler looked unhappy. It appeared that he was the only capitalist among the four, and under the circumstances he did not feel exactly proud of the position. Although sevenpence might do very well for one, it would not be improved by quartering.

"Yes, I know, I daresay," he grumbled. "You're very fond of borrowing, but you're not so fond of paying back again." He trudged on stolidly.

Bailey caught him by the arm. "You don't mean that you're not going to lend me anything, after my asking for you to come out with me, and all?"

"I'll lend you twopence."

"Twopence! What's twopence?"

"It's all you'll get; you can have it or lump it, I don't care; I'm not dead nuts on lending you anything." Wheeler was a little wiry-built boy, and when he meant a thing very much indeed he had an almost terrier-like habit of snapping his jaws—he snapped them now. Bailey trudged by his side with an air of dudgeon; he probably reflected that, after all, twopence was better than nothing. But Ellis and Griffin had their claims to urge. They apparently did not contemplate with pleasure the prospect of tramping to and from the village for the sake of the exercise alone. Ellis began,—

"I say, old fellow, you'll lend me a penny, won't you? I'm always game for lending you."

"Look here, I tell you what it is, I won't lend you a blessed farthing! It's like your cheek to ask me; you owe me ninepence from last term."

"But I expect a letter from home in the morning with some money in it. I'll pay you the ninepence with threepence interest—I'll pay you eighteenpence —you see if I don't. And if you'll lend me a penny now I'll give you twopence for it in the morning. Do now, there's a good fellow, Wheeler; honour bright, I will."

For answer Wheeler put his finger to his eye and raised the eyelid. "See any green in my eye?" he said.

"You're a selfish beast!" replied his friend. And so the four trudged on. Then Griffin made his attempt.

"I'll let you have that knife, Wheeler, if you like."

"I don't want the knife."

"You can have it for threepence."

"I don't want it for threepence."

"You offered me fourpence for it yesterday."

"I've changed my mind."

Charlie pondered the matter in his mind. They were about half-way to their destination, and already bore a closer resemblance to drowned rats than living schoolboys. By the time they had gone there and back again, it would be possible to wring the water out of their clothes; what Mrs. Fletcher would have to say remained to be seen. After they had gone a few yards further, and paddled through about half a dozen more puddles, Charlie began again.

"I'll let you have it for twopence."

"I don't want it for twopence."

"It's a good knife." No answer. "It cost a shilling." Still no answer. "There's only one blade broken." Still no reply. "And that's only got a bit off near the point." Still silence. "It's a jolly good knife." Then, with a groan, "I'll let you have it for a penny."

"I wouldn't give you a smack in the eye for it."

After receiving this truly elegant and generous reply, Griffin subsided into speechless misery. It is not improbable that, so far as he was himself concerned, he began to think that the expedition was a failure.

In silence they reached the village. It was not a village of portentous magnitude, since it only contained thirteen cottages and one shop, the shop being the smallest cottage in the place. The only point in its favour was that it was the nearest commercial establishment to Mecklemburg House. The proprietor was a Mrs. Huffham, an ancient lady, with a very bad temper, and a still worse reputation—among the boys—for honesty in the direction of weights and measures. It must be conceded that they could have had no worse opinion of her than she had of them.

"Them young warmints, if they wants to buy a thing they wants ninety ounces to the pound, and if they wants to pay for it, they wants you to take eightpence for a shilling—oh, I knows 'em!" So Mrs. Huffham declared.

At the door of this emporium parley was held. Ellis suddenly remembered something.

"I say, I owe old Mother Huffham two-and-three." So far as the gathering mist and the soaking rain enabled one to see, Dick's countenance wore a lugubrious expression.

"Well, what of that?"

"Well"—Dick Ellis hesitated—"so long as that brute Stephen isn't about the place I don't mind. He called out after me the other day, that if I didn't pay he'd take the change out of me some other way."

The Stephen referred to was Mrs. Huffham's grandson, a stalwart young fellow of twenty-one or two, who drove the carrier's cart to Kingston and back. His ideas on pecuniary obligations were primitive. Having learned from experience that it was vain to expect Mr. Fletcher to pay his pupils' debts at the village shop, he had an uncomfortable way of taking it out of refractory debtors in the shape of personal chastisement. Endless disputes had arisen in consequence. Mr. Fletcher had on more than one occasion threatened the summary Stephen with the terrors of the law; but Stephen had snapped his fingers at Mr. Fletcher, advising him to pay his own debts, lest worse things happened to him. Then Mr. Fletcher had forbidden Mrs. Huffham to give credit to the boys; but Mrs. Huffham was an obstinate old lady, and treated the headmaster with no more deference than her grandson. Finally, Mr. Fletcher had forbidden the boys to deal with Mrs. Huffham; but in spite of his prohibition an active commerce was carried on, and on more than one occasion the irate Stephen had been moved to violence.

"You should have stopped at home," was Wheeler's not unreasonable reply to Dick's confession. "I don't owe her anything. I don't see what you wanted to come for, anyhow, if you haven't got any money and you owe her two-and-three."

And turning the handle of the rickety door he entered Mrs. Huffham's famed establishment. Bailey, rich in the possession of a prospective loan of twopence, and Charlie Griffin followed close upon his heels. After hesitating for a moment Ellis went in too. To remain shivering outside would have been such a lame conclusion to a not otherwise too satisfactory expedition, that it seemed to him like the last straw on the camel's back. Besides, it was quite on the cards that the impetuous Stephen would be engaged in his carrier's work, and be pleasantly conspicuous by his absence from home.

The interior of the shop was pitchy dark. The little light which remained without declined to penetrate through the small lozenge-shaped windowpanes. Mrs. Huffham's lamp was not yet lit, and the obscurity was increased by the quantity of goods, of almost every description, which crowded to overflowing the tiny shop. No one came.

"Let's nick something," suggested the virtuously minded Griffin. Ellis acted on the hint.

"I'm not going there and back for nothing, I can tell you."

On a little shelf at the side of the shop stood certain bottles of sweets. Dick reached up to get one down. At that moment Wheeler gave him a jerk with his arm. Ellis, catching at the shelf to steady himself, brought down shelf, bottles and all, with a crash upon a counter.

"Thieves!" cried a voice within. "Thieves!" and Mrs. Huffham came clattering into the shop, out of some inner sanctum, with considerable haste for one of her mature years. "Thieves!"

For some moments the old lady's eyes could see nothing in the darkness of the shop. She stood, half in, half out, peering forward, where the boys could just see her dimly in the shadow. They, deeming discretion to be the better part of valour, and not knowing what damage they might not have done, stood still as mice. Their first impulse was to turn and flee, and Griffin was just feeling for the handle of the door, preparatory to making a bolt for it, when heavy footsteps were heard approaching outside, and the door was flung open with a force which all but threw Griffin back upon his friends.

"Hullo!" said a voice; "is anybody in there?"

It was Stephen Huffham. With all their hearts the boys wished they had respected authority and listened to Mr. Shane! There was a coolness and promptness about Stephen Huffham's method of taking the law into his own hands upon emergency which formed the basis of many a tale of terror to which they had listened when tucked between the sheets at night in bed.

Mr. Huffham waited for no reply to his question, but he laid an iron hand upon Griffin's shoulder and dragged him out into the light.

"Come out of that! Oh, it's you, is it?" Charlie was gifted with considerable powers of denial, but he found it quite beyond his power to deny Mr. Huffham's assertion then. "Oh, there's some more of you, are there? How many of you boys are there inside here?"

"They've been a-thieving the things!" came in Mrs. Huffham's shrill treble from the back of the shop.

"Oh, they have, have they? We'll soon see about that. Unless I'm blinder than I used to be, there's young Ellis over there, with whom I've promised to have a word of a sort before to-day. You bring a light, granny, and look alive; don't keep these young gentlemen waiting, not by no manner of means."

Mrs. Huffham retreated to her parlour, and presently re-appeared with a lighted lamp in her hand. This, with great deliberation, for her old bones were stiff, and rheumatism forbade anything like undue haste, she hung upon a nail, in such a position that its not too powerful light shed as great an illumination as possible upon the contents of her shop. Far too powerful an illumination to suit the boys, for it brought into undue prominence the damage wrought by Ellis and his friend. They eyed the ruins, and Mrs. Huffham eyed them, and Mr. Stephen Huffham eyed them too. The old lady's feelings at the sight were for a moment too deep for words, but Mr. Stephen Huffham soon found speech.

"Who did this?" he asked; and there was something in the tone of the inquiry which grated on his hearers' ears.

Had Dick Ellis and his friend deliberately planned to do as much mischief as possible in the shortest possible space of time, they could scarcely have succeeded better. Three or four of the bottles were broken to pieces, and in their fall they had fallen on a little glass case, the chief pride and ornament of Mrs. Huffham's shop, which was divided into compartments, in one of which were cigars, in another reels of cotton and hanks of thread, and in a third such trifles as packets of hair-pins, pots of pomade, note-paper and envelopes, and a variety of articles which might be classified under the generic name of "fancy goods." The glass in this case was damaged beyond repair; the sweets from the broken bottles had got inside, and had become mixed with the cigars, and the paper, and the hair-pins, and the pomade, and the rest of the varied contents.

Mr. Stephen Huffman not finding himself favoured with an immediate reply to his inquiry, repeated it.

"Who did this? Did you do this?" And he gave Charlie Griffin a shake which made him feel as though he were being shaken not only upside down, but inside out.

"No-o-o!" said Charlie, as loudly as he was able with Mr. Stephen Huffman shaking him as a terrier shakes a rat. "I-I-I didn't! Le-e-eave me alone!"

"I'll leave you alone fast enough! I'll leave the lot of you alone when I've taken all the skin off your bodies! Did you do this?" And Mr. Stephen Huffham transferred his attention to Bailey.

"No!" roared Bertie, before Huffman had time to get him fairly in his grasp. Mr. Huffman held him at arm's length, and looked him full in the face with an intensity of scrutiny which Bertie by no means relished.

"I suppose none of you did do it; nobody ever does do these sort of things, so far as I can make out. It was accidental; it always is."

His voice had been so far, if not conciliatory, at least not unduly elevated. But suddenly he turned upon Ellis with a roar which was not unlike the bellow of a bull. "Did you do it?"

Ellis started as though he had received an electric shock.

"No-o!" he gasped. "It was Wheeler!"

"Oh, it was Wheeler, was it?"

"It wasn't me," said Wheeler.

"Oh, it wasn't you? Who was it, then? That's what I want to know; who was it, then?" Mr. Huffham put this question in a tone of voice which would have been eminently useful had he been addressing some person a couple of miles away, but which in his present situation almost made the panes of glass rattle in the windows. "Who was it, then?" And he caught hold of Ellis and shook him with such velocity to and fro that it was difficult for a moment to distinguish what it was that he was shaking.

"It—was—Whe-e-eler!" gasped Ellis, struggling with his breath.

"Now, just you listen to me, you boys!" began Mr. Huffham. (They could scarcely avoid listening to him, considering that he spoke in what was many degrees above a whisper.) "I'll put it this way, so that we can have things fair and square, and know what we're a-doing of. There's a pound's damage been done here, so perhaps one of you gentlemen will let me have a sovereign. I'm not going to ask who did it; I'm not going to ask no questions at all: all I says is, perhaps one of you young gentlemen will let me have a sovereign." He stretched out his hand as though he expected to receive a sovereign then and there; as it happened he stretched it out in the direction of Bertie Bailey.

Bertie looked at the horny, dirt-grimed palm, then up in Mr. Huffham's face. A dog-fancier would have said that there was some scarcely definable resemblance to the bull-dog in the expression of his eyes. "You won't get a sovereign out of me," he said.

"Oh, won't I? we'll see!"

"We will see. I'd nothing to do with it; I don't know who did do it. You shouldn't leave the place without a light; who's to see in the dark?"

"You let me finish what I've got to say, then you say your say out afterwards. What I say is this—there's a pound's worth of damage done—"

"There isn't a pound's worth of damage done," said Bertie.

Mr. Huffham caught him by the shoulder. "You let me finish out my say! I say there is a pound's worth of damage done; you can settle who it was among you afterwards; and what I say is this, either you pays me that pound before you leave this shop or I'll give the whole four of you such a flogging as you never had in all your days—I'll skin you alive!"

"It won't give me my money your flogging them," wailed Mrs. Huffham from behind the counter. "It's my money I wants! Here is all them bottles broken, and the case smashed—and it cost me two pound ten, and everything inside of it's a-ruined. It's my money I wants!"

"It's what I wants too; so which of you young gents is going to hand over that there sovereign?"

"Wheeler's got sevenpence," suggested Griffin.

"Sevenpence! what's sevenpence? It's a pound I want! Which of you is going to fork up that there pound?"

"There isn't a pound's worth of damage done," said Bertie; "nothing like. If you let us go, we'll get five shillings somehow, and bring it you in a week."

"In a week—five shillings! you catch me at it! Why, if I was once to let you outside that door, you'd put your fingers to your noses, and you'd call out, 'There goes old Huffham! yah—h—h!'" And he gave a very fair imitation of the greeting which the sight of him was apt to call forth from the very youths in front of him.

"If they was the young gentlemen they calls themselves they'd pay up, and not try to rob an old woman what's over seventy year."

"Now then, what's it going to be, your money or your life? That's the way to put it, because I'll only just let you off with your life, I'll tell you. Look sharp; I want my tea! What's it going to be, your money, or rather, my old grandmother's money over there, an old woman who finds it a pretty tight fit to keep herself out of the workhouse—"

"Yes, that she do," interpolated the grandmother in question.

"Or your life?" He looked in turn from one boy to the other, and finally his gaze rested on Bailey.

Bertie met his eyes with a sullen stare. "I tell you I'd nothing to do with it," he said.

"And I tell you I don't care that who had to do with it," and Mr. Huffham snapped his fingers. "You're that there pack of liars I wouldn't believe you on your oath before a judge and jury, not that I wouldn't!" and his fingers were snapped again. He and Bailey stood for a moment looking into each other's face.

"If you hit me for what I didn't do, I'll do something worth hitting for."

"Will you?" Mr. Huffham caught him by the shoulder, and held him as in a vice.

26

"Don't you hit me!"

Apparently Mrs. Huffham was impressed by something in his manner. "Don't you hit 'un hard! now don't you!"

"Won't I? I'll hit him so hard, I'll about do for him, that's about as hard as I'll hit him." A look came into Mr. Huffham's face which was not nice to see. Bailey never flinched; his hard-set jaw and sullen eyes made the resemblance to the bulldog more vivid still. "You pay me that pound!"

"I wouldn't if I had it!"

In an instant Mr. Huffham had swung him round, and was raining blows with his clenched fist upon the boy's back and shoulders. But he had reckoned without his host, if he had supposed the punishment would be taken quietly. The boy fought like a cat, and struggled and kicked with such unlooked-for vigour that Mr. Huffham, driven against the counter and not seeing what he was doing, struck out wildly, knocked the lamp off its nail with his fist, and in an instant the boy and the man were struggling in the darkness on the floor.

Just then a stentorian voice shouted through the glass window of the rickety door,—

"Bravo! that's the best plucked boy I've seen!"

Chapter IV

<u>A LITTLE DRIVE</u>

Those within the shop had been too much interested in their own proceedings to be conscious of a dog-cart, which came tearing through the darkening shadows at such a pace that startled pedestrians might be excused for thinking that it was a case of a horse running away with its driver. But such would have been convinced of their error when, in passing Mrs. Huffham's, on hearing Mr. Stephen bellowing with what seemed to be the full force of a pair of powerful lungs, the vehicle was brought to a standstill as suddenly as a regiment of soldiers halt at the word of command. The driver spoke to the horse,—

"Steady! stand still, old girl!" The speaker alighted. Approaching Mrs. Huffham's, he stood at the glass-windowed door, observing the proceedings within; and when Mr. Stephen, in his blind rage, struck the lamp from its place and plunged the scene in darkness, the unnoticed looker-on turned the handle of the door and entered the shop, shouting, in tones which made themselves audible above the din,—

"Bravo! that's the best plucked boy I've seen!" And standing on the threshold, he repeated his assertion, "Bravo! that's the best plucked boy I've seen." He drew a box of matches from his pocket, and striking one, he held the flickering flame above his head, so that some little light was shed upon what was going on within. "What's this little argument?" he asked.

Seeing that Mr. Huffman was still holding Bailey firmly in his grasp, "Hold hard, big one," he said; "let the little chap get up. You ought to have your little arguments outside; this place isn't above half large enough to swing a cat in. Granny, bring a light!"

As the match was just on the point of going out he struck another, and entered the shop with it flaming in his hand. Mrs. Huffham's nerves were too shaken to allow her to pay that instant attention to the new-comer's orders which he seemed to demand.

"Look alive, old lady; bring a light! This old band-box is as dark as pitch."

Thus urged, the old lady disappeared, presently reappearing with a little table-lamp in her trembling hands.

"Put it somewhere out of reach—if anything is out of reach in this dog-hole of a place. I shouldn't be surprised if you had a little bonfire with the next lamp that's upset."

Mrs. Huffman placed it on a shelf in the extreme corner of the shop, from which post of vantage it did not light the scene quite so brilliantly as it might have done. Mr. Stephen and the boy, relaxing a moment from the extreme vigour of discussion, availed themselves of the opportunity to see what sort of person the stranger might chance to be.

He was a man of gigantic stature, probably considerably over six feet high, but so broad in proportion that he seemed shorter than he actually was. A long waterproof, from which the rain was trickling in little streams, reached to his feet; the hood was drawn over his head, and under its shadow was seen a face which was excellently adapted to the enormous frame. A huge black beard streamed over the stranger's breast, and a pair of large black eyes looked out from overhanging brows. He was the first to break the silence.

"Well, what is this little argument?" Then, without waiting for an answer, he continued, addressing Mr. Huffham, "You're rather a large size, don't you think, for that sized boy?"

"Who are you? and what do you want? If there's anything you want to buy, perhaps you'll buy it, and take yourself outside."

The stranger put his hand up to his beard, and began pulling it.

"There's nothing I want to buy, not just now." He looked at Bailey. "What's he laying it on for?"

"Nothing."

"That's not bad, considering. What were you laying it on for?" This to Huffham.

"I've not finished yet, not by no manner of means; I mean to take it out of all the lot of 'em. Call themselves gents! Why, if a working-man's son was to behave as they does, he'd get five years at a reformatory. I've known it done before today."

"I daresay you have; you look like a man who knew a thing or two. What were you laying it on for?"

"What for? why, look here!" And Mr. Huffham pointed to the broken bottles and the damaged case.

"And I'm a hard-working woman, I am, sir, and I'm seventy-three this next July; and it's hard work I find it to pay my rent: and wherever I'm to get the money for them there things, goodness knows, I don't. It'll be the workhouse, after all!" Thus Mrs. Huffham lifted up her voice and wept.

"And they calls themselves gents, and they comes in here, and takes advantage of an old woman, and robs her right and left, and thinks they're going to get off scot free; not if I know it this time they won't." Mr. Stephen Huffham looked as though he meant it, every word.

"Did you do that?" asked the stranger of Bailey.

"No, I didn't."

"I don't care who did it; they're that there liars I wouldn't believe a word of theirs on oath; they did it between them, and that's quite enough for me."

"I suppose one of you did do it?" asked the stranger.

Bailey thrust his hands in his pockets, looking up at the stranger with the dogged look in his eyes.

"The place was pitch dark; why didn't they have a light in the place?"

"Because there didn't happen to be a light in the place, is that any reason why you should go smashing everything you could lay your hands on? Why couldn't you wait for a light? Go on with you! I'll take the skin off your back!"

"How much?" asked the stranger, paying no attention to Mr. Stephen's eloquence.

"There's a heap of mischief done, heap of mischief!" wailed the old lady in the rear.

"How am I to tell all the mischief that's been done? Just look at the place; a sovereign wouldn't cover it, no, that it wouldn't."

"There isn't five shillings' worth of harm," said Bertie. "If you were to get five shillings, you'd make a profit of half a crown."

The stranger laughed, and Mr. Huffham scowled; the look which he cast at Bertie was not exactly a look of love, but the boy met it without any sign of flinching.

"I'll be even with you yet, my lad!" Mr. Stephen said.

"If I give you a sovereign you will be even," suggested the stranger.

Mr. Stephen's eyes glistened; and his grandmother, clasping her old withered palms together, cast a look of rapture towards the ceiling.

"Oh, deary me! deary me!" she said.

"It's a swindle," muttered Bertie.

"Oh, it's a swindle, is it?" snarled Mr. Stephen. "I'd like to swindle you, my fighting cock."

30

"You couldn't do it," retorted Bertie.

The stranger laughed again. Unbuttoning his waterproof, and in doing so distributing a shower of water in his immediate neighbourhood, out of his trousers pocket he took a heavy purse, out of the purse he took a sovereign, and the sovereign he handed to Mr. Stephen Huffham. Mr. Stephen's palm closed on the glittering coin with a certain degree of hesitation.

"Now you're quits," said the stranger, "you and the boy."

"Quits!" said Bertie, "it's seventeen-and-sixpence in his pocket!"

Mr. Stephen smiled, not quite pleasantly; he might have been moved to speech had not the stranger interrupted him.

"You're pretty large, and that's all you are; if this boy were about your size, he'd lay it on to you. I should say you were a considerable fine sample of a—coward."

Mr. Stephen held his peace. There was something in the stranger's manner and appearance which induced him to think that perhaps he had better be content with what he had received. After having paused for a second or two, seemingly for some sort of reply from Mr. Huffham, the stranger addressed the boys.

"Get out!" They went out, rather with the air of beaten curs. The stranger followed them. "Get up into the cart; I'm going to take you home to my house to tea." They looked at each other, in doubt as to whether he was jesting. "Do you hear? Get up into the cart! You, boy," touching Bailey on the shoulder, "you ride alongside me."

Still they hesitated. It occurred to them that they had already broken their engagement with the credulous Mr. Shane, broken it in the most satisfactory manner, in each separate particular. They were not only wet and muddy, looking somewhat as though they had recently been picked out of the gutter, but that half-hour within which they had pledged themselves to return had long since gone. But if they hesitated, there was no trace of hesitation about the stranger.

"Now then, do you think I want to wait here all night? Tumble up, you boy." And fairly lifting Wheeler off his legs, he bore him bodily through the air, and planted him at the back of the trap. And not Wheeler only, but Griffin and Ellis too. Before those young gentlemen had quite realized their position, or the proposal he had made to them, they found themselves clinging to each other to prevent themselves tumbling out of the back of what was not a very large dog-cart. "You're none of you big ones! Catch hold of each other's hair or something, and don't fall out; I can't stop to pick up boys. Now then, bantam, up you go."

And Bertie, handled in the same undignified fashion, found himself on the front seat beside the driver. The stranger, big though he was, apparently allowed his size to interfere in no degree with his agility. In a twinkling he was seated in his place by Bertie.

"Steady!" he cried. "Look out, you boys!" He caught the reins in his hands; the mare knew her master's touch, and in an instant, even before the boys had altogether yet quite realized their situation, they were dashing through the darkening night.

It was about as cheerless an evening as one could very well select for a drive in an open vehicle. The stranger, enveloped in his waterproof, his hood in some degree sheltering his face, a waterproof rug drawn high above his knees, was more comfortable than the boys. Bailey, indeed, had a seat to sit upon and a share of the rug, but his friends had neither seat nor shelter.

Perhaps, on the whole, they would have been better off had they been walking. The imperfect light and the hasty start rendered it difficult for them to have a clear view of their position. The mare—which, had it been lighter and they versed in horseflesh, they would have been able to recognise as a very tolerable specimen of an American trotter—made the pace so hot that they had to cling, if not to each other's hair, at least to whatever portion of each other's person they could manage to get hold of. Even then it was only by means of a series of gymnastic feats that they were able to keep their footing and save themselves from being pitched out on to the road.

They had not gone far when Griffin had a disaster.

"I've lost my hat!" he cried. Wind and pace and nervousness combined had loosened his headgear, and without staying to bid farewell to his head, it disappeared into the night.

The stranger gave utterance to a loud yet musical laugh.

"Never mind your hat! Can't stop for hats! The fresh air will do you good, cool your head, my boy!" But this was a point of view which did not occur to Griffin; he was rather disposed to wonder what Mr. Shane and Mrs. Fletcher would say.

"I wish you wouldn't catch hold of my throat; you'll strangle me," said Wheeler, as the vehicle dashed round a sharp turn in the road, and the hatless Griffin made a frantic clutch at his friend to save himself from following his hat.

"I—can't—help—it," gasped his friend in reply. "I wish he wouldn't go so fast. Oh—h!"

The stranger laughed again.

"Don't tumble out! we can't stop to pick up boys! Hullo! what are you up to there?"

The trio in the rear were apparently engaged in a fight for life. They were uttering choking ejaculations, and struggling with each other in their desperate efforts to preserve their perpendicular. In the course of their struggle they lurched against the stranger with such unexpected violence that had he not with marvellous rapidity twisted round in his seat and caught them with his arm, they would in all probability have continued their journey on the road. At the same instant, with his disengaged hand he brought the horse, who seemed to obey the directions of its master's hand with mechanical accuracy, to a sudden halt.

"Now, then, are you all right?"

They were very far from being all right, but were not at that moment possessed of breath to tell him so. Had they not lost the power of speech they would have joined in a unanimous appeal to him to set them down, and let them go anywhere, and do anything, rather than allow them to continue any longer at the mercy of his too rapid steed. But the stranger seemed to take their involuntary silence for acquiescence. Once more they were dashing through the night, and again they were hanging on for their bare lives.

"Like driving, youngster?" The question was addressed to Bailey. "Like horses? Like a beast that can go? Mary Anne can give a lead to a flash of lightning and catch it in two T's."

"Mary Anne" was apparently the steed. At that moment the trio in the rear would have believed anything of Mary Anne's powers of speed, but Bailey held his peace. The stranger went on.

"I like a drive on a night like this. I like dashing through the wind and the darkness and the rain. I like a thing to fire my blood, and that's the reason why I like you. That's the reason why I've asked you home to tea. What's your name?"

"Bailey, sir."

"I knew a man named Bailey down in Kentucky who was hanged because he was too fond of horses—other people's, not his own. Any relation of yours?" Bertie disclaimed the soft impeachment.

"I don't think so, sir."

"There's no knowing. Lots of people are hanged without their own mothers knowing anything about it, let alone their fathers, especially out Kentucky way. A cousin of mine was hanged in Golden City, and I shouldn't have known anything about it to this day if I hadn't come along and seen his body swinging on a tree. As nice a fellow as man need know, six-feet-one-and-three-quarters in his stockings—three-quarters of an inch shorter than me. They explained to me that they'd hanged him by mistake, which was some consolation to me, anyway, though what he thought of it is more than I can say. I cut him down, dug a hole seven foot deep, and laid him there to sleep; and there he sleeps as sound as though he'd handed in his checks upon a feather bed."

Bailey looked up at the speaker. He was not quite sure if he was in earnest, and was anything but sure that the little narrative which he rolled so glibly off his tongue might not be the instant coinage of his brain. But something in the speaker's voice and manner attracted him even more than his words; something he would have found it difficult to describe.

"Is that true?" he asked.

The stranger looked down at him and laughed.

"Perhaps it is, and perhaps it isn't." He laughed again. "Wet, youngster?"

"I should rather think I am," was Bertie's grim response. All the stranger did was to laugh again. Bailey ventured on an inquiry. "Do you live far from here?" He was conscious of a certain degree of interest as to whether the stranger was driving them to Kentucky; he, too, had Mr. Shane and Mrs. Fletcher in his mind's eye. "Shane'll get sacked for this, as sure as fate," was his mental observation. He was aware that at Mecklemburg House the sins of the pupils not seldom fell upon the heads of the assistant-masters.

"Pain's Hill," was the answer to his question. "Ever heard of Washington Villa?" Bertie could not say he had.

"I am George Washington Bankes, the proprietor thereof. Yes, and it isn't so long ago that if any one had said to me that I should settle down as a country gentleman, I should have said, 'There have been liars since Ananias, but none quite as big as you.'"

Bailey eyed him from a corner of his eye. His father was a medical man, with no inconsiderable country practice. He had seen something of country gentlemen, but it occurred to him that a country gentleman in any way resembling his new acquaintance he had not yet chanced to see.

"You at the school there?"

Taking it for granted that he referred to Mecklemburg House, Bertie confessed that he was.

"Why don't you run away? I would."

Bertie started; he had read of boys running away from school in stories of the penny dreadful type, but he had not yet heard of country gentlemen suggesting that course of action as a reasonable one for the rising generation to pursue.

"Every boy worth his salt ought to run away. I did, and I've never done a more sensible thing to this day." In that case one could not but wonder for how many sensible things Mr. George Washington Bankes had been remarkable in the course of his career. "I've been from China to Peru, from the North Pole to the South. I've been round the world all sorts of ways; and the chances are that if I hadn't run away from school I should never have travelled twenty miles from my old mother's door. Why don't you run away?"

Bertie wriggled in his seat and gasped.

"I—I don't know," he said.

"Ah, I'll talk to you about that when I get you home. You're about the best plucked lad I've seen, or you wouldn't have stood up in the way you did to that great hulking lubber there; and rather than see a lad of parts wasting his time at school—but you wait a bit. I'll open your eyes, my lad. I'll give you some idea of what a man's life ought to be! Books never did me any good, and never will. I say, throw books, like physic, to the dogs—a life of adventure's the life for me!"

Bertie listened open-eyed and open-mouthed; he began to think he was in a waking dream. There was a wildness about his new acquaintance, and about his mode of speech, which filled him with a sort of dull, startled wonder. There was in the boy, deep-rooted somewhere, that half-unconscious longing for things adventurous which the British youngster always has. Mr. Bankes struck a chord which filled the boy almost with a sense of pain.

"A life of adventure's the life for me!" Mr. Bankes repeated his confession of faith, laughing as he did so; and the words, and the voice, and the manner, and the laugh, all mixed together, made the boy, wet as he was, glow with a sudden warmth. "A life of adventure's the life for me!"

The drive was nearly ended, and during the rest of it Mr. Bankes kept silence. Wheeler's hat had followed Griffin's, but he had not mentioned it; partly because, as he thought, he would receive no sympathy and not much attention, and partly because, in his anxiety to keep his footing in the trap, and get out of it with his bones whole, it would have been a matter of comparative indifference to him if the rest of his clothing had followed his hat. But he, too, mistily wondered what Mr. Shane and Mrs. Fletcher would say.

Fortunately for his peace of mind, and the peace of mind of his two friends, the good steed, Mary Anne, brought them safely to the doors of Washington Villa. Fond of driving as they were, as a rule, they were conscious of a distinct sense of relief when that drive was at an end.

Chapter V

AN EVENING AT WASHINGTON VILLA

Washington Villa appeared, from what one could see in the darkness, to be a fairly sized house, standing in its own grounds. Considerable stabling was built apart from, but close to the house, and as the trap dashed along the little carriage-drive numerous loud-voiced dogs announced the fact of an arrival to whomever it might concern. The instant the vehicle stopped, the hall door was opened, and a little wizened, shrunken man came down the steps. Mr. Bankes threw him the reins.

"Jump out, you boys, and tumble into the house. Welcome to Washington Villa." Suiting the action to the word, and before his young friends had clearly realized the fact of their having arrived at their destination, he had risen from his seat, sprung to the ground, and was standing on the threshold of the door. The boys were not long in following suit.

"Come this way!" Striding on in front of them, through a hall of no inconsiderable dimensions, he led them into a room in which a bright fire was blazing, and which was warm with light. A pretty servant girl made a simultaneous entrance through a door on the other side of the room. "Catch hold." Tearing rather than taking off his waterproof and hood, he flung them to the maid. "Where are my slippers?" The maid produced a pair from the fender, where they had been placed to warm; and Mr. Bankes thrust his feet into them, flinging his boots off on to the floor. "Tea for five, and a good tea, too, and in about less time than it would take me to shoot a snake."

The maid disappeared with a laugh on her face; she was apparently used to Mr. Bankes, and to Mr. Bankes' mode of speech. Then, after having attended to his own comfort, the host turned his attention to his guests.

"Well, you're a nice lot of half-drowned puppies. By right, I ought to hang you up in front of the kitchen fire to dry."

His guests shuffled about upon their feet with not quite a graceful air. It was true that they looked in about as miserable a condition as they very well could do; but considering the circumstances under which they had travelled, it was scarcely to be wondered at. Had Mr. Bankes travelled in their place, he might have looked like a half-drowned puppy too.

"But a wetting will do you good, and as for mud, why, I don't care for mud. I've swallowed too much of it in my time to stick at a trifle. When I was a boy, I was the dirtiest little blackguard ever seen. Now, then, is that tea ready? Come along."

And off he strode into the hall, the boys following sheepishly in the rear. Wheeler poked Bailey in the side with his elbow, and Bailey poked Griffin, and they each of them poked the other, and they grinned. Their feelings were altogether too much for speech. What Mr. Shane and Mrs. Fletcher would think and say—but that was a matter on which they would not improbably be able to speak more fully later on. A more unguestlike-looking set of guests could hardly be conceived. Not only were their boots concealed beneath thick layers of mud, but they were spattered with mud from head to foot; their hands and faces were filthy, and their hair was in a state of untidiness better imagined than described. They had their everyday clothes on; their trousers were in general too short in the leg, and their coats too short in the sleeves; while Griffin was radiant with a mighty patch in the seat of his breeches of a totally different material to the original cloth. It was fortunate that Mr. Bankes did not stick at trifles, or he would never have allowed his newly-discovered guests to enter his well-kept residence.

They followed their host into a room on the other side of the hall, and the sight they saw almost took their breath away. A table laden with more delicacies than they remembered to have seen crowded together for a considerable space of time was, especially after the fare to which they were accustomed at Mecklemburg House, a spectacle calculated at any time to fill them with a satisfaction almost amounting to awe. But to come out of such a night to such a prospect! To come to feast from worse than famine! The revulsion of feeling was considerable, and the aspect of the guests became even more sheepish than before.

"Sit down, and pitch in. If you're as hungry as I am, you'll eat the table, legs and all."

The boys needed no second invitation. In a very short space of time host and guests alike were doing prodigies of execution. The nimble-handed servant-maid found it as much as she could do to supply their wants. On the details of the feast we need not dwell. It partook of the nature of a joke to call that elaborate meal tea. By the time it was finished the four young gentlemen had not only ceased to think of what Mrs. Fletcher and Mr. Shane might say, but they had altogether forgotten the existence of Mecklemburg House Collegiate School; and even Charlie Griffin was prepared to declare that he had thoroughly enjoyed that nightmare journey from Mrs. Huffham's to the present abode of bliss. The meal had been no less to the satisfaction of the host than of his guests.

"Done?" They signified by their eloquent looks as much as by their speech that they emphatically had. "Then let's go back to the other room." And they went.

A peculiarity of this other room was that all the chairs in it were arm-chairs; and in four of not the least comfortable of these arm-chairs the boys found themselves seated at their ease. Over the fire-place, arranged in the fashion of a trophy, were a large number of venerable-looking pipes. Taking one of these down, Mr. Bankes proceeded to fill it from a tobacco jar which stood in a corner of the mantelshelf. Then he lit it, and, planting himself in the centre of the hearthrug, right in front of the fire, he thrust his hands into his pockets and looked down upon his guests, a huge, black-bearded giant, puffing at his pipe.

"Had a good feed?"

They signified that they had.

"Do you know what I brought you here for?"

The food and the warmth combined had brought them into a state of exceeding peace, and they were inclined to sleep. Why he had brought them there they neither knew nor cared; they were beyond such trifling. They had had a good meal, the first for many days, and it behoved them to be thankful.

"I'll tell you. I brought you here because I want to get you, the whole lot of you, to run away."

His listeners opened their eyes and ears. Bailey had made some acquaintance with his host's character before, but his three friends stared.

"Every boy worth his salt runs away from school. I did, and it was the most sensible thing I ever did in my life."

When Mr. Bankes thus repeated the assertion which he had made to Bailey in the trap, his hearers banished sleep and began to wonder.

"What's the use of school? What do you do there? What do you do at that tumble-down old red-brick house on the Cobham road? Why, you waste your time."

This assertion, if, to a certain extent, true, as it applied to the establishment in question, was a random shot as applied to schools in general.

"Shall I tell you what I learnt at school? I learnt to hate it, and I haven't forgotten that lesson to this day; no, and I shan't till I'm packed away with a lot of dirt on top of me. My father," Mr. Bankes took his pipe out of his mouth, and pointed his remarks with it as he went on, "died of a broken heart, and so should I have done if I hadn't cut it short and run away."

No man ever looked less like dying of a broken heart than Mr. Bankes did then.

"A life of adventure's the life for me!"

They were the words which had thrilled through Bertie when he had heard them in the trap; they thrilled him again as he heard them now, and they thrilled his companions too. They stared up at Mr. Bankes as though he held them with a spell; nor would that gentleman have made a bad study for a wizard.

"A life of adventure's the life for me! Under foreign skies in distant lands, away from the twopenny-halfpenny twaddle of spelling-books and sums, seeking fortune and finding it, a man in the midst of men, not a finicking idiot among a pack of babies. Why don't you run away? You see me? I was at school at Nottingham; I was just turned thirteen: I ran away with ninepence-halfpenny in my pocket. I got to London somehow; and from London I got abroad, somehow too; and abroad I've picked up fortune after fortune, thrown them all away, and picked them up again. Now I've had about enough of it, I've made another little pile, and this little pile I think I'll keep, at least just yet awhile. But what a life it's been! What larks I've had, what days and nights, what months and years! Why, when I think of all I've done, and of what I might have done, rotted away my life, if it hadn't been for that little bolt from school,—why, when I think of that, I never see a boy but I long to take him by the scruff of the neck, and sing out, 'Youngster, why don't you do as I have done, cut away from school, and run?'"

Mr. Bankes flung back his head and laughed. But whether he was laughing at them, or at his own words, or at his recollections of the past, was more than they could say. They looked at each other, conscious that their host was not the least part of the afternoon's entertainment, and somewhat at a loss as to whether he was drawing the long bow, taking them to be younger and more verdant than they were, or whether he was seriously advancing an educational system of his own.

He startled them by putting a question point-blank to Bailey, one which he had put before.

"Why don't you run away?"

"I—I don't know!" stammered Bertie. Then, frankly, as the idea occurred to him, "Because I never thought of it."

Mr. Bankes laughed. His constant tendency to laughter, with or without apparent reason, seemed to be his not least remarkable characteristic.

"Now you have thought of it, why don't you run away?"

Bailey turned the matter over in his mind.

"Why should I?"

His friends looked at each other, thinking the conversation just a trifle queer.

"Why ever should he run away?" asked Griffin.

"And wherever would he run to?" added Wheeler.

Dick Ellis said nothing, but possibly he thought the more. Mr. Bankes directed his reply directly at Bailey.

"I'll tell you why you ought to run away; because that's the shortest cut into a world into which you will never get by any other road. I'll tell you where you ought to run to, out of this little fleabite of an island, into the lands of golden dreams and golden possibilities, my lad; where men at night lay themselves down poor, and in the morning rise up rich."

Mr. Bankes, warming with his theme, began to gesticulate and stamp about the room, the boys following him with all their eyes.

"I hate your huggermuggering existence; why should a lad of parts huggermugger all his life away? When I saw you stand up to that great lout, I said to myself, 'That lad has grit; he's just the very spit of what I was when I was just his age; he's too good to be left to muddle in this old worn-out country, to waste his time with books and sums and trash.' I said to myself, 'I'll lend him a helping hand,' and so I will. I'll show you the road, if I do nothing else; and if you don't choose to take it, it's yourself's to blame, not me.

"When I was out in Colorado, at Denver City, there was a boy came along, just about your age; he came along from away down East. He was English; he'd got himself stowed away, and he'd made his way to the promised land. He took a spade one day, and he marked out a claim, and that boy he worked it, he did, and it turned up trumps; there wasn't any dirt to dig, because pretty nearly all that his spade turned up was virgin silver. He sold that claim for 10,000 dollars, money down, and he went on and prospered. That boy is now a man; he owns, I daresay, half a dozen silver mines, and he's so rich,—ah, he's so rich he doesn't know how rich he is. Now why shouldn't you have been that boy?"

Mr. Bankes paused for a reply, but his listeners furnished none. Griffin was on the point of suggesting that Bailey was not that boy because he wasn't; but he refrained, thinking that perhaps that was not quite the sort of answer that was wanted.

"I knew another boy when I was going up from the coast to Kimberley, Griqualand West. Do you boys know where that is?"

This sudden plunge into geographical examination took his guests aback; they did not know where Griqualand West was; perhaps they had been equally misty as to the whereabouts of Denver City, Colorado.

"It's in South Africa. Ah, that's the way to learn geography, to travel about and see the places,—pitch your books into the fire!"

"And is the other place in South Africa?" queried Griffin.

Mr. Bankes gave him a look the like of which he had never received from Mr. Fletcher; a look of thunder, as though he would have liked to pick him up, then and there, and pitch him after the books into the fire.

"Denver City, Colorado, in South Africa?" he roared. "Why, you leather-headed noodle, where were you at school? If I were the man who taught you, I'd flog you from here to Dublin with a cat-o'-nine-tails, rather than I'd let you expose your ignorance like that!"

The sudden advent among them of an explosive bomb might have created a little more astonishment than this speech, but not much. Griffin felt that he had better abstain from questioning, and let his host run on.

"Denver City is in the United States of America, in the land of the stars and bars, as every idiot knows! As I was saying, before that young gentleman wrote himself down donkey—and he looks it, every inch of him!—as I was saying, when I was going up from the coast to Kimberley, there was a boy who used to do odd jobs for me; he hadn't sixpenny-worth of clothes upon his back! I lost sight of him; five years afterwards I met him again. It was like a tale out of the *Arabian Nights*, I tell you! That ragged boy that was, when I saw him again five years afterwards, he reckoned to cover what any half-dozen men might have put down, and double it afterwards. And look at the life he'd led! It's no good my talking about it here, you'd hardly believe me if I told you half the things he'd done. Don't you believe any of your adventure books. There aren't half the adventures crowded into any book which that lad had seen. Yes, a life of adventure was the life for him, and he'd had it, too!"

Mr. Bankes returned to his post of vantage in front of the fire. In his excitement he had smoked his pipe to premature ashes; he refilled and lighted it. Then he addressed himself to Bailey, marking time as he went on by beating the palm of his right hand against his left.

"I say, don't let a day be wasted—days lost are not recovered; now's your time, and now's your opportunity; don't let the week's end find you huggermuggering in that old school. Go out into the world! learn to be a man!

Try your courage! Put your powers to the test! Search for the golden land! Let a life of adventure be the life for you! As for you," Mr. Bankes turned with ominous suddenness towards Charlie Griffin, "I don't say that to you; what I say to you is this: write home to your mother for a good supply of flannel petticoats, and wrap yourself up warm, and let your hair grow long, and take care of your complexion. You're a beauty boy, one of the sort who didn't ought to be trusted out after dark alone, and who's sure to have a fit if he sees the moon!"

It is a question if this sudden change of subject made Griffin or his friends the more uncomfortable. Thinking that Mr. Bankes intended a joke, and that it would be ungrateful not to laugh, Ellis attempted a snigger; but a sudden gleam from his host's eyes in his direction brought his mirth to an untimely ending.

"What are you laughing at?" asked Mr. Bankes. Ellis kept silence, being most unwilling to confess that he did not know. Mr. Bankes addressed himself again to Bailey.

"It is you I am advising to do as I did, to try a fall with the world and to back yourself to win, not such things as those."

Under this heading he included Bertie's three friends, with an eloquent wave of his hand in their direction.

"It wants a boy to make a man, not a farthing sugar stick! You'll have cause to bless this evening all your life, and to bless me, too, if you take the tip I've given you. Don't you listen to those who talk to you about the hardships you will meet. What's life without hardships, I should like to know; it's hardships make the man! I'm not advising you to wrap yourself up in cotton-wool; leave cotton-wool to mutton-headed dummies;" this with a significant glance in the direction of Bailey's friends. "Rather I tell you this, you back yourself to fight, and fight it out, and fight to win, and win you will! Run away to-night, to-morrow, I don't care when, so long as it's within the week. There's nothing like striking the iron while it's hot, and set the clock a-going which will never stop until it strikes the hour of victory won and fortune made! A life of adventure's the life for me, and it's the life for you, and the sooner you begin it the longer it will last and the sweeter it will be."

There was something in Mr. Bankes' tone and manner, when he chose to put it there, which, in the eyes of his present audience, at any rate, had all the effect of natural eloquence. His excitement excited them, and almost he persuaded them to believe in the reality of his golden dreams. Bailey, indeed, sat silent, spellbound. Mr. Bankes, by no means a bad judge of character, had not mistaken the metal of which the boy was made, and every stroke he struck, struck home. As was not unnatural, Mr. Bankes' eloquence had a very much more mixed effect on Bailey's friends. Their host gave a sudden turn to their thoughts by taking out his watch.

"Eleven o'clock! whew-w-w!" This was a whistle. "They'll think you've run away already! Ha! ha! ha! I'm not going to have you boys sleep here, so the sooner you go the better. Now then, out you go!"

His guests sprang to their feet as he made a movement as though he would turn them out with as much precipitation as he had lifted them into the trap. And, indeed, the manner of their departure was not much more ceremonious. Before they quite knew what was happening, he had hustled them into the hall; the hall-door was open; they were the other side of it, and Mr. Bankes, standing on the doorstep, was ordering them off his premises.

"Now then, clear out of this! The dogs will be loose in half a second; you'd better make tracks before they take it into their heads to try their teeth upon your legs."

The door was shut, and they were left standing in the night, endeavouring to realize whether their adventure of the night had been actual fact, or whether they had only dreamed it.

Chapter VI

AFTERWARDS

But Wheeler's first observation brought them back to *terra firma* with a plunge.

"It's my belief that fellow's a howling madman."

They cast a look over their shoulder to see if the fellow thus referred to was within hearing of this courteous speech, and then, with one accord, they made for the entrance to Washington Villa, not pausing till they stood clear of its precincts on the road outside.

Then Wheeler made another observation.

"This is a jolly lark!"

Ellis and Griffin laughed, but Bailey held his peace. A thought struck Griffin.

"I say, I wonder what old Mother Fletcher'll say? She'll send herself into fits! Fancy its being eleven o'clock! Did you ever hear of such a set-out in all your lives? And I've no more idea of where we are than the man in the moon."

"I know," said Bailey. He began to trudge on a few feet in front of them.

It still rained—a steady, soaking drizzle—and a haze which hung about the air made the night darker than it need have done. Griffin and Wheeler, minus caps, were wholly at the mercy of the weather.

"I shouldn't be surprised," muttered Griffin, "if I didn't catch a death of cold after this."

And, indeed, such was a quite possible consummation of the evening's pleasure. The boys trudged on, following Bailey's lead. But Wheeler's feelings could only find relief by venting themselves in speech.

"Did you ever hear anything like that chap? I never did, never! Fancy his going on with all that stuff about running away. I should like to catch myself at it,—running away! He's about the biggest liar ever I heard!"

"And didn't he snap me up!" said Griffin. "Did you ever see anything like it? How was I to know where the beastly place was? I don't believe there is such a place."

"He's cracked!" decided Ellis. Then, despite the rain, the young gentleman began snapping his fingers and cutting capers in the middle of the muddy road. "He's cracked! cracked! Oh lor', I never had such a spree in all my life!"

Then the three young gentlemen put their hands to their sides and roared with laughter, stamping about the road to save themselves from choking. But Bailey trudged steadily on in front.

"And didn't he give us a blow-out!"

A shout of laughter. "Ho, ho, ho! ha, ha, ha!"

"And didn't he tell some busters!"

Another chorus, as before.

"I wonder if he ever did run away himself, as he said he did?" This remark came from Ellis, and his friends checked their laughter to consider it. They then for the first time discovered that Bailey was leaving them in the rear.

"You're a nice sort of fellow," shouted Ellis after him. "Let's catch him up! What's his little game, I wonder? Let's catch him up!"

They scampered after him along the road, soon catching him, for Bertie, who was not hurrying himself, was only a few yards in advance. Ellis slipped his arm through his.

"I say, Bailey, do you think he ever ran away from school himself?"

"What's it got to do with me?" was Bertie's reply.

"Whatever made him go on at you like that? He must have taken you for a ninny to think you were going to swallow all he said! Fancy you running away! I think I see you at it! Running away to Huffham's and back is about your style. Why didn't you ask him for a tip? He seemed to be so uncommon fond of you that if I'd been you I'd have asked for one. You might have said if he made it large enough you'd run away; and so you might have done—to old Mother Huffham's and back." And Ellis nudged him in the side and laughed. But Bailey held his peace.

Wheeler gave the conversation a different turn.

"How are you fellows going to get in?" He referred to their effecting an entrance into Mecklemburg House.

"Knock at the door, of course, and pull the bell, and dance a break-down on the steps, and make a shindy generally, so as to let 'em know we've come." These suggestions came from Griffin. Wheeler took up the parable.

"And tell old Mother Fletcher to let us have something hot for supper, and to look alive and get it, and make it tripe and onions, with a glass of stout to follow. I just fancy what she'd say."

"And tell her," continued Griffin, "that we've been paying a visit to a nice, kind gentleman, who happens to be raving mad."

"And she'd be pleased to hear that he advised us all to run away, and waste no time about it. Where did he advise us to go to? The land of golden dreams? Oh, my crikey, don't I see her face!"

Bailey made a remark of a practical kind.

"We can get in fast enough, there are always plenty of windows open." It is not impossible that the young gentleman had made an entrance into Mecklemburg House by some such way before.

"It's easy enough to get in," said Ellis, "but what are we to say in the morning? It'll take about a week to dry my things, and about a month to get the mud off."

"I shouldn't be surprised if old Shane got sacked," chuckled Wheeler.

"It will be jolly hard lines if he does," said Ellis.

"Oh, what's the odds? he shouldn't have let us go!" Which remark of Wheeler's was pretty good, considering the circumstances under which Mr. Shane's permission had been obtained.

Just then Bailey stopped, and began to peer about him in the night.

"Have you lost your way?" asked Ellis. "That'll be the best joke of all if you have. Fancy camping out a night like this! We shan't quite be drowned by the morning, but just about almost."

"I'm going to cut across this field," said Bailey. "It's ever so far round by the road, but we shall get there in less than no time if we go this way."

The suggestion tickled Ellis.

"Fancy cutting across fields on a night like this! Oh, my gracious! what will old Mother Fletcher say?"

Bailey climbed over a gate, and the others clambered after him. It might be the shortest cut, but it was emphatically the dirtiest.

"Why, if they haven't been ploughing it!" cried Griffin, before they had taken half a dozen steps.

Apparently they had, and very recently too. The furrows were wide and deep, the soil seemed to be a stiffish clay; walking was exercise of the most hazardous kind. There was an exclamation from some one; but as it appeared that Griffin had only fallen forward on to his nose, his friends were too much occupied with their own proceedings to pay much heed.

"I have lost my shoe!" declared Wheeler, immediately after. "Oh, I'm stuck in the mud; I believe I'm planted in this beastly field."

"Never mind your shoe, since you've lost your hat already," said Ellis, with ready sympathy. "You might as well leave all the rest of your things behind you, for all the use they'll be after this little spree is over."

"I don't know what Bailey calls a short cut," grumbled Griffin. "At the rate I'm going it'll take me about a couple of hours to do a hundred yards."

"We shall be home with the milk," said Ellis.

"I've lost my other shoe!" cried Wheeler.

"No, have you really, though?"

"I believe I have, but I don't know whether I have or whether I haven't; all I know is, I've got about a hundred pounds of mud sticking to my feet. I wish Bailey was at Jericho with his short cuts!"

"This is nicer than that old lunatic," sang out Dick Ellis. "Don't I wish old Mother Fletcher could see us now."

"I don't know what you call nice," said Griffin. "You'd call it nice if you had your eyes and nose and mouth bunged up. I'm down again!"

"You needn't pull me with you," remonstrated Ellis.

But Griffin did. Feeling that he was going, he made a frantic clutch at Ellis, who was just in front of him, and the two friends embraced each other on the treacherous ground. Ellis' tone underwent a sudden change.

"I'll pay you out for this!"

"I couldn't help it," protested Griffin.

"Couldn't help it! What do you mean, you couldn't help it? Do you mean to say you couldn't help catching hold of me, and dragging me down into this beastly ditch?"

"It isn't a ditch; it's a furrow."

"I don't know what you call a furrow. I know I'm sopping wet, and where my hat's gone to I don't know."

"What's it matter about your hat? I've lost mine ever so long ago! I wish I'd stopped at home, and never bothered old Shane to let me out. I know whoever else calls this a spree, I don't; spree indeed!"

48

When they had regained their feet, and were cool enough to look about them, they found that the others were out of sight, and apparently out of hearing too.

"Blessed if this isn't a go! If they haven't been and gone and left us. Hollo!" Ellis put his hand to his mouth, that his voice might carry further; but no answer came. "Ba-a-ailey! Ba-a-ailey!" But from Bailey came no sign. "This is a pretty state of things! wherever have they gone? If this is a game they think they're having, it's the meanest thing of which I ever heard, and I'll be even with them, mark my words. Which way did they go?"

"How should I know? I don't even know which way we came. How's a fellow to know anything when he can't see his hand before his face in a place like this? It's my belief it's one of Bailey's little games."

"Ba-a-ailey!" Ellis gave another view-halloo. In vain, only silence answered. "Well, this is a go! If it hadn't been for you I shouldn't have been in this hole."

"I wish I'd never bothered old Shane to let me out!"

"Bother old Shane, and bother you too! I don't know where I am any more than Adam."

"I'm sure I don't."

"It's no good standing here like a couple of moon-struck donkeys. I sink in the mud every time I put my foot to the ground; we shall be over head and heels by the time the morning comes. I'm going straight ahead; it must bring us somewhere, and it seems to me it don't much matter where."

Minus his hat, not improved in person by his contact with the ground, nor in temper by the desertion of his friends, Dick Ellis renewed his journeying. Griffin found some difficulty in keeping up with him. How many times they lost their footing during the next few minutes it would be bootless to recount. Over mud, through mire, uphill, downhill, they staggered wildly.

"I wonder how large this field is," observed Ellis, after about ten minutes of this sort of work. "It seems to me we've gone about six miles."

"It seems to me we've gone sixty," groaned his friend.

"Talk about short cuts! Fancy bringing a fellow into the middle of a ploughed field on a pitch-dark, rainy night, and leaving him to find his way alone! I say, Ellis, supposing we lose our way?"

"Supposing we lose our way!" shouted Dick. "I guess we've lost it! What an ass you are! What do you think we're doing here, if we haven't lost our way? Do you think I'd stop in a place like this if I knew a way of getting out of it?" Just then he emphasized his remarks by sitting down in the mud, and remaining seated where he was. "I can't get up; I believe I'm stuck, and here I'll stick; and in the morning they'll find me dead: you mark my words, and see if they don't."

The terror of the situation moved Griffin almost to tears.

"Let's shout," he said.

"What's the good of shouting?"

"I don't know," said Griffin.

"Then what an ass you are!" With difficulty Ellis staggered to his feet. "It's my belief I've got about an acre of land fastened to the seat of my breeches. I should like to know how I'm to walk and carry that about."

They staggered on. A few yards further on they heard the sound of wheels upon a road.

"There's the road!" cried Griffin, rapture in his voice. The sound gave him courage. He quickened his pace, and hastened on. Suddenly there was a splash, a cry of terror, then all was silence.

"What's the matter?" cried Ellis, startled he scarcely knew at what. There was no reply. "Griffin, where are you? What's the matter?"

There was a sound as of a splashing of water, and a stifled voice exclaimed,—

"Help! I am drowning! He-elp!"

Ellis pulled up short, and only just in time, for the ground seemed all at once to come to an end. He stood on the edge of a declivity, and in front of him was he knew not what. It was so dark, he could not see his hand in front of him. There was only the sound as of some one struggling in water, and faint cries for help. For an instant his legs seemed to refuse their office, his knees gave way from under him, and his tongue clave to the roof of his mouth. Then he became conscious of wheels moving along a road which was close at hand. The sound gave him courage, and he shouted with the full force of his lungs,—

"Help! help!"

To his intense satisfaction, an immediate answer was returned.

"Hollo!" a gruff voice replied; "who's that a-calling?" "I!—

here!—in the field! There's some one drowning."

"Hold hard! I'll bring you a light."

A moment's pause; then in front of him a light was seen dimly approaching through the night. Never before had a light been so heartily welcome to Master Richard Ellis.

"Where are you?"

"Here! Take care where you're coming; there's a pond, or something, just in front of you."

The new-comer approached, keeping a wary eye upon the ground as he advanced. Ellis saw it was a carter, and that he carried an old-fashioned round lantern in his hand, with a lighted candle stuck in the socket. The carter held the lantern above his head, standing still, and peering through the night. The man was visible to the boy, but the boy, shrouded in the blackness of the night, was invisible to the man.

"Where are you?" he asked, seeing nothing in the gloom.

"Never mind me; Griffin's drowning in a pond, or something."

The splashing continued.

"I'm drowning! He-elp!"

The carter stooped forward, so that the light fell on the ground. Then Ellis perceived that between the man and himself was a little pond, into which the over-anxious Griffin had managed to fall.

"There ain't no water there," said the carter. "Where are you? Come out of it. There ain't enough water to drown a cat."

Griffin, perceiving that the fact was as the carter stated, proceeded to betake himself to what was, in comparison, dry land. But though not drowned, a more pitiable sight could scarcely be presented. He had fallen head-foremost into the filthy pool; the water was trickling down his head and face, and his countenance was plastered with an unsavoury coating of green slime.

"What are you? a boy?" inquired the carter. "Well, you're a pretty sight, anyhow!"

For answer Griffin burst into tears. Ellis, who had by this time found his way round the pond, joined in the criticism of his friend.

"Well, I am blessed!" In spite of his own plight, he was almost moved to mirth. "Won't old Mother Fletcher take it out of you! I wouldn't be in your shoes for a pound."

"Who's she? and who are you?" asked the carter.

"Have you ever heard of Mecklemburg House?"

"What, the school? Be you from the school? Well, you're a pretty couple, the pair of you. What little game are you up to now—running away? Won't they lay it into you!" The carter grinned; he was not aware that corporal punishment was interdicted at Mecklemburg House, and already seemed to see the "laying in" in his mind's eye.

"We—weren't running—away!" wept Griffin. "We've lost our way."

"Lost your way! Well, I never! That's a good one!" The carter seemed to doubt the statement.

"We have lost our way," said Ellis.

"Look here! for a couple of pins I'll take you by the scruff of your necks and walk you back myself, if you come any of your games on me."

From his tone and manner the carter seemed to be indignant. Griffin stared —as well as he could through his tears and the slime—and Ellis stared, being both at a loss to understand his indignation.

"Coming with your tales to me, telling me you've lost your way, with the school just across the road."

His hearers stared still more.

"You don't mean it?" Ellis said. "Why, if—I don't believe—why, if this isn't old Palmer's field, which he was only ploughing yesterday, and if you haven't tumbled into old Palmer's pond! Well, if we aren't a couple of beauties!"

Griffin stared at Ellis, and the carter stared at both of them. The fact was beginning to dawn upon these young gentlemen, the startling fact, that they had been all the time in a country with every inch of which they were acquainted, and that it was only the darkness which had confused them. As the carter had said, Palmer's field—which was the name by which it was known to the boys—was right in front of Mecklemburg House, and, in consequence, the school, instead of being, as they supposed, a mile or so away, was just across the road. When they had fully realized this fact, the young gentlemen gave a simultaneous yell of satisfaction, and without wasting any time in compliments and thanks, dashed through the open gate, and out of sight, leaving the carter to the enjoyment of his own society.

"Well," was the comment of that worthy, when he perceived the full measure of ingratitude which was entailed by this unlooked-for flight, "if I ever helps another being out of a ditch I'll let him know. Not even the price of half a pint!" Then he shouted after them, "I hope the schoolmeaster'll tan the hide from off you. I would if I were him."

Possibly the expression of this pious wish in some degree relieved his feelings, for he followed the boys, though at a much more decorous pace, through the gate. When he reached the road, he stopped for a moment and looked around him, but there were no signs of any one in sight—the birds had flown. So, muttering beneath his breath what were probably not blessings, he returned to his charge, a huge vehicle, drawn by four perspiring horses, and which was loaded with market produce. Climbing up to his seat, he started his horses and continued his journey through the night. But though he was not aware of it, the young gentlemen who had treated him with such ingratitude had not come to the end of their adventure.

The front gate of Mecklemburg House stood wide open, and they unhesitatingly dashed inside. But no sooner were they in the grass-grown courtyard than a thought struck Griffin.

"I wonder if Bailey and Wheeler have come back?"

"I don't know, and I don't care," said Ellis.

But the interchange of speech brought them back to the sense of their situation.

"How are you going to get in?" asked Griffin.

"Through the schoolroom window; it's always open," replied his friend.

But this always was a rule liable to exceptions, for on this occasion the particular window referred to happened to be shut. However, to understand all that was to follow, it is necessary to bring this chapter to an end.

Chapter VII

THE RETURN OF THE WANDERERS

While Bailey and his friends were spending the evening in the company of Mr. George Washington Bankes, the principal of Mecklemburg House was in a condition in which principals are very seldom supposed to be, a condition very closely allied to tears.

Mr. Fletcher was a tall, thin man, whose height was altogether out of proportion to his width. He was afflicted with a chronic stoop, and had a way, in walking, of shuffling, rather than stepping from foot to foot, which was scarcely dignified. His face was not unpleasing; there was a mildness in his eye and a sweetness about his infrequent smile which spoke of a gentler nature than the typical pedagogue is supposed to have.

The Philistines were upon him now; the battle, which he had long been feebly eluding, rather than boldly facing, had closed its ranks, and in the mere preamble to the fray he had immediately succumbed. It would have been better, perhaps, if he had been made of sterner stuff, but, unless he could have been entirely changed into another man, sooner or later the end was bound to come. Mr. Fletcher was ruined, and with him Mecklemburg House Collegiate School was ruined too.

He had been on a forlorn hope to town. A certain creditor, in return for money advanced, held a bill of sale on all the contents of the academy. Necessary payments had not been made, and he had threatened to swoop down upon the ancient red-brick house, and make a clearance of every desk and stool, every pot and kettle, every bed and bolster the premises contained. To appease this personage, Mr. Fletcher had journeyed up to town, and had journeyed up in vain. The fiat had gone forth that to-morrow, the day after, any day or any hour—in the middle of the night, for all he knew—hard-hearted strangers might and would arrive, and, without asking with your leave or by your leave, would strip Mecklemburg House of every movable it contained.

This was what it had come to after five-and-twenty years! When his father died he had been left a comfortable sum of ready money, untarnished credit, and a flourishing school; of all which nothing was left him now.

The principal and his wife were seated in their own sitting-room, trying to look the matter boldly in the face. Mr. Fletcher, sitting with his elbows on the table, covered his face with his hands. Mrs. Fletcher, a hard-featured woman,

54

had her arm about his neck, and strove to comfort him. Her ideas of comfort were of a material sort.

"Come, eat your supper, now do. You've had nothing to eat all day, and when you've eaten a bit things will look brighter, perhaps."

Mr. Fletcher turned his care-worn face up to his wife.

"Jane, things will never look bright to me again."

The man's voice trembled, and the woman turned her face away, perhaps unwilling to let him see that in her eyes were tears. The principal got up and began to walk about the room. His stoop was more pronounced than usual, and his shuffling style of movement more ungainly.

"I'm just a failure, that's what I am, a failure. The world's moved on, and I've stood still. I'm exactly where my father was, and in schools and schoolmasters there's a difference of a hundred years between his time and this. I'm not fit for keeping school in these new times. I don't know what I am fit for. I'm fit for nothing but to die!"

"And if you die, what's to become of me?"

"And if I live, what'll happen to you then?"

"It'll happen to me that I'll have you, and do you think that's nothing?"

"Jane, it's worse than nothing! You ought to have been the man instead of me. I shall be a clog to you and a burden; you're fit for fifty things, and I'm not fit for one! I could not make a decent clerk. I'm very certain I could not pass the examination required of a teacher in a board-school; I doubt if I ever could have reached that standard. I'm very certain I could not now. Times are changed in matters of education. People used to be satisfied with a twentieth part of what they now require. When I am turned out of the house in which I was born, and in which I have lived my whole life long, as I shall be in the course of a day or two, and you are turned out with me, wife, there will be fifty openings you will be fitted to fill, while I shall only be fit to carry circulars from house to house, or a sandwich-board through the streets."

"It's no use talking in that way, Beauclerk; it only breaks my heart to hear you, and it does no good. We must make up our minds to do something at once, and the great thing is, what? Now come and eat your supper, or you'll be ill; you know how you suffer if you go hungry to bed."

"I may as well become accustomed to it, because I shall have to go hungry very soon."

"Beauclerk!—what is the use of going on like that?—do you want to break my heart?"

"Wife, I believe mine's broken."

Mr. Fletcher leaned his face against the wall just where he was standing, his long, lean frame shaken with his sobbing.

"Beauclerk! Beauclerk! don't! don't!"

Hard-faced Mrs. Fletcher went to her husband, and took him in her arms, and soothed him as though he were a child of five. Mr. Fletcher looked up. His face was ghastly with the effort he made at self-control.

"I think I will have some supper; perhaps it will do me good,"

Husband and wife sat down to supper. There were the remains of a leg of mutton, a little glass jar half-filled with pickled cabbage, a small piece of cheese, and bread. Mrs. Fletcher put some mutton on her husband's plate, and a smaller portion on her own. Mr. Fletcher swallowed one or two mouthfuls, but apparently it went against the grain.

"I can't eat it," he said, pushing away his plate; "I'm not hungry."

"Won't you have some cheese? it's very nice cheese."

"I'm not hungry," repeated her husband.

His wife held her peace; she continued eating, not, perhaps, because she was hungry, but possibly because she wished, in doing something, to find a momentary relief from the necessity of thinking. Mr. Fletcher sat drawing patterns with his fork upon the tablecloth.

"I shall write to the parents in the morning. In fact, I ought to write to them to-night, but I don't feel up to it. I shall tell them that I am ruined, root and branch, stock and stone; that Mecklemburg House Collegiate School is a thing of the past, and that they had better remove their sons immediately, and let them have the means to travel with, because I have none."

"When did Booker say he would distrain?"

Booker was the creditor who held the bill of sale.

"He didn't specify the exact hour and minute, but it'll only be a question of an hour or two in any case. We can't pay and the things must go."

"But you have received money from some of the boys in advance."

Mr. Fletcher got up, and began to pace the room again.

"I have received money from most of them. Jane, what am I to do? As you know very well, I have received from more than half the boys the term's fees in advance. I am not clear that they could not prosecute me for obtaining money by means of false pretences; but, in any case, I shall feel that I have played the part of a dishonest man. Why didn't I say frankly at the beginning of the term, I am ruined, ruined hopelessly! and gone down at once without a pretence of struggling through another term?"

"We have struggled through so many, we could not tell we should not be able to struggle again."

"At any rate, we haven't. Before we're halfway through the term we're beaten, and I have received money on what was very much like false pretences. Then there are Mr. Till and Mr. Shane; they're entitled to a term's salary, if they could not lay claim to a term's notice too."

Mrs. Fletcher's face grew cold and hard, and there was an unpleasant glitter in her eyes.

"I shouldn't trouble myself about them; a more helpless lout than Mr. Shane, as you call him, I never saw, and to my mind Mr. Till never has been worth his salt. This morning, when he was left in charge, the school was like a bear-garden; I had to go in half a dozen times to ask what the noise was about. It's my belief that if you had had proper assistance you wouldn't be in the state you are in now."

Mr. Fletcher sighed.

"That is not the question, my dear; I owe them the money, and they ought to be paid. I know that they are both almost, if not quite penniless, and if I do not pay them something I doubt whether they will have the means to take them up to town. Remember, too, that this is the middle of term, and that how long they will be without even the chance of getting another situation goodness only knows."

"And are you better off? Have you better prospect of a situation? Beauclerk, before you pay either of those men a penny you will have to speak to me; I will not be robbed by them."

"If I would I have nothing to pay them with, so there is an end of it, my dear."

"Do you know what Mr. Shane's latest performance has been?" Struck by something in his wife's tone, Mr. Fletcher glanced at her with inquiry in his eyes. "I have not told you yet, because I have been too much upset by the news which you have brought to tell you anything,—goodness knows we have enough of our own to bear without having to bear the brunt of that clown's blunders too."

Seeing that his wife's eloquence bade fair to carry her away, Mr. Fletcher interposed a question.

"What has Mr. Shane been doing?"

"Doing! I'll tell you what he has been doing,—and you talk of robbing yourself to give him money! He let four of those boys go out in the rain this afternoon, when I expressly told him not to; and it would seem as if he has let them go for good, for they are still out now."

Her husband looked at her, not quite catching the meaning of her words.

"Still out now?"

"Yes, still out now. Bailey, Griffin, Wheeler and Ellis went out this afternoon, in all the rain and fog, with Mr. Shane's permission; and out they've stopped, for they're not back yet."

"Not back yet! Jane, you cannot mean it. Why, it's nearly midnight." Mr. Fletcher looked at his venerable silver watch, which had come to him, with the rest of his possessions, from his father. "What's that?"

Husband and wife listened. The silence which reigned without had been broken by a crash from the schoolroom, a crash which bore a strong family resemblance to the sound made by the upsetting of a form.

"It's those boys!" said Mrs. Fletcher. "They're getting through the window."

She hurried off to see, her husband following closely after. All the lights were out; save the sitting-room which they had left, all the house was dark. She called to him to bring the lamp. Returning, he snatched it from the table and went after her again.

They entered the schoolroom, Mr. Fletcher acting as lamp-bearer. Directly the door was opened they were conscious of a strong current of air within the room. Mrs. Fletcher went swiftly forward, picking her way among the desks and forms, and the cause of the noise they had heard and the draught they felt was soon apparent. The furthest window was wide open. In front of it a form was overturned upon the floor, a form which some one effecting a burglarious entrance through the window in the dark had unwittingly turned over. The lady's quick eye caught sight of a figure crouching behind a neighbouring desk. It did not take her long to drag a young gentleman out by the collar of his coat.

"Well—upon—my—word!"

Her astonishment was genuine, and excusable; few more disreputable figures ever greeted a lady's eye.

"Is this Bailey?"

It was Bailey. Perhaps at that moment Bailey rather wished it wasn't; but the surprise of his sudden capture had bereft him of the power of speech, and he was unable to deny his identity. The lady did nothing else but stare. Suddenly somebody else made his appearance at the window, a head rose above the window-sill, and a meek, modest voice inquired,—

"Please, ma'am, may I come in?"

The new-comer was Edward Wheeler. The lady's astonishment redoubled.

"Well—I—never!"

Taking this exclamation to convey permission, Wheeler gradually raised himself the necessary height, and finally, after a few convulsive plunges to prevent himself from slipping back again, scrambled through the window and stood upon the floor. Wheeler presented a companion picture to his friend. As he had lost his hat at an early hour of the evening, he, perhaps, in some slight details, bore away the palm from Bailey. Mrs. Fletcher stared at them both in blank amazement; in all her experience of boys she never had seen anything quite equal to these two. Mr. Fletcher, lamp in hand, came up to join in the inspection.

"Where have you boys been?" he asked.

"Out to tea," said Bailey.

Mrs. Fletcher sniffed disdainfully.

"Out to tea! Don't tell me that! I should think you've been out to tea in a ditch!"

Mr. Fletcher carried on the examination.

"How dare you tell me you've been to tea! Where have you boys been?"

"We have been out to tea," said Bailey.

"And where, sir, have you been having tea, that you come back at this hour, and in such a plight as that?"

"Washington Villa," answered Bailey.

"Washington Villa! And where's Washington Villa? But never mind that, I shall have something to say to you in the morning. Where are those other boys? Where are Griffin and Ellis?"

"They're coming," muttered Bailey.

Just then they came. While Mr. Fletcher hesitated, in doubt what to do or say, a voice, unmistakably Ellis', was heard without.

"Is that you, Bailey? Won't I pay you out for this, you cad! We might have got drowned for all you cared. Here's Griffin got half-drowned as it is."

Thrusting her head out of the window, Mrs. Fletcher replied to the wanderer; a reply, doubtless, as unexpected as undesired.

"If Mr. Fletcher did as I wished him, he'd give each of you boys a good round flogging before you went to bed, a lot of disobedient, ungrateful, untruthful, and untrustworthy scamps!"

Possibly this was enough for Ellis, for he subsided and was heard no more, but a sound of weeping arose. It was the grief of Charlie Griffin. Placing the lamp upon a desk, Mr. Fletcher put his head out of the window beside his wife's.

"I'm not going to open the hall door for you at this time of night. Your friends came through the window, and you can follow your friends."

They followed their friends, Ellis coming first; Griffin, with not unnatural bashfulness, preferring to keep in the background. Mrs. Fletcher's uplifted hands and cry of astonishment greeted Ellis, who was indeed a notable example of the possibilities of dirt as applied to the person, but Griffin's entry was followed by the silence of petrified amazement.

His friends' attempts at disfigurement were altogether unsuccessful as compared to the success which had attended his. They were dandies compared to him. It was difficult at a first glance to realize that he was a boy, or indeed a human being of any kind. He was covered with a combination of weeds, green slime, particoloured filth, and yellow clay; the water dripped from the more prominent portions of his frame; his clothes were glued to his limbs; he was hatless; his face and hair were plastered with the aforesaid slime; and, to crown it all, he was convulsed with a sorrow which lay too deep for words.

"Griffin!" was all that the headmaster's wife could gasp. "Charlie Griffin!"

"Where have you been?" asked Mr. Fletcher.

"I've been in the pond," gasped Griffin, half choked with mud and tears.

"In the pond? What pond?"

"Pa-almer's po-ond!"

"Palmer's pond! What were you doing in there? What I'm to do with you boys is more than I can say!" Mr. Fletcher sighed. "There's one thing, I shan't have to do with you much longer." This was muttered half beneath his breath.

"What are we to do with them, my dear?" This was a question to his wife.

"Don't ask me; I don't know what we're to do with them. I should think that boy"—here she pointed an accusatory finger at Griffin—"had better go back to Palmer's pond. He appears to be fond of it, and it's the only place he's fit for." Griffin was moved to wilder tears. "He had better take his things off where he stands, and throw them out into the yard; they'll never be good for anything again, and he shan't go upstairs with them on. And all four of them"—this with sudden vivacity which turned attention away from Griffin —"must have a bath before they think of going to bed between my sheets. A pretty state of things to have to get baths ready at this time of night!"

"Griffin, you had better take off your things," said Mr. Fletcher mildly, when his wife had finished. "I don't know what your father will say when he hears of the way in which you treat your clothing."

Mrs. Fletcher returned to her sitting-room, and Griffin unrobed himself, flinging each separate article of clothing into the yard as he took it off. Then a procession, headed by Mr. Fletcher, started for the bath-room. After a few moments' contact with clean, cold water, the young gentlemen, presenting a more respectable appearance, were escorted to their bedroom, Mr. Fletcher remaining while they put themselves to bed. Having assured himself that they actually were between the sheets, "I will speak to you in the morning," he said, and disappeared.

When the boys had satisfied themselves that he was out of hearing, their tongues began to wag. Griffin was still whimpering.

"It's all through you, Bailey, I got into this row."

Something suspiciously like a chuckle was the only answer which came from Bailey's bed.

"I say, did you really tumble into Palmer's pond?" inquired Wheeler.

"Of course I did! How could I help it when you couldn't see your hand before your face?"

Wheeler buried himself in the bedclothes and roared with laughter.

"You wouldn't have laughed if it had been you," continued the outraged Griffin. "I was as nearly drowned as anything. I should have been if it hadn't been for a fellow with a lantern."

"Go away! drowned!" scoffed Bailey, unconsciously repeating the carter's words; "why, there isn't enough water to drown a cat!"

"What did you go and leave us for like that?" asked Ellis.

"Do you think I was going to mess about in the rain all night while you two were squabbling on top of each other in the mud?"

"I call it a mean thing to do!"

"Who cares what you call it?"

"And if it weren't so jolly late, I'd give you something for yourself."

"Oh, would you? You'd give me something for myself! I like that! You wait till the morning, and then perhaps I'll give you something for yourself instead!"

Unconscious of the compliments which his affectionate pupils were bandying from one to the other, Mr. Fletcher returned to his wife, seated in the parlour. His whole air was one of depression, as of one who had no longer spirit enough to fight with fortune.

"Well, it will be over to-morrow!" he said. "I don't think I'm much good at school-keeping; I'm not strong enough; I'm not sufficiently able to impress my influence on others." Going to the mantelshelf he leaned his head upon his hand. "I suspect I've failed as a schoolmaster because I deserved to fail."

Then, forgetting the heroes of the night, his wife began to comfort him.

Chapter VIII

PREPARING FOR FLIGHT

That night Bertie Bailey dreamed a dream. In fact, he dreamed several dreams; his slumber-time was passed in dreamland, journeying from dream to dream.

He dreamed of the Land of Golden Dreams; of Mr. Bankes and Washington Villa; of a boy traversing a road which ran right around the world; of tumbling into ponds and scrambling out of them; of some mysterious country, peopled by a race of giants, to which there came a boy, who, single-handed, brought them low, and claimed the country for his own, and the soil of that land consisted of gold and silver, with judicious variations of precious stones. In his dreams he saw weapons flashing in the air, and he heard the sound of strange instruments of music.

Just before he woke he dreamed the most vivid dream of all. A moment before all had been a chaos of bewilderment, but all at once he found himself alone, in the centre of some wild place, not quite sure what sort of place it was, nor where, nor of anything about it, but he knew that it was wild. A voice was heard in the air, and he knew that it was the voice of Mr. George Washington Bankes. The voice kept repeating, "A life of adventure's the life for me!" and every time the words were uttered the boy's heart leapt up within him, and he went bounding on. The one voice became several, the world was full of voices, yet he knew that they all belonged to the original Mr. George Washington Bankes; and over and over again they repeated the same refrain, "A life of adventure's the life for me!" till the whole world was alive with it, and birds and beasts and sticks and stones caught up the same refrain, "A life of adventure's the life for me!" and the boy's heart was filled with a great and wondrous exultation. But all at once the voices ceased; all was still; and the boy found that he was standing in front of a mighty mountain, which filled the world with darkness, and barred the way in front of him. And he was beginning to be afraid, when out of the silence and the darkness came, in a still small whisper—which he knew to be the whisper of Mr. George Washington Bankes—the words, "A life of adventure's the life for me!" and they put courage into his heart, and he stretched out his arm and touched the mountain, and, behold! at his touch it was cleft asunder, and in its bosom were all the treasures of the earth.

But it was unfortunately at this point that he awoke. It was not unnatural that for some moments he should have refused to have acknowledged the fact

—to confess that he really was awake, and that it had been nothing but a dream.

It was broad daylight. The sun was peeping through the windows, along the edges of the ill-fitting blinds. It was nothing but a dream. As he began to realize the fact of the gleaming sunshine, even he was obliged to admit that it had been nothing but a dream. He turned in his bed with a dissatisfied grunt.

"I never dreamed anything like that before, nothing half so real! It seemed as if I had only to put out my hand to touch that mountain now."

But it only seemed, for there was no mountain there, only a coverlet, and a sheet, and a blanket or two, and a bolster, and a mattress, and a bed. Bertie lay on his back, with his eyes closed, attempting, by an effort of his will, to bring back the vanished dream. And to some extent he succeeded, for as he lay quiescent he seemed to hear, ringing in his ears, the words he had heard in his dream—

"A life of adventure's the life for me!"

He seemed so certainly to hear them that, just as they had done in his dream, they filled him with a sudden fire. Thoroughly aroused, he sat up in bed, grasping the bedclothes with eager hands. And to himself he said, half beneath his breath, "A life of adventure's the life for me!"

The other boys were still asleep in the little iron bedsteads on either side of him, but he made no attempt to recompose himself to slumber. He remained sitting up in bed, his knees huddled up to his chin, engaged in a very unwonted act for him, the act of thinking.

The events of the night before were vividly before him, but principally among them, a giant in the foreground, was the figure of Mr. George Washington Bankes.

"Why don't you run away?" Mr. Bankes' question rang in his ears.

"A life of adventure's the life for me!" Those other words of Mr. Bankes, which had been with him through the dream-haunted night, still danced before his eyes.

Than Bertie Bailey a less romantic-looking youth one could scarce conceive. But history tells us that some of the greatest heroes of romance, real, live, flesh-and-blood heroes, who actually at some time or other did exist, were anything but romantic in their persons. Perhaps Bailey was one of these. Anyhow, stowed away in some out-of-the-way corner of his unromantic-looking person was a vein of romance of the most pronounced and unequivocal kind.

His range of reading was not wide, yet he had his heroes of fiction none the less. They were rather a motley crew, and if he had been asked the question, say in an examination paper, "Who is your favourite hero? give a short sketch of his life," he would have hesitated once or twice before he would have written Dick Turpin, Robin Hood, Robinson Crusoe, or Jack the Giant-Killer. Perhaps he would have hesitated still longer before he had attempted to sketch the life of any one of them. Yet, had he told the truth, the gentleman selected would have been one of these.

Possibly in the act of selection his greatest difficulty would have lain. He never could quite make up his mind which of the four gentlemen named above he liked the best. There were points about Dick Turpin which struck his fancy. He would rather have ridden that ride to York than have had ten thousand pounds. It would have been worth his while to have been Dick Turpin if only to possess that horse of horses, Black Bess, the coal-black steed of his heart's desire, though it may be mentioned in passing that up to the present moment Bertie Bailey had never figured upon a horse's back. He had once ridden a donkey from Ramsgate to Pegwell Bay, but a donkey was not Black Bess.

On the other hand, there was no part of England with which he was better acquainted—theoretically—than the glades of Sherwood Forest. To have lived in those glades with Robin Hood, Bailey would heave a great sigh at the prospect; ah, that he only could! Yet certainly one had only to speak of the desert island, and of Robinson Crusoe on its lonely shore, for Bertie to feel a wild longing to plough the distant main, a longing which was scarcely consistent with his desire for the glades of Sherwood Forest. It is the fashion to sneer at fairy tales, and to speak of them as though they were beneath the supposititious dignity of the common noun boy, and certainly the marvellous history and adventures of Jack the Giant-Killer belong to the domain of the fairies. Possibly Bertie would have been himself ashamed to own his partiality for that hero of the nursery; and yet, to have had Jack's courage and strength and skill, to have slaughtered giants and taken castles and rescued maidens—Bertie sometimes dreamt of himself as another Jack, and then always with a rapture too deep for words.

Perhaps his real, ideal, and favourite hero would have consisted of a judicious combination of the four—something of Dick Turpin, and something of Robin Hood, and something of Robinson Crusoe, and something of Jack the Giant-Killer. Take all these somethings and mix them well together, and you would have had the man for Bailey. Emphatically, although almost unconsciously, in all his waking dreams, a life of adventure had been the life for him.

Mr. George Washington Bankes had applied the match to the powder. As he thought of all that gentleman had said, even in the cool of the morning, all his soul was on fire. Seeing him in his nightshirt of doubtful cleanliness, and with his touzled hair, you might not have supposed that there was fire in his soul, but there was. Run away! He had heard of boys running away from school before to-day.

Boys had run away from Mecklemburg House, and there were stories of one who, within quite recent times, had made a dash for liberty. Some said he had got as far as Windsor, some said Dorking, before he had changed his mind and decided to come back again. But he had come back again. Bailey made up his mind that when he ran away he would never come back again; never! or, at any rate, not till he had traversed the world in several different directions, as Mr. George Washington Bankes had done.

It had already become a question of *when* he ran away. With that quickness in arriving at a decision which, so some tell us, is the sure sign of a commanding intellect, he had already decided that he would; there only remained the question of time and opportunity.

"Why don't you run away?" Mr. Bankes had asked. Yes, why, indeed? especially if one had only to run away to step at once into the Land of Golden Dreams!

When the boys took their places in the schoolroom after breakfast, prepared for morning school, a startling announcement was made to them by Mr. Fletcher. Bailey and his friends had expected that something would be said to them on the subject of their escapade of the night before; but so far, so far as those in authority were concerned, their expectations had been disappointed. They had been sufficiently cross-examined by their fellow-pupils, and in spite of a slight suggestive foreboding of something unpleasant to come, when they perceived how their proceedings appeared in the eyes of their colleagues, they were almost inclined to look upon themselves somewhat in the light of heroes. Griffin, indeed, had not heard the last of the pond, and it was not of the tragic side of his misadventure that he heard the most. There were some disagreeable remarks made by personal friends who would not see that he had run imminent risk of being drowned. He almost began to wish that he had been.

"You wouldn't have laughed at it then," he said. But they laughed at it now.

But neither from Mr. Till, nor from Mr. Shane, nor from Mr. Fletcher, nor from the far more terrible Mrs. Fletcher, had either of the young gentlemen heard a word.

And just when they were preparing for morning school Mr. Fletcher made his startling announcement.

At first the quartett thought, not unreasonably, that his remarks were going to have particular reference to them and to their misdoings, but they were wrong. The headmaster was seated at his desk, in a seemingly more than usually preoccupied mood; but he too often was preoccupied in school, so they paid no heed, and got out their books and slates, and other implements of study, with the ordinary din and clatter. Suddenly he spoke.

"Boys, I want to speak to you."

The boys looked at him, and the quartett looked at each other. Mr. Fletcher did not raise his head, but with his eyes fixed on the desk in front of him continued to speak as though he found considerable difficulty in saying what he had to say.

"I have had heavy losses lately in carrying on the school. Some of you know that the number of boys has grown smaller by degrees and beautifully less."

There was a faint smile about Mr. Fletcher's mouth which did not quite betoken mirth.

"But I do not complain. I should not have mentioned it, only"—he paused, raised his head, and looked round the room, his eyes resting for a moment on each of the boys as they passed—"only when one has no boys one can keep no school. I have found, very certainly, that without boys school cannot keep me—my wife and I. Our wants are not large—they have grown even smaller of recent years—but to satisfy the most modest wants something is required, and we have nothing."

Again he paused, and again something like the ghost of a smile flitted across his face. By this time the boys were listening with their eyes and ears, and Mr. Shane and Mr. Till listened with the rest.

"I am a ruined schoolmaster. I should not have told you this—it is not a pleasant thing to have to tell—only my ruin is so complete, and so near. It will necessitate your returning home at once. Mecklemburg House will no longer be able to offer shelter to either you or I, and I—I was born here; you will perhaps be able to go with lighter hearts. I have communicated with your parents. You must pack your things at once; some of you will, perhaps, be fetched in an hour or two. I have advised your parents that you had better be all of you removed by to-morrow morning at the latest. Under these circumstances there will, of course, be no morning school; nor, indeed, in Mecklemburg House any more school at any time."

Perhaps, in that schoolroom, the silence had never been so marked as it was when Mr. Fletcher ceased. The boys looked at each other, and at their master, scarcely understanding what it was that he had said, and by no means certain that they were entitled to believe their ears. No morning school! Mecklemburg House ceased to exist! Pack up! Going home at once! These things were marvellous in their eyes. There were those among them who had not failed to see the way in which things were tending, who knew that Mecklemburg House was very far from being what it was, that the glory was departed; but for such a thunderclap as this they were wholly unprepared. Pack up! Going home at once! The boys could do nothing else but stare.

"You will disperse now, and go into the playground. Put your books away quietly You will be called in as you are wanted to assist in packing."

They put their books away. It was unnecessary to bid them do it quietly; their demeanour had never been so decorous. Then they filed out silently, one after the other, and the headmaster and his ushers were left alone.

One boy there was who walked out of that schoolroom as though he were walking in a dream. This was Bailey. It was all wonderful to him. He was watching for an opportunity to fly—he knew not why, he knew not where; but that is by the way. He had only begun to watch an hour or two ago, and here was the opportunity thrust into his hand. He never doubted for an instant that here was the opportunity thrust into his hand.

It was now or never. He had reasons of his own for knowing that when he had left Mecklemburg House he had left boarding-school for ever. He might have a term or two at a day-school, but what was the use of running away from a school of that description? It was heroic to run away from boarding-school, but from day-school—where was the heroic quantity in that? No, it was now or never, and Bertie Bailey resolved it should be now. So in a secluded corner of the playground he matured his adventurous scheme; for even he was not prepared to rush through the playground gate and dash into the world upon the spot.

"I must get some money."

So much he decided. It may be mentioned that he arrived at this decision first of all. It may be added that his consciousness of the desirability of getting money was not lessened by the fact that he possessed none now; no, not so much as a specimen of the smallest copper coinage of the realm.

"I must try to borrow some from some of the chaps." He was aware that this was not a hopeful field. "But a fellow can't go without any money at all; even Mr. Bankes said he had ninepence-halfpenny." He remembered every word which Mr. Bankes had said. "Wheeler had sevenpence, and he promised to lend me twopence, but he's such a selfish beast I shouldn't be surprised if he's changed his mind. Besides, I ought to have more than twopence, or sevenpence, either. Perhaps he might lend me the lot; he's not a bad sort sometimes. Anyhow, I'll try."

He tried. Slipping his arm through Wheeler's he drew him on one side. He approached the matter diplomatically.

"I say, Wheeler, I know you're a trump."

This sort of diplomacy was a mistake; Wheeler was at once on the alert.

"What are you buttering me up for? Don't you think you're going to get anything out of me, because you just aren't; so now you know it."

This was abrupt, not to say a little brutal, perhaps. Bailey perceived the error he had made; he changed his tone with singular presence of mind.

"Look here, Wheeler, I want you to lend me that sevenpence of yours."

"Then you'll have to want; I like your cheek!"

"Lend me sixpence."

"I won't lend you a sight of a farthing."

"You promised to lend me twopence."

"Oh, did I? Then I won't. I'm going to buy sevenpenn'orth of cocoanut candy, and perhaps I'll give you a bit of that, though I don't promise, mind; and it'll only be a little bit, anyhow."

"But look here, I want it for something—I do, I really do, or else I wouldn't ask you for it."

"What do you want it for?" asked Wheeler, struck by something in the other's tone.

"Oh! for something particular."

"What do you want it for? If you tell me, perhaps I'll lend it."

This was a bait; but Bailey did not trust his friend so completely as he might have done. He suspected that if he told him what it really was wanted for, the story might be all over the playground in a minute; and it was possible that his friends might not view his intended flight from the heroic point of view from which it appeared to him. So he temporized.

"If you'll lend me the sevenpence first, I'll tell you afterwards."

"You catch me at it! What do I want to know what you want it for? I know I want it myself, and that's quite enough for me."

Wheeler turned away; Bailey caught him by the arm.

"Lend me the twopence which you promised."

"I won't lend you a brass farthing."

Bertie felt the moment was not propitious. It occurred to him that he might pick a quarrel with his friend and fight him, and that when he had fought him long enough his friend might see things in a different light, and a loan might be arranged. But of this he was by no means certain. He was not clear in his own mind as to the amount of hammering which would be required to bring about a conversion. He had never measured his strength with Wheeler; and it even occurred to him that he might be the hammered one, and not his friend. On the whole, he thought that he had better leave that scheme untried; sevenpence might be bought too dearly.

Baffled in one quarter he tried another. In quest of money he buttonholed all the school. But this, again, was a mistaken step. It soon got about that Bailey was in search of some one to devour, and, in consequence, those who were worth devouring took the hint—they by no means showed themselves anxious to be devoured. In spite of his repeated efforts, he only met with one success, and that was one of which he was scarcely entitled to be proud.

Willie Seymour, Bailey's cousin, has been already mentioned. He was the youngster who led Mr. Shane's German grammar on its final road to ruin. A little pale-faced boy, certainly not more than nine years old, and without even the strength of his years.

Bertie caught him by the jacket.

"Now then, where's that money of yours?"

His temper was not improved by the want of confidence his friends had shown, and this was not a case in which he thought delicacy was required.

"What money? Bertie, don't! you're hurting my arm!"

"Yes, and I'll hurt it, too! Where's that money of yours? I know you've got some."

"I've only got one and fivepence. Mamma sent it me last week to buy a birthday present. It was my birthday, you know."

"Oh, was it! Then I'll buy you a birthday present—something spiffing. Fork it up!"

"But, Bertie—"

"Fork it up!"

"It's in my desk."

"Then just you let me see your desk. It's never safe to leave money in your desk; it might get stolen."

And Bailey dragged his relative indoors. It may be mentioned that Willie's mother (Bertie's aunt) had particularly commended her lad to Bertie's care. This was the first symptom of a careful disposition he had shown.

Chapter IX

THE START

With tears and sighs Willie Seymour produced his desk for his relative's inspection. It was a little rosewood desk which his mother had given him to keep his papers in, and envelopes, and his own particular pens, and his stamps, and his money, and his treasures. Bailey proceeded to inspect it.

"Where's the key?"

"Don't take the money, Bertie. Mamma sent it me to buy a birthday present with, and I've spent sevenpence already. It was two shillings she sent."

"Oh, you've spent sevenpence, have you! Then I've half a mind to give you a licking for spending such a lot. Do you think your mother sent you money to chuck about all over the place? She told me to look after you, and so I will. Give me the key."

From a miscellaneous collection of odds and ends, which bulged out the pockets of his knickerbockers, the key was produced.

"Don't take the money, Bertie!"

Bailey unlocked the desk with a magisterial air.

"If your mother knew that you'd spent sevenpence, what d'ye think she'd say to me? She'd say, 'I told you to look after him, and here you let him go chucking the money I sent him to buy a birthday present into his stomach, and making himself as ill as I don't know what! Is that the way to buy a birthday present? Nice affectionate lad you are!'"

At this point Bailey, having discovered the one and fivepence, held it in his hand.

"I shall put this money into my pockets, and I shall take care of it for you, and when you want it, you come to me and ask for it. D'ye hear?"

At this point he slipped the money into his trousers pocket.

Willie wept.

"What are you snivelling for? If you don't stop I'll take care of your desk as well. Now I think of it, Wheeler wants just such a desk as this. I shouldn't be surprised if he gave me sevenpence for it; it would just come in handy."

Bailey subjected the desk to a critical examination.

"I'll tell Mr. Fletcher if you take my desk away."

"What, sneak, would you? As it happens, I don't care for you or Mr. Fletcher either."

Bertie tucked the desk under his arm and moved to the door. Willie flung his head upon his arms and burst into a passion of tears. At the door Bertie turned and surveyed the child.

"Here, take your desk. Think I want the thing!"

He flung the desk towards his cousin. Falling on the edge of a form, it burst open, and the contents were thrown out of it. Leaving Willie to make the best of a bad case, and pick up his ill-used property, Bertie marched away with the one and fivepence in his pocket.

That one and fivepence was all the cash he could secure. He made one or two efforts in the course of the day to increase his capital by the addition of a penny or two, but the efforts were in vain. None of the smaller boys had any money; some of the seniors he suspected were in possession of funds, but in face of their refusal to oblige him with a temporary loan he did not feel justified in taking them by the throats and putting into practice any theory of their money or their life. He suspected he might get neither; sundry knocks and bruises he might be the richer for, but they were riches for which he had no longing. One particularly gallant attack he made upon a suspected seat of capital does not deserve to go unchronicled.

The suspected seat of capital was Mr. Shane. Chancing to pass the schoolroom on his way downstairs, a glimpse he caught of some one within brought him to a standstill. He entered; he shut the door behind him for precaution's sake, being unwilling that his friends should intrude upon what he perceived might be a delicate interview.

In a corner of the schoolroom was Mr. Shane. He sat with his elbows resting on the desk and his head resting on his hands. So absorbed was he in his own meditations that he paid no heed to Bailey's entrance. Bertie watched him in silence for a moment or two, then he made his presence known.

"I say, Mr. Shane."

Mr. Shane started and looked up. His face was very pale, there were traces of what were suspiciously like tears about his eyes, and his whole appearance was as of one who had received a sudden blow. Without speaking he stared at Bailey, whose presence evidently took him by surprise. Seeing that the other held his peace, Bertie came to the point.

"Can you lend me a shilling or two?"

"Lend you a shilling or two!"

73

"I daresay you'll think it like my cheek to ask you, and so it is; but—I'm in an awful hole, I really am. I know I've not been such a civil beggar as I might have been, but—I never meant any harm; and—I'm sorry about that grammar, I really am; I'd buy you another if I'd got the money, upon my word I would —I don't know what I wouldn't do for you if you'd lend me a shilling or two —especially if you'd make it three."

In spite of himself Bertie grinned, and his eyes glistened at the idea of spoiling the usher. Mr. Shane stared at him, as well he might. He spoke with a sort of little pause between each word, as though he were doubtful if he had heard aright.

"You want me to lend you a shilling or two?—me?"

"Yes. I'll let you have it back as soon as, I can, and I'm in an awful hole, or I wouldn't ask you. Do lend it me!"

Mr. Shane stood up, with a curious agitation in his air.

"I haven't got it."

"Not got it I Not got a shilling or two! Oh, I say, come!"

"I haven't got a penny in the world."

"Not got a penny in the world! Oh, I say, aren't you piling it on!"

"Not a penny; not a penny in the world; not one. I'm a beggar!"

Mr. Shane's agitation was so curious, and the air with which he proclaimed himself a beggar was so wild, that Bertie's surprise grew apace. He wondered whether, as he might himself have phrased it, the usher had a tile loose in his head.

"See!" Mr. Shane turned his coat-tail pockets inside out. There was nothing in them. "See!" He followed suit with the pockets in his trousers. They also were void and empty. "Nothing! nothing! not a sou! Mr. Fletcher engaged to pay me sixteen pounds a year. There's fifteen shillings owing from last term. I couldn't afford to buy myself a pair of boots when I came back. Look at my boots." Mr. Shane held up his boots, one after the other. Bertie stared at them; they were very much the worse for wear. "And now he tells me that I'm to leave this very day, leave in the very middle of the term, without a penny-piece. He says he cannot let me have a penny-piece. I've worked hard for my money; he knows I've worked hard for my money; he knows I've been cruelly used; and yet he sends me away in the middle of the term a beggar, and with fifteen shillings owing from last term. What am I to do! My mother lives at Braintree. I can't walk all the way to Braintree in Essex, especially in such boots as these; and she hasn't any money to give me when I get there, and I can't get another situation in the middle of the term. It's cruel, cruel, cruel! I'm a beggar, and I shall have to go to the workhouse and sleep in the casual ward, and break stones before they let me leave in the morning. It's wicked cruelty! I don't care who hears me say it, so it is!"

Mr. Shane's agitation, though real enough, was also sufficiently grotesque. With his pockets turned inside out, and his collar and necktie all awry, he paced about the schoolroom, swinging his arms, speaking in his thin, cracked tones, the tears running down his cheeks, half choked with passion. It was the grotesque side of the usher's woe which appealed to Bailey.

"You don't mean to say Mr. Fletcher won't pay you your wages?"

"I do, I do! He says he hasn't got it; he says he doubts if he has five shillings to call his own. What right has he to engage an usher if he has not got five shillings of his own? How does he expect to pay me, and fifteen shillings owing from last term? How am I to walk to Braintree in Essex in these boots without a penny in my pocket? and what will my mother say when I get home—if I ever do get home—with no money in my pocket, and turned out of a situation in the middle of a term? It's a cruel, wicked shame, and I'll shout it out in the middle of the road! I don't care what they say, I will! I won't go without my money, if it's only the fifteen shillings left owing from last term!"

"Then I suppose you can't lend me a shilling or two?"

"Lend you a shilling or two! How can I? It's for you to advance a loan to me. Bailey, you've been a wicked boy to me ever since I came, and now to come and ask me to lend you money! You're all wicked about the place."

"I've got one and fivepence." Bailey held the money in his hand.

"One and fivepence! Bailey, it's your duty to lend me that one and fivepence. You can't want money, your parents will send you the means to take you home. And here am I without a penny. How am I to walk all the way to Braintree in Essex in these boots without a penny in my pocket? It is a wicked thing that I should ever have been induced to accept such a situation. It's your duty to make amends for your uniform bad conduct, and to sympathise with me in my distress. You ought to lend me that one and fivepence. Won't you lend it to me, Bailey?"

Bertie went through the familiar pantomime of putting his fingers to his nose.

"Me lend you one and fivepence—ax your grandmother! You must think me jolly green."

He thrust the hand which still held the one and fivepence into his trousers pocket, and turning on his heel marched with an air of great deliberation to the door. At the door he turned, and again addressed the usher.

"If I were you, old Shane, I'd go to Fletcher, and I'd say, 'Fork up, Fletcher, or I'll give you one in the eye;' and then if he didn't fork up I'd give him a couple of good fine black ones. He'd look nice with a couple of black eyes, would Fletcher; and, if you like, I'll come with you now and see you do it."

He paused; but seeing that Mr. Shane gave no immediate signs of acting on this useful hint he went on,—

"You haven't got the spirit of an old dead donkey. You'd let anybody have a kick at you. You're a regular all-round Molly, Shane."

With this frank expression of heart-felt sympathy for Mr. Shane's distress he left the room, and banged the door behind him. His enterprise, though displaying boldness, had been a failure; he had not succeeded in adding to his capital. As he walked away from the schoolroom he meditated upon the matter.

"One and fivepence isn't much—not to run away with—but Mr. Bankes said he'd only ninepence-halfpenny; I'm better than that. Still, I'd like another shilling or two; one and fivepence doesn't go far, stretch it how you will. But if I can't get more I'll make it do, somehow. If Mr. Bankes managed with ninepence-halfpenny I don't see why I shouldn't do with one and fivepence. Something is sure to turn up directly I am off."

It occurred to him that perhaps Mr. Bankes might have had something else besides his ninepence-halfpenny—something in the shape of food, valuables, or extra clothing, or some other unconsidered trifle of that kind. Bertie perceived that if he put into execution his plan of immediate flight he would have to go as he was, with his one and fivepence and nothing else. He had a misty recollection of having read somewhere of a young gentleman, just such another hero as himself, who started on his exploration of the world with baggage in the shape of a red cotton handkerchief, which contained a clean shirt, some bread and cheese, and, if his memory served him, a pair of socks which his little sister had neatly darned for him on the night before his setting out.

Bertie would have to start without even this amount of luggage. Nor could he understand that he would be much worse off on that account; the bread and cheese might be useful—if he remembered rightly, the young gentleman referred to had eaten his bread and cheese about ten minutes after starting— but for the shirt and socks he could perceive no use whatever. He had a sort of idea that either those sort of things would not be required, or else that they could be had for asking when he was once out in the world.

But his chief fear was, and it kept him on tenter hooks throughout the day, that his grand exploit would be nipped in the bud, altogether frustrated, by his being prematurely fetched home. He lived at Upton, a little town in Berkshire, not twenty miles away. It would not take long for Mr. Fletcher's communication to reach his home, and it was quite within the range of possibility that a messenger would be immediately despatched to fetch him. In that case he would sleep that night in a paternal bed, and farewell to the Land of Golden Dreams.

The flitting had already commenced. By the afternoon some of the boys, who lived close by, had already gone. The packing progressed briskly. He had seen with his own eyes his boxes locked and corded. It was with very mixed sensations that he had himself assisted at the process. Within those well-worn receptacles was he locking and cording the Land of Golden Dreams! At the mere thought of such a thing he could have shed unheroic tears. At any moment he might be called, he might be greeted by a familiar face, he might be whirled away in a cab at the rate of four or five miles an hour, with his luggage on the roof of the vehicle, and then—farewell to the Land of Golden Dreams.

He might have put an end to his uncertainty by starting at once on his progress through the world. But he had made up his mind that that was not the thing. To run away in broad daylight, like an urchin who had stolen a twopenny loaf, with half a dozen yelping curs at his heels and not impossibly the country folks all grinning—who could connect romance with such an undignified departure? No, night was the thing for him—silent, mysterious night; and, above all, the witching hour. That was the time for romance! Under the cold white moon, and across the moonlit meadows, when all the world was sleeping—then he could conceive a flight into the world of mystery and of magic, and of Lands of Golden Dreams. So he had decided that as nearly as possible midnight should be the moment for his adventures to begin.

The choice of such an hour put difficulties in his way. First of all, there was the difficulty of being sure of the time. He did not himself possess a watch, and he could not rely upon some distant church clock informing him of the passage of the night. Fortunately he remembered that Tom Graham, who slept in a bed next door but one to his, possessed a watch. He would time his departure by Tom Graham's watch. Then there was the difficulty of egress —how was he to get away? In his strong desire to play the more heroic part, he would have liked to have dropped from the window of his bedroom some thirty-five feet on to the paving-stones of the courtyard below. But then he reflected that he would not improbably break his neck, and it would be just as well not to begin his adventures by doing that; that sort of thing would come in its proper place a little later on. He might knot his sheets together, and form an impromptu rope, and descend by means of that: there were charms about the idea which commended themselves to him. He had seen a picture somewhere of a gallant youth descending by means of such a rope a tower apparently a mile or two in height; it was an unpleasant night and the youth was whirled hither and thither by the tempestuous winds. Had his bedroom been a couple of miles from the ground, why then—Bailey smacked his lips, and his eyes glistened—but as it wasn't he discarded the idea. He sighed to think that they build none of those lofty towers now—at least, so far as he was aware.

No; for the present it was sufficient to get away. Let him first get clear away, and then he would have adventures fast enough. He decided that the old familiar schoolroom window would suffice for the occasion. He would get out of that.

But the chief difficulty he had to face was the terrible risk which existed of his being fetched away. One boy after another went; hour after hour passed; a bare handful of young gentlemen remained. They had dinner, such as it was; but Bertie had lost his appetite, and was for the nonce contented with meagre fare. They had tea, which was postponed to the latest possible hour, and which when it came consisted of a liquid which such boys as partook of it declared was concocted of the tea leaves which had remained at breakfast, and which was accompanied by thick slices of unbuttered bread. But Bertie never grumbled; he ate his bread and he drank his tea without suggesting anything against its quality.

The evening passed. The number of boys was still more diminished, yet for Bailey no one came. The clock pointed to an hour at which it was declared that no one could come now—it was half-past nine. The usual hour for bed was half-past eight, but the boys had been kept up in the expectation and possible hope that at Mecklemburg House it would not be necessary for them to go to bed at all. Now they were ordered to their rooms.

Bertie could have danced, and sung, and stood on his head, and comported himself generally like a juvenile madman; but he refrained, His time was coming; he would be able to comport himself as he liked in two hours and a half, but at present the word was caution.

It was arranged that all the boys who remained should sleep in the same room. There were only five: Edgar Wheeler, Tom Graham, little Willie Seymour, a boy whose parents were in India named Hagen, and commonly called Blackamoor, and Bertie Bailey. The first into bed was Bailey. Not a word was to be got out of him edgeways. He was a model of good behaviour. He even pressed the others to hurry into bed, to go to sleep, to let him sleep. They slept long before he did. He lay awake tingling all over. He listened to their regular respirations—Hagen was a loud snorer and always set up a signal of distress—and when he was sure they were asleep he hugged himself in bed. Then he sat up, being careful to make as little noise as possible, and in the darkness peered at his sleeping comrades. Their gentle breathing and Hagen's stentorian snores were music in his ears. Then he lay back in bed again, biding his time.

He heard a clock strike the half-hour—half-past ten. It was a church clock. He wondered which. The night was calm, and the sound travelled clearly through the air; it might have been a long way off. And then—then he went to sleep.

It was not at all what he intended—very much the other way. He had supposed that he had only to make up his mind to lie awake till twelve o'clock to do it. But he was wrong; the strain at which he had kept his faculties through the day had told upon him more than he had supposed.

He awoke with a start—with a consciousness that something was wrong. He listened for a moment, wondering what strange thing had roused him. Then he remembered with a flash. The time had gone and he had slept.

With a half-stifled cry he sprang up in bed. What time was it? Had he really slept? Only for a minute or two, he felt sure. He groped his way to Graham's bed. That young gentleman slept with his watch beneath his pillow; Bailey was awkward in his attempts to get at it without waking the sleepy owner.

He got it, and took it to the window that he might see the time. Half-past two! soon it would be light—Bertie was almost inclined to think it was getting lighter now. He gave a cry of rage, and the watch dropped from his hand to the floor. Startled, he turned to see if the sleepers were awakened by the noise. He held his breath to listen. They slumbered as before. He picked up the watch and placed it on the mantelshelf, not caring to run the risk of rousing Graham by replacing it beneath his pillow. As he did so, he noticed that the glass was broken, shattered in the fall.

With great rapidity he dressed himself, only pausing for a moment to see that the one and fivepence was safe. His slippers were packed; he had come to bed in his boots. Holding them in his hand, in his stockinged feet he stole across the room, carefully turned the handle of the door, went out, and shut the door behind him.

He met with no accident on his way to the schoolroom. Within five minutes of his leaving his bed he was standing among the desks and forms. The blinds had not been drawn: the moonlight flooded the room—at any rate, the moon had not gone down. He was going to carry out so much of his plans —he was to fly through a moonlit world. Perhaps after all the little accident which had caused him to shut his eyes was not of much importance. Certainly, the sleep had refreshed him; he felt capable of making for the Land of Golden Dreams without requiring to pause upon the way.

Among the moonlit desks and forms he put his boots on; laced them up; then, with a careful hand, slipped the hasp of the familiar window, raised the sash, got out, and lowered himself to the ground. It was only when he was on the ground that he remembered that he was without a cap. He put his hand into the inner pocket of his jacket and produced an old cricket cap which he had privately secured when he was supposed to be assisting at the packing.

Then he started for the Land of Golden Dreams.

Chapter X

ANOTHER LITTLE DRIVE

He ran across the courtyard, glancing up at the silent house behind him. In the moonlight Mecklemburg House looked like a house of the dead. Through the gate, and out into the road; then, for a moment, Bertie paused.

"Which way shall I go?"

He stood, hesitating, looking up and down the road. In his anxiety to reach the Land of Golden Dreams he had not paused to consider which was the road he had to take to get there. Such a detail had not occurred to him. He had taken it for granted that the road would choose itself; now he perceived that he had to choose the road.

"I'll go to London—something's sure to turn up when I get there. It always does. In London all sorts of things happen to a fellow."

His right hand in his pocket, clasping his one and fivepence, he turned his face towards Cobham. He had a vague idea that to reach town one had to get to Kingston, and he knew that through Cobham and Esher was the road to Kingston. If he kept to the road the way was easy, he had simply to keep straight on. He had pictured himself flying across the moonlit fields; but he concluded that, for the present, at any rate, he had better confine himself to the plain broad road.

The weather was glorious. It was just about that time when the night is about to give way to the morning, and there is that peculiar chill abroad in the world which, even in the height of summer, ushers in the dawn. It was as light as day—indeed, very soon it would be day; already in the eastern heavens were premonitory gleams of the approaching sun. But at present a moon which was almost at the full held undisputed reign in the cloudless sky. So bright were her rays that the stars were dimmed. All the world was flooded with her light. All was still, except the footsteps of the boy beating time upon the road. Not a sound was heard, nor was there any living thing in sight with the exception of the lad. Bertie Bailey had it all to himself.

Bertie strode along the Cobham road at a speed which he believed to be first rate, but which was probably under four miles an hour. Every now and then he broke into a trot, but as a rule he confined himself to walking. Conscious that he would not be missed till several hours had passed, he told himself that he would have plenty of time to place himself beyond reach of re-capture before pursuit could follow. Secure in this belief, every now and then he stopped and looked about him on the road.

He was filled with a sense of strange excitement. He did not show this in his outward bearing, for nature had formed his person in an impassive mould, and he was never able to dispossess himself of an air of phlegm. An ordinary observer would have said that this young gentleman was constitutionally heavy and dull, and impervious to strong feeling of any sort. Mr. Fletcher, for instance, had been wont to declare that Bailey was his dullest pupil, and in continual possession of the demons of obstinacy and sulkiness. Yet, on this occasion, at least, Bailey was on fire with a variety of feelings to every one of which Mr. Fletcher would have deemed him of necessity a stranger.

It seemed to him, as he walked on and on, that he walked in fairyland. He was conscious of a thousand things which were imperceptible to his outward sense. His heart seemed too light for his bosom; to soar out of it; to bear him to a land of visions. That Land of Golden Dreams towards which he travelled he had already reached with his mind's eye, and that before he had gone a mile upon the road to Cobham.

Mecklemburg House was already a thing of the past That petty poring over books, which some call study, and which Mr. George Washington Bankes had declared was such a culpable waste of time, was gone for ever. No more books for him; no more school; no more rubbish of any kind. The world was at his feet for him to pick and choose.

By the time he had got to Cobham he was making up his mind as to the particular line of heroism to which he would apply himself. The old town, for Cobham calls itself a town, was still and silent, apparently unconscious of the glorious morning which was dawning on the world, and certainly unconscious of the young gentleman who was passing through its pleasant street, scheming schemes which, when brought to full fruition, would proclaim him a hero in the sight of a universe of men.

"I'll be a highwayman; I'd like to be; I will be. If a coach and four were to come along the road this minute I'd stop the horses. Yes! and I'd set one of them loose, and I'd mount it, and I'd go to the window of the coach, and I'd say, 'Stand and deliver.' And I'd make them hand over all they'd got, watches, purses, jewellery, everything—I shouldn't care if it was £10,000."

He fingered the one and fivepence in his pocket; the sound of the rattling coppers fired his blood.

"And then I'd dash away on the horse's back, and I'd buy a ship, and I'd man it with a first-rate crew, and I'd sink it in the middle of the sea. And, first of all, I'd fill the long-boat with everything that I could want—guns, and pistols, and revolvers, and swords, and bullets, and powder, and cartridges and things—and I'd get into it alone, and I'd say farewell to the sinking ship and crew, and I'd row off to a desert island, and I'd stop there five-and-twenty years. Yes; and I'd tame all the birds and animals and things, and I'd be happy as a king. And then I'd come away."

He did not pause to consider how he was to come away; but that was a detail too trivial to deserve consideration. By this time Cobham was being left behind; but he saw nothing save the life which was to be after he had left that desert isle.

"I'd go to Sherwood Forest, and I'd live under the greenwood tree, and I'd form a band of robbers, and I'd have them dressed in green, and I'd seize the Archbishop of Canterbury, and I'd make him fight me with single-sticks, and I'd let the beggars go, and I'd give the poor all the booty that I got."

What the rest of the band would say to this generous distribution of their hard-earned gains was another detail which escaped consideration.

"And I'd be the oppressor of the rich and the champion of the poor, and I'd make everybody happy." How the rich were to be made happy by oppression it is difficult to see; but so few systems of philosophy bear a rigorous examination. "And I'd have peace and plenty through the land, and I'd have lots of fighting, and if there was anybody in prison I'd break the prisons open and I'd let the prisoners out, and I'd be Ruler of the Greenwood Tree."

His thoughts turned to Jack the Giant-Killer. By now the day was really breaking, and with the rising sun his spirits rose still higher. The moonlight merging into the sunshine filled the country with a rosy haze, which was just the kind of thing for magic.

"I wish there still were fairies."

If he only had had the eyes no fairyland would have been more beautiful than the world just then.

"No, I don't exactly wish that there were fairies—fairies are such stuff; but I wish that there were giants and all that kind of thing. And I wish that I had a magic sword, and a purse that was always more full the more you emptied it, and that I could walk ten thousand miles a day. I wish that you had only got to wish for a thing to get it—wouldn't I just start wishing! I don't know what I wouldn't wish for."

He did not. The catalogue would have filled a volume.

"But the chief thing for which I'd wish would be to be exactly where I am, and to be going exactly where I'm going to."

He laughed, and thrust his hands deeper in his pockets when he thought of this, and was so possessed by his emotions that he kicked up his heels and began to dance a sort of fandango in the middle of the road. He perceived that it was a pleasant thing to wish to be exactly where he was, and to be so well satisfied with the journey's end he had in view. It is not every boy who is bound for the Land of Golden Dreams; and especially by the short cut which reaches it by way of the Cobham road.

So far he had not met a single human being, nor seen a sign, nor heard a sound of one. But when he had fairly left Cobham in the rear, and was yet engaged in the performance of that dance which resembled the fandango, he heard behind him the sound of wheels rapidly approaching. They were yet a considerable distance off, but they were approaching so swiftly that one's first thought was that a luckless driver was being run away with. When Bertie heard them first he started. His thought was of pursuit; his impulse was to scramble into an adjoining field, and to hide behind a hedge. It would be terrible to be re-captured in the initiatory stage of his journey to the Land of Golden Dreams.

But his alarm vanished when he turned and looked behind him. The vehicle approaching contained a friend. Even at that distance he recognised it as the dog-cart of Mr. George Washington Bankes. The ungainly-looking beast flying at such a terrific pace along the lonely road was none other than the redoubtable Mary Anne.

In a remarkably short space of time the vehicle was level with Bertie. For a moment the boy wondered if he had been recognised; but the doubt did not linger long, for with startling suddenness Mary Anne was brought to a halt.

"Hallo! Who's that? Haven't I seen you before? Turn round, you youngster, and let me see your face. I know the cut of your jib, or I'm mistaken."

Bertie turned. He looked at Mr. Bankes and Mr. Bankes looked at him. Mr. George Washington Bankes whistled.

"Whew—w—w, if it isn't the boy who stood up to the lout. What's your name?"

"Bailey, sir; Bertie Bailey."

"Oh, yes; Bailey! Early hours, Bailey—taking a stroll, eh? What in thunder brings you here this time of day? I thought good boys like you were fast asleep in bed."

Bailey looked sheepish, and felt it. There was something in the tone of Mr. Bankes' voice which was a little trying. Bertie hung his head, and held his peace.

"Lost your tongue? Poor little dear! Speak up. What are you doing here this time of day?"

"If you please, sir, I'm running away."

"Running away!"

For a moment Mr. Bankes started. Then he burst into a loud and continued roar of laughter, which had an effect upon Bertie very closely resembling that of an extinguisher upon a candle.

"I say, Bailey, what are you running away for?"

Under the circumstances Bertie felt this question cruel. When he had last seen Mr. Bankes the question had been put the other way. He had been treated as a poor-spirited young gentleman because he had not run away already. Plucking up courage, he looked up at his questioner.

"You told me to run away."

The only immediate answer was another roar of laughter. Something very like tears came into the boy's eyes, and his face assumed that characteristically sullen expression for which he was famous. This was not the sort of treatment he had expected.

"You don't mean to say—now look me in the face, youngster—you don't mean to say that you're running away because I told you to?"

The last words of the question were spoken very deliberately, with a slight pause between each. Bertie's answer was to the point. He looked up at Mr. Bankes with that sullen, bull-dog look of his, and said,—

"I do."

"And where do you think you're running to?"

"To the Land of Golden Dreams."

There was a sullen obstinacy about the lad's tone, as though the confession was extracted from him against his will.

"To the Land of Golden Dreams! Well! Here, you'd better get up. I'll give you a lift upon the road? and there's a word or two I'd like to say as we are going."

Bertie climbed up to the speaker's side, and Mary Anne was again in motion. The swift travelling through the sweet, fresh morning was pleasant; and as the current of air dashed against his cheeks Bertie's heart began to re-ascend a little. For some moments not a word was spoken; but Bertie felt that Mr. Bankes' big black eyes wandered from Mary Anne to him, and from him to Mary Anne, with a half-mocking, half-curious expression.

"I say, boy, are any of your family lunatics?"

The question was scarcely courteous. Bertie's lips shut close.

"No."

"Quite sure? Now just you think? Anybody on your mother's side just a little touched? They say insanity don't spring to a head at once, but gathers strength through successive generations."

Bailey did not quite understand what was meant; but knowing it was something not exactly complimentary he held his peace.

"Now—straight out—you don't mean to say you're running away because I told you to?"

"Yes, I do."

"And for nothing else?"

Bertie paused for a moment to consider.

"I don't know about nothing else, but I shouldn't have thought of it if you hadn't told me to."

"Then it strikes me the best thing I can do is to turn round and drive you back again."

"I won't go."

Mr. Bankes laughed. There was such a sullen meaning in the boy's slow utterance.

"Oh! won't you? What'll you do?"

In an instant Bertie had risen from his seat, and if Mr. Bankes had not been very quick in putting his arm about him he would have sprung out upon the road. As it was, Mr. Bankes, taken by surprise, gave an unintentional tug at the left rein, and had he not corrected his error with wonderful dexterity Mary Anne would have landed the trap and its occupants in a convenient ditch.

"Don't you try that on again," said Mr. Bankes, retaining his hold on the lad.

"Don't you say you'll drive me back again."

"Here's a fighting cock. There have been lunatics in the family—I know there have. Don't be a little idiot. Sit still."

"Promise you won't drive me back."

"And supposing I won't promise you, what then?"

Bertie's only answer was to give a sudden twist, and before Mr. Bankes had realized what he intended he had slipped out of his grasp, and was sprawling on the road. Fortunately the trap had been brought to a standstill, for had Bertie carried out his original design of springing out with Mary Anne going at full speed, the probabilities are that he would have brought his adventures to a final termination on the spot. Mr. Bankes stared for a moment, and then laughed.

"Well, of all the young ones ever I heard tell of!"

Then, seeing that Bertie had picked himself up, and was preparing to escape by scrambling through a quickset hedge into a field of uncut hay—

"Stop!" he cried. "I won't take you back. I promise you upon my honour I won't. A lad of your kidney's born to be hanged; and if it's hanging you've made up your mind to, I'm not the man to stop you."

The lad eyed him doubtfully.

"You promise you'll let me do as I please?"

"I swear it, my bantam cock. You shall do as you please, and go where you please. I can't stop mooning here all day; jump in, and let's be friends again. I'm square, upon my honour."

The lad resumed his former seat; Mary Anne was once more started.

"Next time you feel it coming on, why, tip me the wink, and I'll pull up. It's a pity that a neck like yours should be broken before the proper time; and if you were to jump out while Mary Anne was travelling like this, why, there'd be nothing left to do but to pick up the pieces."

As Bertie vouchsafed no answer, after a pause Mr. Bankes went on.

"Now, Bailey, joking aside, what is the place you're making for?"

"I'm going to London."

"London. Got any friends there?"

"No."

"Ever been there before?"

"I've been there with father."

"Know anything about it?"

"I don't know much."

"So I should say, by the build of you. I shouldn't be surprised if you know more when you come back again—if you ever do come back again, my bantam. Shall I tell you what generally happens to boys like you who go up to London without knowing much about it, and without any friends there? They generally"—Mr. Bankes, as it were, punctuated these words, laying an emphasis on each—"go under, and they stop under, and there's an end of them."

He paused; if for a reply, in vain, for there was none from Bailey.

"Do you think London's the Land of Golden Dreams? Well, it is; that's exactly what it is—it's the Land of Golden Dreams, and the dreams are short ones, and when you wake from them you're up to your neck in filth, and you wish that you were dead. For they're nothing else but dreams, and the reality is dirt, and shame, and want, and misery, and death."

Again he paused; and again there was no reply from Bertie. "How much money have you got?"

"One and fivepence."

"Is that all?"

"Yes."

"Well! well! I say nothing, but I think a lot. And do you mean to tell me that you're off to London with the sum of one shilling and fivepence in your pocket?"

"You said you ran away with ninepence-halfpenny."

"Well, that's a score! And so I did, but circumstances alter cases, and that was the foolishest thing that ever I did."

"You said it was the most sensible thing you'd ever done."

"You've a remarkable memory—a remarkable memory; and if you keep it up you'll improve as you go on. If I said that, I was a liar—I was the biggest liar that ever lived. I wonder if you could go through the sort of thing that I have done?"

Mr. Bankes' eyes were again fixed on Bertie, as though he would take his measure.

"Most men would have been dead a dozen times. I don't know that I haven't been; I know I've often wished that I could have died just once—that I could have been wiped clean out. God save you, young one, from such a life as mine. Pray God to pull you up in time."

Another pause and then—

"What's your plans?"

"I don't know."

"I shouldn't think you did by the look of you. And how long do you suppose you're going to live, on the sum of one and fivepence?"

"I don't know."

"Well, I should say that with economy you could manage to live two hours —perhaps a little more, perhaps a little less; that's to say, an hour before you have your dinner and an hour after. Some could manage to stretch it out to tea, but you're not one. And when the money's gone how do you suppose you're going to get some more?"

"I don't know."

"Now don't you think that I'd better turn Mary Anne right round, and take you back again? You've had a pleasant little drive, you know, and the morning air's refreshing."

"I won't go, and you promised that you wouldn't."

"You'll wish you had about this time to-morrow; and perhaps a little before. However, a promise is a promise, so on we go. Know where you are?"

Bailey did not; Mr. Bankes had turned some sharp corners, and having left the highroad behind was guiding Mary Anne along a narrow lane in which there was scarcely room for two vehicles to pass abreast.

"These are the Ember lanes. There's East Molesey right ahead, then the Thames, then Hampton Court, and then I'll have to leave you. I've come round this way to stretch the old girl's legs." This was a graceful allusion to Mary Anne. "My shortest cut would have been across Walton Bridge, as I'm off to Kempton to see a trial of a horse in which I'm interested; so when I get to Hampton Court I'll have to go some of my way back again. Now make up your mind. There isn't much time left to do it in. Say the word, and I'll take you all the way along with me, and land you back just where you started. Take a hint, and think a bit before you speak."

Apparently Bertie took the hint, for it was a moment or two before he answered.

"I'm not going back."

"Very well. That's the last time of asking, so I wish you joy on your journey to the Land of the Golden Dreams."

Chapter XI

THE ORIGINAL BADGER

As Mr. Bankes spoke, Mary Anne dashed over the little bridge which spans the Mole, and in another second they were passing through East Molesey. Nothing was said as they raced through the devious village street. The world in East Molesey was just beginning to think of waking up. A few labourers were visible, on their road to work. When they reached the river, some of the watermen were preparing their boats, putting them ship-shape for the day, and on Tagg's Island there were signs of life.

Over Hampton Court Bridge flew Mary Anne; past the barracks, where there were more signs of life, and where Hussars were recommencing the slightly monotonous routine of a warrior's life, and then the mare was brought to a sudden standstill at the corner of the green.

"The parting of the ways—you go yours, and I go mine, and I rather reckon, young one, it won't be long before you wish there'd been no parting, and we'd both rolled on together. Which way are you going to London?"

"I thought about going through Kingston."

"All right, you can either go through Bushy Park here, or you can go Kingston way. But don't let me say a word about the road you go, especially as it don't seem to me to matter which it is—round by the North Pole and Timbuctoo for all I care, for you're in no sort of hurry, and all you want is to get there in the end."

"Can't I get to Kingston by the river?"

"Certainly. You go through the barrack yard there, and through the little gate which you'll see over at the end on your right, and you'll be on the towing-path. And then you've only got to follow your nose and you'll get to Kingston Bridge, and there you are. The nearest is by Frog's Walk here, along by the walls, but please yourself."

"I'd sooner go by the river."

"All right."

Mr. Bankes put his hand into his trousers pocket, and when he pulled it out it was full of money.

"Look here, it seems that I've had a hand in this little scrape, though I'd no more idea you'd swallow every word of what I said than I had of flying.

90

You're about as fine a bunch of greens as ever I encountered, and that's the truth. But, anyhow, I had a hand, and as I'm a partner in the spree I'm not going to sort you all the kicks and collar all the halfpence. And I tell you"— Mr. Bankes raised his voice to a very loud key, as though Bailey was arguing the point instead of sitting perfectly still—"I tell you that for a boy like you to cut and run with the sum of one and fivepence in his pocket is a thing I'm not going to stand. No, not on any account, so hold out your hand, you leather-headed noodle, and pocket this."

Bertie held out his hand, Mr. Bankes counted into it five separate sovereigns.

"Now sling your hook!"

Before Bertie had a chance to thank him, or even to realize the sudden windfall he had encountered, Mr. Bankes had caught hold of him, lifted him bodily from his seat, and placed him on the road. Mary Anne had started, and the trap was flying past the Cardinal Wolsey, on the Hampton Road. Left standing there, with the five sovereigns tightly grasped in his palm, Bailey decided that Mr. Bankes had rather a sudden way of doing things.

He remained motionless a minute watching the receding trap. Perhaps he expected, perhaps he hoped, that Mr. Bankes would look round and wave him a parting greeting; but there was nothing of the kind. In a very short space of time the trap was out of sight and he was left alone. Just for that instant, just for that first moment, in which he realized his solitude, he regretted that he had not acted on his late companion's advice, and pursued the journey with Mary Anne. Then he looked at the five pounds he held in his hand.

"Well, here's a go!"

He could scarcely believe his eyes. He took up each of the coins separately and examined it. Then he placed them in a low on his extended palm, and stared. Their radiance dazzled him.

"Catch me going back while I've got all this, I should rather like somebody to see me at it. Five pounds!" Here was a long-drawn respiration. "Fancy him tipping me five pounds! I call that something like a tip. Won't I spend it! Just fancy having five pounds to spend on what you like! Well, I never did!"

"Hallo, you boy, got anything nice to look at?"

Bertie turned. A soldier, in a considerable state of undress, was standing a few yards behind him, watching his proceedings.

"What's that to you?" asked Bertie.

He put both his hands into his trousers pockets, keeping tight hold on the precious sovereigns, and turning, walked up the barrack yard. As he passed, the soldier grinned; but Bertie condescended to pay no heed.

"If I'd had a fortune left to me, I'd stand a man a drink, if it was only the price of half a pint."

This was what the soldier shouted after Bertie. One or two of the troopers who were engaged in various ways, and who were all more or less undressed, looking very different from the dashing pictures of military splendour which they would shortly present upon parade, stared at the boy as he went by, but no one spoke to him.

Once on the towing-path, he turned his face Kingston-wards and hastened on. These five sovereigns burnt a hole in his pocket. When his capital had been represented by the sum of one and fivepence he had been dimly conscious that it would be necessary to be careful in his outlay. He had even outlined a system of expenditure. But five pounds!

They represented boundless wealth. He had been once presented by a grateful patient of his father's with a tip of half a sovereign. That was the largest sum of which he had ever been in possession at one and the same time, and no sooner had the donor's back been turned than his mother had confiscated five shillings of that. She declared that it was intended the half-sovereign should be divided among his brothers and sisters, and the five shillings went in the division. But five pounds! What were five shillings, or even half a sovereign, to five pounds.

If Mr. George Washington Bankes had desired to dissipate whatever effect his words of warning might have had he could not have chosen a surer method. As the possessor of five pounds, Bertie's belief in the land of golden dreams was stronger than ever. The pieces of golden money had as good as transported him thither upon the spot.

His spirits rose to boiling-pitch as he walked beside the river. The sunshine flooded all the world, and danced upon the glancing waters, and filled his heart with joy. As he looked up, the words, "five pounds," seemed streaming in radiant golden letters across the sunlit sky.

Nearly opposite Ditton church he sat down on the grass to revel in his fancies. The castles which he built, the schemes he schemed, the future he foretold! No one passing by, and seeing a boy with an apparently sullen face, sprawling on the grass, would have had the least conception of the world of imagination in which, at that moment, he lived and moved, and had his being.

He lay there perhaps more than an hour. He might have lain there even longer had not two things recalled him to the world of fact. The first was a growing consciousness that he was hungry; and the other, the crossing of the ferry. The Ditton ferry-boat made its first appearance, with two or three young fellows who had seemingly made the passage with a view of enjoying an early morning bathe on the more secluded Middlesex side. When they got out, Bertie got in. Not that he wanted to go to Ditton, nor that he even knew the name of the place which he saw upon the other side of the water, but that he fancied the row across the stream. When he was in the boat a thought struck him.

"How much will you row me to Kingston for?"

"I can't take you in this boat, this here's the ferry-boat; but I can let you have a boat the other side, and a chap to row you, and I'll take you for—do you want to go there and back?"

"No; I want to stop at Kingston."

"Are you going to the fair there? I hear there's to be a fine fair this time, and a circus, and all."

Bertie had neither heard of the fair nor of the circus; but the idea was tempting.

"I shouldn't be surprised if I did go. How much will you row me for?"

The ferryman hesitated. He was probably debating within himself as to the capacity of the young gentleman's pockets, and also not improbably as to his capacity for being bled.

"I'll row you there for five shillings."

But Bertie was not quite so verdant as he looked.

"I'll give you eighteenpence."

"Well, you're a cool hand, you are, to offer a man eighteenpence for what he wants five shillings for. But I don't want to be hard upon a young gentleman what is a young gentleman. I'll row you there for four; a man's got to live, you know, and it isn't as though you wanted a boat to row yourself."

But Bertie was unable to see his way to paying four. Finally a bargain was struck for half a crown. Then a difficulty occurred as to change, and Bertie entrusted one of his precious sovereigns to the ferryman to get changed at the Swan. Then a boat was launched, a lad not very much older than Bertie was placed in charge, the fare was paid in advance, and a start was made for Kingston.

By the time they reached that ancient town, Bertie was hungry in earnest. The walk, the drive, and now the row in the freshness of the early morning had combined to give him an appetite which, at Mecklemburg House, would have been regarded with considerable disapproval. Now, too, the short commons of the day before were remembered; and as Bertie fingered the money in his pockets he thought with no slight satisfaction of the good things in the eating and drinking line which it would buy.

He was landed at his own request on the Middlesex side of Kingston Bridge, and having generously made the lad who had rowed him richer by the sum of sixpence, he started, with renewed vigour, to cross the bridge into the town. No sooner had he crossed than a coffee-shop met his eye. It was the very thing he wanted. With the air of a capitalist he entered and ordered a sumptuous repast—coffee, bread and butter, ham and eggs. Having made a hearty meal,—and a hearty meal was a subject on which he had ideas of his own, for he followed up the ham and eggs with half a dozen open tarts and a jam puff or two, buying half a pound of sweets to eat when he got outside,— he paid the bill and sallied forth.

It was cattle-market day, and unusual business seemed to be doing. Not only was the market-place crowded with live stock, but they overflowed into the neighbouring streets. For the present, Bertie was content to watch the proceedings. In the position of a capitalist he could travel to London in state and at his leisure. Just now his mind was running on what the ferryman had said about the circus and the fair. He could go to London at any time. It was not a place which was likely to run away. But circuses and fairs were things which were quick to go, and once gone were gone for ever. Bertie resolved that he would commence his journey by seeing both the circus and the fair.

Nor was his resolution weakened by a joyous procession which passed through the Kingston street.

"BADGER'S ROYAL POPULAR COSMOPOLITAN AND WORLD-FAMED HIPPODROME" was an imposing title for a circus, but not more imposing than the glories revealed by that procession.

"*Supported by all the greatest artists in the world chosen from all the nations of the universe*" was the continuation of the title, and, judging from the astonishing variety of ladies and gentlemen who rode the horses, who bestrode the camels, who crowded the triumphal cars, and who ran along on foot distributing handbills among the crowd, it really seemed that the statement was justified by fact. There were Chinamen whose pigtails seemed quite real; there were gentlemen of colour who seemed warranted to wash; there were individuals with beards and moustaches of an altogether foreign character; and there were ladies of the most wondrous and enchanting beauty, dressed in the most picturesque and amazing styles. Bertie Bailey, at any rate, was persuaded that it would be absurd for him to think of going on to town till he had attended at least one performance of Badger's Royal Popular Cosmopolitan and World-famed Hippodrome.

He followed the procession to the fair field. And there, although it was not yet noon, the fair was already in full swing. All those immortal entertainments without which a fair would not be a fair were liberally provided. There were shows, and shooting galleries, and bottle-throwing establishments, and seas upon land, and resplendent roundabouts, and stalls at which were vended goods of the very best quality; and all those joys and raptures which go to make a fair in every part of the world in which fairs are known.

But Bertie cared for none of these things. All his soul was fixed upon the circus. He attended the performance. As befitted a young gentleman of fortune he occupied a front seat, price two shillings. A hypercritical spectator might have suggested that the procession had been the best part of the show. But this was not the case in Bertie's eyes. He was enraptured with the feats of skill and daring which he witnessed in the ring. Only one consideration marred his complete enjoyment. Unfortunately he could not make up his mind whether he would rather be the gentleman who, disdaining all ordinary modes of horsemanship, standing upon the backs of two cream-coloured steeds, with streaming tails, dashed round the ring; or the clown whose business it was—a business which he seemed to think a pleasure—to keep the audience in a roar. He was not so much struck by a gentleman who performed marvels on a flying trapeze; nor by the surefootedness of a lady who walked upon an "invisible wire,"—which was, in this case, a rope about the thickness of Bertie's wrist.

But he quite made up his mind that he would be either the clown or the rider; and that, when he had determined which of these honourable positions he would prefer to fill, he would lose no time in laying siege to one of the ladies of the establishment, and to beg her to be his. But here the same difficulty occurred;—he was not quite certain which. However, by the time the performance was over, and the audience was dismissed, on one point he was assured, he would enlist under the banners of the world-famed Badger. Dick Turpin, Robin Hood, Robinson Crusoe, Jack the Giant Killer, might do for some folks, but a circus was the place for him.

When he regained the open air, and had bidden an unwilling adieu to the sawdust glories, the afternoon was pretty well advanced and the fair was more crowded than ever. But Bertie could not tear himself away from Badger's. He hung about the exterior of the tent as though the neighbourhood was holy ground.

Several other loiterers lingered too; and among them were four or five men who did not look, to put it gently, as though they belonged to what are called the upper classes.

"I've half a mind," said Bertie to himself, "to go inside the tent, and ask Mr. Badger if he wants a boy. But perhaps he wouldn't like to be troubled when there's no performance on."

Bertie's ideas on circus management were rudimentary. Mr. Badger would perhaps have looked a little blue to find himself met with such a request if there had been a performance on.

"What do you think of the circus?"

The question was put by one of the individuals before referred to. He had apparently given his companions the slip, for they stood a little distance off, ostentatiously paying no attention to his proceedings. He was a short man, inclined to stoutness, and Bertie thought he had the reddest face he had ever seen.

"It's not a bad show, is it? And more it didn't ought to be, for the amount of money it cost me to put that show together no one wouldn't believe."

Bertie stared. It dimly occurred to him that it must have cost him all the money he possessed and so left him nothing to throw away upon his clothing, for his costume was distinctly shabby. But the stout man went on affably:—

"I saw you looking round, so I thought as perhaps you took a interest in these here kind of things. Perhaps you don't know who I am?"

Bertie didn't and said so.

"I'm Badger, the Original Badger. I may say the only Badger as was ever known,—for all them other Badgers belongs to another branch of the family."

The Original Badger put his hand to his neck, apparently with the intention of pulling up his shirt collar, which, however, wasn't there. Bertie stared still more. The stout man did not by any means come up to the ideas he had formed of the world-famed Badger.

"You're not the Mr. Badger to whom the circus belongs."

"Ain't I! But I ham, I just ham." The Original Badger's enunciation of the letter was more emphatic than correct.

"And I should like to see the man who says I hain't! I'd fight that man either for beer or money either now or any other time, and I shouldn't care if he was twenty stone. Now look 'ere"—the Original Badger gave Bertie so hearty a slap upon the back that that young gentleman tottered—"What I say is this. I wants a well-built young fellow about your age to learn the riding, and to train for clown, and I wants that young feller to make his first

96

appearance this day three weeks. Now what do you say to being that young feller?"

"I don't think I could learn it in three weeks," was all Bertie could manage to stammer.

"Oh couldn't you? I know better. Now, look 'ere, I'm going to pay that young feller five and twenty pound a week, and find him in his clothing. What do you say to that?"

Bertie would have liked to say a good deal, if he could have only found the words to say it with. Among other things he would probably have liked to have said that he hoped the clothing which was to accompany the five and twenty pounds a week would be of a different sort to that worn by the Original Badger. It would have been a hazardous experiment to have offered five and twenty pence for the stout man's costume.

"Now, look 'ere, there's a house I know close by where you and me can be alone, and we can talk it over. You're just the sort of young feller I've been looking for. Now come along with me and I'll make your fortune for you,—you see if I don't."

Before Bertie quite knew what was happening, the stout man had slipped his arm through his, and was hurrying him through the fair, away from it, and down some narrow streets which were not of the most aristocratic appearance. All the time he kept pouring out such a stream of words that the lad was given no chance to remonstrate, even if he had had presence of mind enough to do it with. But, metaphorically, the Original Badger—to use an expression in vulgar phrase—had knocked him silly.

What exactly happened Bertie never could remember. The Original Badger led him to a very doubtful looking public-house, and, before he knew it, the lad was through the door. They did not go into the public bar, but into a little room beyond. They had scarcely entered when they were joined by three or four more shabby individuals, whom the Original Badger greeted as his friends. If Bertie had looked behind he would have perceived these gentry following close upon his heels all the time.

"This young gentleman's going to stand something to drink. Now, 'Enery William, gin cold."

The order was given by the Original Badger to a shrivelled-up individual without a coat who seemed to act as pot-boy. When this person disappeared, and Bertie was left alone with the Original Badger and his friends, he by no means liked the situation. A more unpleasant looking set of vagabonds could with difficulty be found; and he felt that if these were the sort of gentry who had to do with circuses a circus was not the place for him.

The pot-boy re-appeared with a bottle of water, and a tray of glasses containing gin.

"Two shillings," said the pot-boy.

"All right; the gentleman pays."

"Pay in advance," said the pot-boy.

"Two shillings, captain!"

The Original Badger gave Bertie another of his hearty slaps upon the back. Bertie felt they were too hearty by half. However, he produced a florin, with which the pot-boy disappeared, leaving the glasses on the table.

"I'm going," he said, directly that functionary was gone.

"What, before you've drunk your liquor? You'll never do for a circus, you won't." Bertie felt he wouldn't. "Why, I've got all that business to talk over with you. I'm going to engage this young feller in my circus to do the clowning and the riding for five and twenty pound a week."

The Original Badger cast what was suspiciously like a wink in the direction of his friends. One of these friends handed the glasses round. He lingered a moment with the glass he gave to Bertie before he filled it half-way up with water, then he held it towards the boy. He was a tall, sallow-looking ruffian, with ragged whiskers; the sort of man one would very unwillingly encounter on a lonely road at night.

"Drink that up," he said; "that's the sort of thing for circus riders."

"I don't want to drink the stuff," said Bertie. "Drink it up, you fool!"

The lad hesitated a moment, then emptied the glass at a draught. What happened afterwards he never could describe; for it seemed to him that no sooner had he drunk the contents than he fell asleep; and as he sank into slumber he seemed to hear the sound of laughter ringing in his ears.

Chapter XII

A "DOSS" HOUSE

When he woke it was dark. He did not know where he was. He opened his eyes, which were curiously heavy, and thought he was in a dream. He shut them again, and vainly wondered if he were back at Mecklemburg House or in his home at Upton. He half expected to hear familiar voices. Suddenly there was a crash of instruments; he started up, supporting himself upon his arm, and listened listlessly, still not quite sure he was not dreaming. It was the crash of the circus band; they were playing "God Save the Queen."

Something like consciousness returned. He began to understand his whereabouts. A cool breeze was blowing across his face; he was in the open air; behind him there was a canvas flapping. It was a tent. Around him were discords of every kind. It was night; the fair was in all its glory. He was lying in the fair field.

"Hallo, chappie! coming round again?"

Some one spoke. Looking up, peering through his heavy eyes, he perceived that a lean, ragged figure was leaning over him. Sufficiently roused to dislike further companionship with the Original Badger and his friends, he dragged himself to a sitting posture. The stranger was a lad, not much, if any, older than himself, some ragamuffin of the streets.

"Who are you?" asked Bertie.

"Never mind who I am. I've had my eyes on you this ever so long. Ain't you been a-going it neither. I thought that you was dead. Was it—?"

He gave a suggestive gesture with his hand, as though he emptied a glass into his mouth. Bertie struggled to his feet.

"I—I don't feel quite well."

"You don't look it neither. Whatever have you been doing of?"

Bertie tried to think. He would like to have left his new acquaintance. The Original Badger and his friends had been quite enough for him, but his legs refused their office, and he was perforce compelled to content himself with standing still. He did not feel quite such a hero as he had done before.

"Have you lost anything?"

The chance question brought Bertie back to recollection. He put his hand into his trousers pockets—they were empty. Bewildered, he felt in the pockets of his waistcoat and of his jacket—they were empty, too! Some one had relieved him of everything he possessed, down to his clasp knife and pocket handkerchief. Willie Seymour's one and fivepence, and Mr. Bankes' five pounds, both alike were gone!

"I've been robbed," he said.

"I shouldn't be surprised but what you had. What do you think is going to happen to you if you lies for ever so many hours in the middle of the fair field as if you was dead? How much have you lost?"

"Five pounds."

"Five pounds!—crikey, if you ain't a pretty cove! Are you a-gammoning me?"

Bertie looked at the lad. A thought struck him. He put out his hand and took him by the shoulder.

"You've robbed me," he said.

"You leave me alone! who are you touching of? If you don't leave me alone, I'll make you smart."

"You try it on," said Bertie.

The other tried it on, and with such remarkable celerity, that before he had realized what had happened, Bertie Bailey lay down flat. The stranger showed such science that, in his present half comatose condition, Bailey went down like a log.

"You wouldn't have done that if I'd been all right; and I do believe you've robbed me."

"Believe away! I ain't, so there! I ain't so much as seen the colour of your money, and I don't know nothing at all about it. The first I see of you was about five o'clock. You was a-lying just where you are now, and I've come and had a look at you a dozen times since. Why, it must be ten o'clock, for the circus is out, and you ain't woke up only just this minute. How came you to be lying there?"

"I don't know. I've been robbed, and that's quite enough for me,—my head is aching fit to split."

"Haven't you got any money left?"

"No, I haven't."

"Where's your home?"

"What's that to you?"

"Well, it ain't much to me, but I should think it's a good deal to you. If I was you I'd go home."

"Well, you're not me, so I won't."

"All right, matey, it ain't no odds to me. If you likes lying there till the perlice come and walks you off, it's all the same to me so far as I'm concerned."

"I've got no money; I've been robbed."

"I tell you what I'll do, I ain't a rich chap, not by no manner of means, and I never had five pounds to lose, but I've had a stroke of luck in my small way, and if you really haven't got no home, nor yet no coin, I don't mind standing in for a bed so far as four pence goes."

"I don't know what you mean; leave me alone. I've got no money; I've been robbed."

"So you have, chummy, and that's a fact; so you pick yourself up and toddle along with me; there ain't no fear of your being robbed again if you've nothing to lose."

Bertie half resisted the stranger's endeavour to assist him in finding his feet, but the other managed so dexterously that Bertie found himself accompanying his new friend with a fair amount of willingness. The fair was still at its height; the swings were fuller; the roundabout was driving a roaring trade; the sportsmen in the shooting gallery were popping away; but all these glories had lost their charm for Bertie. It seemed to him that it was all a hideous nightmare, from which he vainly struggled to shake himself free.

Had it not been for occasional assistance, he would more than once have lost his footing. Something ailed him, but what, he was at a loss to understand. All the hopes, and vigour, and high spirits of the morning had disappeared, and with them all his dreams had vanished too. He was the most miserable young gentleman in Kingston Fair.

He kept up an under current of grumbling all the way, now and then making feeble efforts to rid himself of his companion; but the stranger was too wide awake for Bertie to shake him off. Had he been better acquainted with the town, and in a fit state to realize his knowledge, he would have been aware that his companion was leading him, by a series of short cuts, in the direction of the apple-market. He paused before a tumbledown old house, over the door of which a lamp was burning. Bertie shrunk away, with some dim recollection of the establishment into which he had been enticed by the Original Badger and his friends. At sight of his unwillingness the other only laughed.

"What are you afraid of? This ain't a place in which they'd rob you, even if you'd got anything worth robbing, which it seems to me you ain't. This is a doss-house, this is."

So saying he entered the house, the door of which seemed to stand permanently open. The somewhat reluctant Bertie entered with him. No one appearing to receive them, the stranger lost no time in informing the inmates of their arrival.

"Here, Mr. Jenkins, or Mrs. Jenkins, or some one, can I come up?"

In answer to this appeal, a stout lady appeared at the head of a flight of stairs, which rose almost from the threshold of the door. Hall there was none. She was not a very cleanly-looking lady, nor had she the softest of voices.

"Is that you, Sam Slater? Who's that you've got with you?"

"A friend of mine, and that's enough for you."

With this brief response, the stranger, whose name appeared to be Sam Slater, led the way up the flight of stairs.

"Anybody here?" he asked, when he reached the landing.

"Not at present there ain't; I expect they're all at the fair."

"All the better," said Sam.

He followed the lady through a door which faced the landing, pausing for a moment to see that Bertie followed too. Something in Bertie's appearance struck the lady's eye.

"What's the matter with your friend,—ain't he well?" she asked.

"Well, he's not exactly well," responded Sam, favouring Bertie with a curious glance from the corner of his eye.

A man who was seated by a roaring fire, although the night was warm and bright, got up and joined the party. He was in his shirt-sleeves, and he also was stout, and he puffed industriously at a short black clay pipe. He stood in front of Bertie, and inspected him from head to foot.

"He don't look exactly well, not by any means he don't."

The stout man grinned. Bertie staggered. The sudden change from the sweet, fresh air to the hot, close room gave him a sudden qualm. If the stout man had not caught him he would have fallen to the floor.

"Steady! Where do you think you're coming to? You're a nice young chap, you are! If I was you I'd turn teetotal."

Sam Slater interfered.

"You don't know anything at all about it; he's not been drinking; he's been got at, and some one's cleared him of his cash."

"You leave him to me, Jenkins," said the stout lady.

For Bertie had swooned. As easily as though he had been a baby, instead of being the great lad that he was, she lifted him and carried him to another room. When he opened his eyes again he found that he was lying on a brilliantly counterpaned bed. Sam was seated on the edge, the lady was standing by the side, and Mr. Jenkins, a steaming tumbler in his hand, was leaning over the rail at his head.

"Better?" inquired the lady, perceiving that his eyes were open.

For answer Bertie sat up and looked about him. It was a little room, smaller than the other, and cooler, owing to the absence of a fire.

"Take a swig of this; that'll do you good."

Mr. Jenkins held the steaming tumbler towards him. Bertie shrank away.

"It's only peppermint, made with my own hands, so I can guarantee it's good. A barrel of it wouldn't do you harm. Drink up, sonny!"

Thus urged by the lady, he took the glass and drank. It certainly revived him, making him feel less dull and heavy; but a curious sense of excitement came instead. In the state in which he was even peppermint had a tendency to fly to his head. Perceiving his altered looks the lady went on,—

"Didn't I tell you it would do you good? Now you feel another man."

Then she continued, in a tone which Bertie, if he had the senses about him, would have called wheedling—

"Anybody can see that you're a gentleman, and not used to such a place as this. You are a little gentleman, ain't you now?"

Bertie took another drink before he replied. The steaming hot peppermint was restoring him to his former heroic state of mind.

"I should think I am a gentleman; I should like to see anybody say I wasn't."

Either this remark, or the manner of its delivery, made Mr. Jenkins laugh.

"Oh lor!" he said, "here's a three-foot-sixer!"

"Never mind him, my dear," observed the lady, "he knows no better. I knows a gentleman when I sees one, and directly I set eyes on you I says, 'he's a gentleman he is.' And did they rob you of your money?"

"Some one's robbed me of five pounds."

This was not said in quite such a heroic tone as the former remark. The memory of that five pounds haunted him.

"Poor, dear, young gentleman, think of that now. And was the money your own, my dear?"

"Whose do you think it was? Do you think I stole it?"

Under the influence of the peppermint, or harassed by the memory of his loss, Bertie positively scowled at the lady.

"Dear no, young gentlemen never steals. Five pounds! and all his own; and lost it too! What thieves this world has got! Dear, dear, now."

The lady paused, possibly overcome by her sympathy with the lad's misfortune. Behind his back she interchanged a glance with Mr. Jenkins. Mr. Jenkins, apparently wishing to say something, but not being able to find the words to say it with, put his hand to his mouth and coughed. Sam Slater stared at Bertie with a look of undisguised contempt.

"You must be a green hand to let 'em turn you inside out like that. If I had five pounds—which I ain't never likely to have! more's the pity—I'd look 'em up and down just once or twice before I'd let 'em walk off with it like that. I wonder if your mother knows you're out."

"My mother doesn't know anything at all about it; I've run away from school."

Under ordinary circumstances Bertie would have confined that fact within his own bosom; now, with some vague idea of impressing his dignity upon the contemptuous Sam, he blurted it out. Directly the words were spoken a significant look passed from each of his hearers to the other.

"Dear, now," said the lady. "Run away from school, have you now? There's a brave young gentleman; and that there Sam knows nothing at all about it. It's more than he dare do."

"Never had a school to run away from," murmured Sam.

"Did they use you very bad, my dear?"

"It wasn't because of that; I wouldn't have minded how they used me. I ran away because I wanted to find the Land of Golden Dreams."

Mr. Jenkins put his hand to his mouth as if to choke what sounded very like a laugh; Sam stared with a look of the most profound amazement on his face; a faint smile even flitted across the lady's face.

"The Land of Golden Dreams," said Sam. "Never heard tell of such a place."

"You never heard tell of nothing," declared the lady. "You ain't a scholar like this young gentleman. And what's the name of the school, my dear?"

"Mecklemburg House Collegiate School."

Bertie informed them of the name and title of Mr. Fletcher's educational establishment with what he intended to be his grandest air, with a possible intention of impressing them with its splendour.

"There's a mouthful," commented Sam. "Oh my eye!"

The lady's reception of Bertie's information was more courteous.

"There's a beautiful name for a school. And where might it be?"

"It's not very far from Cobham. But I don't live there."

"No, my dear. And where do you live, my lovey?"

The lady became more affectionate in her titles of endearment as she went on. Mr. Jenkins, leaning over the head of the bed, listened with all his ears; but on his countenance was a delighted grin.

"I live at Upton."

"Upton," said the lady, and glanced at Mr. Jenkins behind the bed. Mr. Jenkins winked at her.

"My father's a doctor; he keeps two horses and a carriage; everybody knows him there; he's the best doctor in the place."

"And is your mother alive, my dear?"

"I should rather think she was, and won't she go it when she knows I've run away!"

"Dear now, think of that! I shouldn't be surprised if she was very fond of you, my dear. And I daresay, now, she'd give a deal of money to any one who told her where you were."

"I should think she would. I daresay she'd give—I daresay she'd give—" he searched his imagination for the largest sum of which he could think; he desired to impress his audience with an idea of the family importance and wealth. "I daresay she'd give a thousand pounds." His hearers stared. "But she's not likely to know, for there's no one to tell her."

This statement seemed to tickle Mr. Jenkins and Sam so much, that with one accord they burst into a roar of laughter. Bertie glowered.

"Never mind them, my lovey; it's their bad manners, they don't know no better. I'll soon send them away. Now, out you go, going on with your ridiculous nonsense, and he such a brave young gentleman; I'm ashamed of you;—get away, the two of you."

Mr. Jenkins and Sam obediently went, stifling their laughter on the way. But apparently when they were outside they gave free vent to their sense of humour, for their peals of mirth came through the door.

"Never mind them, my dear; you undress yourself and get into bed, and have a nice long sleep, and be sure you have a friend in me. My name's Jenkins, lovey, Eliza Jenkins, and that there silly man's my husband. By the way, you haven't told me what your name is, my dear."

"My name's Bailey, Bertie Bailey."

"Dear now, and you're the son of the famous Dr. Bailey of Upton. Think of that now."

She left him to think of it, for immediately after Mrs. Jenkins followed her husband and Sam. Bertie, left alone, hesitated for a moment or two as to what he should do. He tried to think, but thought was just then an exercise beyond his powers. The events of the last few hours were presented in a sort of kaleidoscopic picture to his mind's eye. There was nothing clear. He found a difficulty in realizing where he was. As he looked round the unfamiliar room, with its scanty furniture, and that of the poorest and most tawdry class, he found it difficult not to persuade himself that he saw it in a dream.

All the events of the day seemed to have been the incidents of a dream. Mecklemburg House seemed to be a house he had seen in a dream. He seemed to have left it in a dream. That walk along the moonlit road had been a walk in a dream. He had driven with Mr. George Washington Bankes in a dream. He had possessed five pounds in a dream; had lost it in a dream; had been to the circus in a dream; the Original Badger and his friends were the characters seen in a dream—a dream which had been the long nightmare of a day.

One thing was certain, he was sleepy; on that point he was clear. He could hardly keep his eyes open, and his head from sinking on his breast. As in a dream he lazily undressed; as in a dream he got into the bed; and once into the bed he was almost instantly wrapped in a sound and dreamless slumber.

He was awoke by the sound of voices. It seemed to him that he had only slept five minutes, but it was broad daylight; the sun was shining into the room, and, almost immediately after he opened his eyes, the clock of

Kingston church struck twelve. It was high noon.

But he was not yet fully roused. He lay in that delicious state of languor which is neither sleep nor waking. The owners of the voices were evidently not aware that he was even partially awakened. They went on talking with perfect absence of restraint, entirely unsuspicious of there being any listener near. The speakers were Mr. and Mrs. Jenkins.

"It's all nonsense about the thousand pounds; a thousand pence will be nearer the thing; but even a thousand pence is not very far off a five-pound note, and a five-pound note's worth having."

Mr. Jenkins ceased, and Mrs. Jenkins took up the strain. Bertie, lying in his delightful torpor, heard it all; though he was not at first conscious that he was himself the theme of his host and hostess's conversation.

"He says his father keeps two horses and a carriage; he must be tidy off. If his mother's fond of him, she wouldn't mind paying liberal to hear his whereabouts. If you goes down and tells her how you took him in without a penny in his pockets, not so much as fourpence to pay for his bed—which it's against our rule to take in anybody who doesn't pay his money in advance—and how he was ill and all, there's no knowing but what she wouldn't pay you handsome for putting her on his track and all."

"It's worth trying anyhow. Dr. Bailey, you say, is the name?"

"He says his own name is Bertie Bailey, and his father's name is Dr. Bailey."

Bertie pricked up his ears at the sound of his name, and began to wonder.

"And his home is Upton? There don't seem no railway at this here Upton. Slough seems the nearest station, because I asked them at the booking office, and there's a tidy bit to walk."

"Don't you walk it. You take a cab and drive. Make out as how there wasn't no time to lose, and as how you thought the mother's heart was a longing for her son. Do the thing in style. If there don't nothing else come of it they'll have to pay your expenses handsome."

"I'm not going all that way for my expenses, so I'll let them know! They'll have to make it worth my while before I tell them where to lay their finger on the kid."

Bertie wondered more and more. He still lay motionless, but by now he was wide awake. It dawned upon him what was the meaning of the conversation. Mr. and Mrs. Jenkins were apparently about to take advantage of his incautious frankness to betray him for the sake of a reward. He had a dim recollection of having blurted out more than he intended; and, on the strength of the information he had thus obtained, Mr. Jenkins was going to pay a little visit to his home.

"Don't you be afraid," went on the lady, "I tell you they'll pay up handsome. You and me, perhaps, wouldn't make much fuss if one of our young 'uns was to cut and run, but gentlefolks is different. It isn't likely that a lady can like the thought of a boy of hers knocking about in the gutter, and trying his luck in the ditch. Just you put your hat on, and you go straight to this here Upton, and you see if it isn't the best day's work you've ever done. I'll go fast enough, if you've not started soon."

Mr. Jenkins did not seem to like this idea at all; his tone was a little sulky.

"You needn't put yourself out, Eliza; I'm a-going."

"Then why don't you go, instead of standing wool gathering there?"

"You don't know his address. What am I to ask for when I get to this here Upton?"

"Why, ask for Dr. Bailey; it's only a little place. You'll find he's as well known as the church clock, and perhaps better."

"And about the boy; what are you going to do when he wakes up?"

"I'll look after him. Don't you trouble your head about the boy; you'll find him here when you come back as safe as houses."

"All right, Eliza, I'm off; and by to-night, I shouldn't be surprised if Master Bertie Bailey, Esquire, was returned to his fond parent's arms."

His tone was jocular; but the expression of his countenance was not exactly genial when Master Bertie Bailey sat up in bed, as he did at this identical moment, and looked his host and hostess in the face.

Chapter XIII

IN PETERSHAM PARK

Bertie looked at Mr. and Mrs. Jenkins, and Mr. and Mrs. Jenkins looked at him, and husband and wife looked at one another.

"And have you had a nice sleep, my dear?"

Bertie vouchsafed no reply to the lady's question, continuing to look at her with his characteristically dogged look in his eyes.

"And how long have you been awake, my dear? Have you only just now woke?"

Bertie threw the clothes from off him, and turned to Mr. Jenkins.

"I won't go home, even if you do go and tell my mother, you old sneak!"

This uncomplimentary epithet was applied to Mr. Jenkins with such sullen ferocity, that that gentleman started and looked even more discomfited than he had done before. Bertie got out of bed and stood upon the floor.

"Give me my clothes, and let me go; you've no right to keep me here."

Mr. Jenkins was apparently speechless, but his quicker-witted wife was voluble enough.

"Certainly, my dear. No one wants to keep you, lovey. You pay us what you owe and you're as free as the air!"

"I don't owe you anything."

"Not anything for a young gentleman like you; it's only six shillings, my dear."

"Six shillings!"

"Yes, six shillings. Would you like your bill, my dear? Jenkins, go and get the young gentleman his bill."

"You're a lot of thieves!"

"Oh, thieves are we? Very well, if you like to think us so, my dear. But I shouldn't have thought that a young gentleman like you would have liked to rob poor people of the money he owes for his board and lodging. And if you talk about thieves, my dear, Jenkins will go for a policeman, and a policeman will soon show you who's the thief, if you don't pay us what you owe, my lovey. And I shouldn't be surprised if, when he heard as how you'd runned away, the policeman wasn't to take and lock you up at once, my pet. Now, Jenkins, you come along with me, and while I makes up the young gentleman's bill you go and fetch a policeman, because as he thinks we're thieves, he do."

While the lady delivered herself of this voluble string of observations she had gradually approached the door. Before Bertie had perceived her design, she had pushed her husband through the door, and was through herself; the door was shut, the key turned in the lock, and Bertie was a prisoner.

"Now we'll see who's thieves!" the lady was heard to observe outside. "Now, Jenkins, you go and get a policeman this instant minute, and mind you bring a good big one, too!"

Very few boys would be so foolish as to, what is rather erroneously termed run away; sneak away would perhaps be the correct phrase. If in any given million we were to put it that there is one such being, we should perhaps be stating a larger average than actually exists. But we may be pretty sure, that for even that young gentleman the adventures which had befallen Bertie Bailey at the very outset would have been quite sufficient; he would have devoted the small remainder of his energies to running, *i.e.*, sneaking, back again.

But Bertie Bailey was made of sterner stuff; he was of those young gentlemen who have to learn their lessons a good many times over before they can get the meaning of what they have learnt into their heads. Those who reach the end of this story will find that he did learn his lesson to the end, and that it was a terrible lesson too, but the ending was not yet.

So soon as he understood that he was a prisoner, Bertie cast about for some method of escape. In his heart he could not but allow that the commencement of his journey had not been so successful as he had intended that it should be. But he was naturally slow to admit a failure. And to think that the ingenious Mr. and Mrs. Jenkins should make capital out of his misfortunes; that was an idea he by no means relished.

Fortunately, the lady had left his clothes behind. It occurred to Bertie that she might perceive her error and return to fetch them. To prevent any likelihood of that he put them on. Then he looked about to find a path to freedom.

The window immediately caught his eye. It was a very little one, in the fashion of a double lattice, which opened outwards. But Bertie resolved that it was large enough for him. He opened it carefully and peeped out. It was apparently a window at the side of the house, looking out upon a narrow passage-way.

Had Mr. and Mrs. Jenkins known the character of their guest, they would never have been so foolish as to think the bird was safe while he had the command of that convenient window. It was only some ten or twelve feet above the ground, and to Bertie the drop was nothing.

He lost no time in putting it to the test. First peering up and down the narrow passage, to see that no one was in sight and that no other window commanded a view of his operations, he brought the only chair the room contained up to the window and commenced to climb through it, feet foremost. The operation was a delicate one, but the size of the window precluded any other mode of egress. Even as it was, when he was about half way through he discovered that he was stuck fast. For a few disagreeable moments he feared that he would have to remain in that uncomfortable position till Mrs. Jenkins returned to secure her prey.

He wriggled and twisted, but for a time in vain. Suddenly, however, he did more than he intended; for the result of a desperate effort was to precipitate him so rapidly backwards that he was only just able to grasp the old-fashioned, narrow, wooden window sill with his right hand in time to prevent himself from falling in a heap upon the ground. He hung for a second, to give himself chance to recover from the shock, then he loosened his hold, and, dropping, alighted on his feet upon the ground; and no sooner was he on the ground than, without waiting to see if there was any one about, he dashed helter skelter down the passage at the top of his speed.

He was not pursued. On that point his mind was soon at rest. Mr. and Mrs. Jenkins were probably too much engaged with other matters to think of the possibility of their guest effecting his escape. The passage led, by a succession of devious turnings, into the Richmond Road. When he reached the main thoroughfare Bertie ceased to run.

Under the railway arch, past the shops, past the cricket field, into the lanes beyond, went Bertie. He had had nothing to eat that morning, he had not a farthing in his pocket; he had no conception where money was to come from unless it tumbled from the skies; yet he went unhesitatingly forward, as though all the world was at his feet, and all its wealth was in his pocket.

Past Ham Common into Petersham, and now he began to think that perhaps he was a little hungry. Delicious recollections of the morning meal of yesterday floated through his mind. A dish of ham and eggs he would have welcomed as a dish worthy of the gods; but there were no ham and eggs for him just then.

The road was dusty; the previous rains had disappeared, and the mud was turned to dust. By the time he reached Bute House he had made up his mind that the dust and heat combined were a little more than he quite relished. By then, too, he had no doubt but that he was hungry and thirsty too.

Suddenly the sound of voices fell upon his ear; of children's voices, of their laughter, of their cries of pleasure as they called to one another. He looked through the rails into Petersham Park. The park was full of children. There was some huge school treat, and in hundreds they were passing here and there. Up the hill, and along the valley, among the trees, and in the nooks and dells, as far as the eye could penetrate, there were children moving. He entered, and advancing some distance from the outer wall, he lay down upon the grass.

When he had lain there some time there were races started. Little boys and big raced for prizes. Those in charge of the multitude of children arranged the sports.

"Here's a race for a shilling!" shouted one such person in authority. He held a leather bag above his head. There was a shout from the boys who crowded round him. The prize was of unusual magnitude. All the prizes seemed to be in money,—twopence, threepence, fourpence had been their value until now—and no sooner were they won than the winners rushed to spend their prizes at the stalls of fruit and sweets, the proprietors of which plied a roaring trade. When the race for a shilling was announced there was a shout from a multitude of throats.

"Now then, why don't you have a try to win? you're big enough. Lying there as if you're half asleep; jump up, and show them how fast your feet can travel!"

A young man was standing by Bertie, looking down at him, evidently unaware that he was not an original member of the noisy crowd.

"Jump up! Why don't you go in for the race? Are you ill?"

"I'm not ill."

Without another word Bertie got up and joined the host of boys who were preparing to run. There were probably a hundred, and the directors of the sports had considerable difficulty in arranging a fair start. The race was confined to the bigger ones; there were no starts allowed, and they were all supposed to start from the same line. But the competitors had not the nicest sense of honour, and each endeavoured to steal a yard from his friend. Finally they were got into something like a proper line.

The distance to be run was about two hundred yards. The course was not a very regular one, as some were up the hill, and some were down; the breadth of the level ground was not sufficient to contain them all. Two persons stood in a line to mark the winning-post, and between them they stretched a cord. The one on the right held the shilling in a bag.

Several false starts were made. In their anxiety to be first the competitors could not manage to stand still. Half a dozen times they broke away, and had to be called back again. At last they were off. The course was from the park and towards the road, the winning-post being about a dozen yards from the school house at the gate.

The race was short, and, so far as the majority of the competitors were concerned, by no means sharp. Quite a third were out of it in the first six yards; half the remainder were beaten in a dozen, and before half the distance was covered there were only four or five who had a chance of winning. Among these was Bailey. He was not over fast on his feet as a rule, but never had the inducement to make the best possible speed been so strong before. He was running for his dinner, and, for all he knew, his tea and supper too.

In the last fifty yards the race resolved itself into a struggle of three. In front was a tall, lanky boy, who, so far as length of limb was concerned, ought to have left the others at the post. But his condition was not equal to his build; he went puffing and panting along. Obviously it would take him all he knew to last it out. About a couple of yards behind him, and almost side by side with Bertie, was a slightly-built lad, who was straining every nerve to keep his place. The freshest of the three was Bailey.

Yet the lanky youth looked like winning. He lumbered and blundered along, but his long legs enabled him to cover at a single stride the ground which they had to take two steps to cover. The boy by Bertie's side had just given up the struggle with a gasp, when the lanky lad caught his foot in a hole and went headlong to the ground. Like a flash Bertie put on a spurt and dashed victorious in. The prize-holder held out the leather bag, and Bertie caught it as he passed.

But the lanky youth, disappointed in his expectations, having puffed himself for nothing, beheld the reward of his endeavours snatched from his grasp with a burning sense of injury. Struggling to his feet he gave his emotions words.

"It ain't fair! Who's he? He ain't one of us! He's a stranger!"

Instantly the words were caught up by a host of disappointed competitors.

"He's a stranger! What's he want running races along with us? and winning of the prizes?"

The individual who had so hastily yielded up the reward of victory, turned to Bertie.

"Aren't you one of our boys?"

But Bertie did not wait to give an answer. The shilling of which he had gained possession meant so much to him, that he instinctively felt that to wait to explain exactly who he was would be a waste of time. He had been told to run, he had run, he had fairly won, he had been handed the shilling as his by right; it meant dinner, supper, everything to him; he was not going to stop to argue the point as to who he was. So when the over hasty-individual put the question to him, his only answer was to take to his heels and run.

Instantly a crowd was after him.

"Stop him! stop him! He's a stranger! He's not one of us!"

But if he had run fast before, he ran faster now. He was through the gate before any one was near him, dashing across the road, and under the shadow of the "Star and Garter."

But the chase was relinquished almost as soon as it was begun. The person who had held the shilling stopped it.

"Never mind, boys; he won the race, so let him take the prize. Perhaps he wants it more than we do. I daresay we can find another shilling, and next time we'll be a little more particular."

The crowd returned into the park again.

Bertie pursued his way. When he saw that the chase had stopped he slowed a little, soon contenting himself with rapid walking. He was very hot; the perspiration stood in great beads upon his face; his clothing had an inclination to stick to his limbs. And he was very thirsty; his throat was parched and dry. He was hungry too; his long abstinence began to tell; he felt he could not go much farther without something to eat and drink.

Along the Lower Road, past Petersham fields, past Buccleuch House, into Richmond town. The town was crowded. The afternoon was well advanced. The fine weather had brought people out into the streets. Hill Street and George Street were crowded with both pedestrians and carriages. Richmond can be both gay and lovely on a sunny afternoon. It was then. The untidy, dusty, perspiring boy looked out of place in that big bright crowd, made up as it was for the most part of well-dressed people.

Once or twice he stopped and looked into the confectioners' shops, but from their appearance they were evidently beyond his means. If he had only been still the possessor of five pounds he might have ruffled it with the best of them, but a shilling would not go far in those well-filled emporiums of confectionery and nice-looking but unsubstantial odds and ends, and he so hungry too. He was beginning to fear that Richmond was not the place for him, and that he would have to go hungry and thirsty, when he reached the coffee palace in the Kew Road.

Here he thought he might venture in; and he did. He had a bloater and some bread-and-butter, and a cup of coffee, and there was not much change left in his pocket after that. But it was a sufficiently hearty meal, and the choice of materials did credit to his judgment. He left the shop with his hunger satisfied, feeling brighter and fresher altogether, and with fivepence in his pocket clutched tightly with his right hand. Those coppers were exceeding precious in his eyes.

He set out to walk to London. He knew that Richmond was not very far from London, and had a general idea that he had to keep straight on. He had lingered over his meal, taking his time and resting, and watching the other customers enjoying theirs, so that it was about six o'clock when he rose and went. A curious spirit of adventure possessed him still. The bull-dog nature of the boy was roused, and it was with an implicit faith in the future that he went straight on.

Until he reached Kew Bridge all was easy sailing; there was a straight road, and he went straight on. But at Kew Bridge he pulled up, puzzled. He had crossed the river at Hampton Court, and again at Kingston, and apparently here was another bridge to cross. It seemed to him that things were getting mixed. Ignorant of the convolutions of the Thames, of its manifold twists and turns, he began to wonder whether he had not after all gone wrong, when he found the river in front of him again.

By the bridge lingered two or three of the flower-sellers who haunt the neighbourhood of Kew Gardens. He addressed himself to one of them.

"Am I right for London?"

"Of course you is, over the bridge, turn to the right, and go straight on. Won't you buy a bookay? Only this one left; ain't sold none all day,—flowers only just fresh,—only sixpence, sir."

The man kept up by Bertie's side, supported by one or two of his colleagues, proffering their wares.

"I haven't any money."

"Don't say that, sir,—I'm a poor chap, sir,—I am indeed, sir,—very 'ard to stand all day and not sell nothing—just this one, sir—you shall have it for fivepence."

"I tell you I haven't any money."

"Leave the gentleman alone, Bill. Don't you see he's a-going home to his ma?"

His colleagues dropped off, firing a parting shot; but the man whom Bertie had originally addressed kept steadily on, sticking close to his side. They crossed the bridge together. The sun was beginning to go home in the west, majestically enthroned in a bank of crimson clouds. The waters were tinted by his departing rays.

"Just this one, sir—take pity on a poor chap, now do, sir—you've got a nice home to go to, and a ma and all, and here's me, what hasn't earned a copper all the day, with nothing to eat and drink, and not a bed to lay me 'ead upon—buy this one, sir—you shall have it for fourpence."

"I haven't any money."

They went down the bridge together, the man still sticking to Bertie's side.

"If I was a gentleman, and a poor chap came to me, and asked me to buy a bookay, I wouldn't tell him I'd got no money, and me a hard-working chap what hasn't tasted food for a couple of days, and hasn't seen a bed for a week —just this one, sir—you shall have it for threepence, and that's less than it cost me, it is indeed, sir—won't you have it for threepence?"

"I tell you I haven't any money."

The man stopped, allowing Bertie to wend his way alone, but his voice still followed after.

"Oh, you haven't any money, haven't you? would you like me to lend you half-a-crown or a suvering? I'm sure I'm game. 'Ow much does your ma allow you a week? a hapenny and a smack on the 'ead? If I was you I'd ask your nurse to take you out in the pram, and buy you lollipops,—go on, you mealy-faced young 'umbug!"

Bertie almost wished he had not asked the way, but had been content to blunder on unaided. The flower-seller's voice was peculiarly audible; the passers by were more amused than Bertie was. It was his first experience of the characteristic eloquence of a certain class of Londoner; he would have been content if it had been his last. He went on, feeling somewhat smaller in his own esteem.

Past the "Star and Garter," along the Kew road, never a very cheerful thoroughfare. Bertie thought it particularly cheerless then. Through Gunnersbury, and Chiswick, and Turnham Green, past the green itself, past Duke's Avenue, which is already a caricature of its former self, and threatens to be an avenue no more. Past where, not so very long ago, the toll bar used to stand, though there is no memorial of its presence now. Past the carriage manufactory; past the terminus of that singular railway which boasts of a single carriage and a single engine,—said railway being two if not three miles long. Into King Street, Hammersmith, and when he had got so far upon his journey the lad began to tire.

The evening was closing in. The lamps were lighted; the shops were ablaze with gas; the streets were crowded. But Bertie did not know where he was; he was standing on strange ground. He wondered, rather wearily, if this were London; but after his recent experience with the vendor of bouquets he was afraid to ask. He was hungry again, and began to look into the shop windows with anxious eyes. Fivepence would not go far.

He tramped wearily on, right through King Street. At a costermonger's stall he bought a pennyworth of apples, and munched them as he went. His capital was now reduced to fourpence, and night was come, and he was on the threshold of the great city—that Land of Golden Dreams.

Chapter XIV

IN TROUBLE

Through the Broadway, along the Hammersmith Road, on, and on, and on. Every step he took made the next seem harder. He was conscious that he could hardly walk much more. The crowd, the lights, the strangeness of the place, confused him. He wondered where he was. Was this London? and was it nothing else but streets? and was this the Land of Golden Dreams?

When he reached the Cedars, where the great pile of school buildings is now standing, he saw, peering through the railings, a little arab of the streets. To him he applied for information.

"Is this London?"

The urchin withdrew his head from between the two iron rails through which he had managed to squeeze it, and eyed his questioner. He was a little lad, smaller than Bertie, hatless, shoeless, in a ragged pair of trousers which were several sizes too large for him, and which were rolled up in a bunch about his ankles to enable him to put his feet far enough through to touch the ground.

"What, this? this 'ere? no, this ain't London."

"How far is it then?"

"How far is it? what, London? It just depends what part of London might you be wanting?"

"Any part; I don't care."

The urchin whistled. His small, keen eyes had been reading his questioner all the time, and Bertie was conscious of a sense of discomfort as he observed the curious gaze. In some odd way he felt that this little lad was bigger and stronger, and older than himself; that he looked down at him, as it were, from a height.

"Say, matey, where might you be going to? You don't look as though you knowed your way about, not much, you don't."

The cool tone of superiority irritated Bertie. Tired and weary as he was, and a little sick at heart, he was not going to allow a little shrimp like this to look down on him.

"If you won't tell me the way, why, that's enough. I don't want any of your cheek."

Bertie moved on, but the other called after him.

"You needn't turn rusty, you needn't; I didn't mean no harm. I'm going to London, I am, and if you like you can come along o' me."

The urchin was by his side again. Bertie looked at him with disgusted eyes. He had not set out upon his journey with the intention of travelling with such tag-rag and bobtail as this lad. So far the society into which he had fallen had been of an unfortunate kind; he had had enough of Sam Slater, and of Sam Slater's sort.

"I'm not going with you; I'm going by myself."

"Alright, matey, every bloke's free to choose his pals."

The urchin turned a series of catherine-wheels right under Bertie's nose. Then, with a whistle of unearthly shrillness, he set off running, and disappeared into the night. Bertie was left no wiser than before.

He dragged along till he reached Addison Road A gentleman in evening dress came across the road, smoking a cigar. He was of middle age, irreproachably attired, with nothing of Sam Slater about him.

"If you please, sir, can you tell me how far it is to London?"

The gentleman stopped short, puffing at his cigar.

"What's that?"

Bertie repeated his inquiry. For answer, the gentleman took him by the shoulder, led him to a neighbouring lamp-post, and looked him in the face.

"What are you doing here? You look respectable; you're from the country, aren't you?"

Bertie hesitated; he remembered the effect produced by his incautious frankness on Mr. and Mrs. Jenkins.

"Speak up; you have got a tongue, haven't you? What are you doing here? run away from home?"

The lad, giving a sudden twist, freed himself from the gentleman's grasp, and ran off as fast as his legs could carry him. The stranger, puffing at his cigar as he stood under the lamp-post, laughed as he peered after the retreating boy. But Bertie, despite his weariness, still ran on. He dimly wondered, whether he bore about with him some outward sign by which any one could tell he was a runaway. He made up his mind that he would ask no more questions if he ran the risk of meeting such home thrusts in reply.

He wandered onwards till he reached Kensington Gardens, and then the

Albert Hall. There was a concert going on, and the place was all lit up. He stared with amazement at the enormous building, imperfectly revealed in the darkness of the night. Carriages and cabs were going to and fro. Some one touched him on the shoulder. It was a gorgeous footman, with powdered hair, in splendid livery. His magnificence dazzled him.

"I say, you boy, do you know Thurloe Square?"

"No, sir."

"What do you mean? are you gettin' at me? You take a message for me to Thurloe Square, and there'll be a bob when you get there."

"But I don't know Thurloe Square; I'm a stranger, sir."

"A stranger, are you? Then what do you mean by standing there, as though you was born just over the way? Get on out of it! I shouldn't be surprised if you was after pockethandkerchiefs;—what's your little lay? I'll tell the policeman to keep an eye on you, telling me you don't know Thurloe Square; —oh yes, I jest dersay!"

The footman appeared to be angry; Bertie slunk away. He crossed the road to the park; a gate was open; people were going in and out. He entered too. It looked quiet inside; perhaps there was grass to sit upon. He went up towards the Serpentine, and had not gone far when he came to a seat. On this he sat. Never was seat more welcome; it was ecstasy to rest. He was dimly conscious of what was going on; before he knew it he was fast asleep.

Time passed; still he slept. A perfect sleep untroubled by dreams. Some one else approached the seat, some one in the last stage of raggedness, so exhausted that he seemed hardly able to drag one foot behind the other. He, too, sat down; he, too, fell fast asleep.

Some one else approached,—a woman with a baby and a watercress basket. The baby was crying faintly; the woman tried to comfort it, speaking to in a droning monotone:

"I've nothing to give you, bairn," she said; "I've nothing to give you, bairn! God help us all!"

A policeman came along. When he reached the seat he stopped, and flashed the bull's-eye lantern in the faces of the sleepers. The woman woke up instantly, perhaps used to such a visitation.

"I'm going, sir; I only sat down for a moment to rest awhile."

The baby began to cry again.

"I've nothing to give you, bairn," she said; "I've nothing to give you, bairn! God help us all!"

It seemed to be a stereotyped form of speech. She got up, with the baby and her basket, and walked away, the baby crying as she went. The policeman remained behind, flashing his bull's-eye.

"Now then, this won't do, you know; wake up, you two."

He took the ragged sleeper by the shoulder, and shook him; he seemed to wake in a kind of stupor, and staggered off without a word. The policeman turned to Bertie.

"Now then!"

The lad woke with a start; he thought some one was playing tricks with him.

"What do you want?"

"I want you to clear out of this, that's what I want."

Opening his eyes Bertie was for a moment dazzled by the glaring light; then he saw at the back the policeman's form, looming grim and awful. Possessed by a sudden fear, he sprang to his feet, and ran as for his life.

"Now I wonder what you've been up to?" murmured the policeman. "I don't remember seeing your face before; I should say you was a new hand, you was."

Bertie ran, without knowing where he was running to; across the road, under a rail. He found himself upon the grass. It was quite dark, mysterious, strange. He could hardly be followed there, so he thought at least, and strolled more slowly on. But he was very tired still, and, yielding to his weariness, when he had gone a little farther, he sat down upon the grass to rest.

And this was the Land of Golden Dreams! this was his entrance into the promised land! A gentle breeze murmured through the night; there was a sound as of rippling grass and of rustling leaves; he could see no stars; a heavy dew was falling; the grass was damp; it was chilly; the breeze blew cold; he shivered with hunger and with cold. His head was nodding on his breast; almost unconsciously he lay full length upon the sodden grass, and again fell fast asleep.

But this time it was not a dreamless slumber; it was a continued nightmare. He was oppressed with horrid visions, with continuous strugglings against hideous forms of terror. Unrefreshed he woke. It was broad day; but there had come a sudden change of weather, the skies were overcast and dull. His limbs were aching; he was stiff, and wet, and cold; he was soaked to the skin; his clothes stuck to his body. Shivering, he struggled to his feet, rising with pain.

The place was deserted. Three was a solitary horseman in the distance; the horseman and the lad were the only living things in sight.

It began to drizzle; the wind had risen; it whistled in the air. The fine weather had departed as though never to return. Bertie's teeth were chattering; he felt dull and stupid, ignorant of what he ought to do.

He began walking through the rain across the grass. How cold he was, and oh! how hungry. He must have something to eat, and something warm to drink. He thought of his money; he felt for his fourpence; it was gone!

The discovery stunned him. He could not realize the fact at once, but searched in each of his pockets laboriously, one after the other. He turned them inside out; felt for holes through which it might have fallen. He remembered that he had put it in the right hand pocket of his trousers; he examined it again and again, in a sort of stupor. In vain; it was gone!

He retraced his steps. It might have fallen out of his pockets in the night; he fell upon his knees and searched. There was no sign of it about. He was without a sou, and he was so hungry and so cold, and it was raining, and he was wet to the skin.

He could not realize his loss. He wandered stupidly on, stopping at times, feeling in his pockets again and again. It could not be gone. But there was no money there. This was his Land of Golden Dreams; this was the object of his journey; this was the result of his dash into the world; he was cold, and he was hungry, and he saw no signs of anything to eat.

At last he left the park behind. He went out by the Piccadilly gate, as miserable a figure as any to be seen, stained with mud, soaked with wet, hungry and forlorn. It was early. The early omnibuses were bringing crowds of business men to town. The drivers were muffled in their mackintoshes, the outside passengers crouched beneath their umbrellas. Everything and every one looked cold, and miserable, and wet; Bertie looked worst of all, for he looked hungry too.

How hungry! There had been moments at Mecklemburg House when hunger had made itself felt, but never hunger such as this. The very worst meal Mr. Fletcher had ever set before his pupils—and his system of dietary was not his strongest point—Bertie would have welcomed as a feast. Even a dry crust of stale bread would have been welcome; a cup of the wishy-washiest tea would have been nectar of the gods.

He was footsore too. As he wandered by the Piccadilly mansions and approached the shops, he became conscious that his feet were blistered. It was a discomfort to be obliged to put them to the ground. His right foot, in particular, had a blister on the heel, and another on the ball of the foot. It seemed to him that every moment these were getting larger. He would have liked to have taken his boot and sock off and examine his injuries. He was aware, too, that he was dirty; more than two days had passed since he had come in contact with soap and water. Once upon a time he had had a vague idea that it was a glorious sport of the heroic character to be dirty; now he would have liked to have had a wash. But he could neither wash nor examine his feet in the middle of Piccadilly.

The presence of the shops caused him an additional pang. The display of costly goods in their windows seemed to add to his misery. Even the possession of his fourpence, as compared to the value of such treasures, would have placed him at a disadvantage.

But without it he was poor indeed. He was fascinated by the fruit shops; all the fruits of the earth, those in season and those out, seemed gathered there. He glued his nose to the window and looked and longed.

"Now then, what are you doing there? move on out of that!"

A policeman, in a shiny cape, from which the wet was dripping, roughly shouldered him on. He was not even allowed to look. This was not at all the sort of thing he had expected. His idea of his entry into the great city had been altogether different. He was to come as the king of boys, if not of men; as something remarkable, as a heaven-born conqueror; something to be talked of; the centre of all eyes directly he was seen. To sleep upon the sodden grass, to be penniless, cold, wet, and hungry, to be shouldered by policemen, to be bidden to move on, these things had not entered into his calculations when that night at Mecklemburg House he had dreamed those golden dreams.

He struggled on; his feet became more painful; he was limping; rest he must. He turned down a bye-street, and then down a friendly entry, and leaned against the wall. Was this what he had come for, to lean in the rain against a wall, and to be thankful for the chance of leaning? He had not read in lives of Robin Hood, and Turpin, and Crusoe, and Jack the Giant-Killer, of episodes like this. But then, perhaps, his acquaintance with the histories of those gentlemen was not so perfect as it might have been.

Suddenly he heard the sound of rapidly approaching footsteps. Some one was coming along the side-street as though racing for his life. A lad about his own age came darting round the corner in such terrific haste that he almost ran into Bertie's arms.

"Catch hold! here's a present for you."

The runner gasped out the words, without pausing in his flight. Like an arrow from a bow he darted on, leaving Bertie standing there. To his amazement Bailey found that he had thrust something in his hand; his surprise was intensified when he discovered what it was,—it was a purse. The runner had turned another corner and was already out of sight.

Bertie, in his bewilderment, could do nothing else but gaze. Such unexpected generosity, coming at such a moment, was so astonishing that it was almost as though the gift had fallen from the skies. A good fat purse! It was like the stories after all. He could feel that it was heavy; he almost thought that he could feel that it was full. Suppose it were full of gold! Had it fallen from the skies?

All this occupied an instant. The next he was conscious that some one else was coming up the street; apparently some one else in equal haste; apparently more than one. Cries rang in his ears; he could not quite distinguish the words which were shouted, but at their sound, for some reason, a cold chill went down his back.

Some one came round the corner; some one who seized him as though he were some wild thing.

"Got you, have I! thought you'd double, did you, and slip out when I'd run past? Artful, but it didn't quite do,—not this time, at any rate."

His captor shook him as a terrier shakes a rat. It was a policeman, a huge, bearded fellow, six feet high. Bertie was like a plaything in his hands. On hearing some one coming, the boy, without any thought of what he was doing, had slipped the hand which held the purse behind his back. The policeman was down on it at once.

"What's that you've got there?"

He twisted the boy round, revealing the hand which held the purse. He took it away.

"Oh, that's it, is it? You hadn't got time to throw it away, I suppose, or perhaps you thought it was too good to lose—worth running a little risk for, eh? Well, you've run the risk just once too often."

By this time others had come into the entry, and now Bertie recognised the words which he had heard. What they had been shouting was, "Stop thief!"

The new comers showed a lively interest in the captive. A man, who looked like a respectable mechanic, reckoned him up.

"That's not the boy," he said.

"Oh, isn't it? It doesn't look like it, not when he was hiding here, and holding the purse in his hand!"

The policeman held up the purse with an air of smiling scorn.

"Had he got the purse? Well, whether he had or whether he hadn't, all I can say is he isn't the boy who took it; I'm willing to take my oath to that. He was a different-looking sort of boy altogether, and I was standing as close to him as I am to you."

"I never took the purse," said Bertie, with dogged lips and dogged eyes. He realized that great trouble had come upon him, as he writhed and twisted in the policeman's hand. "It was given to me."

"Yes, I daresay, and by a particular friend, no doubt. You come along with me, my lad, and tell that tale elsewhere."

The policeman began to drag the lad along the entry.

"The boy will go quietly, I daresay, if you give him a chance," observed the man who had previously spoken. "However it may be about the purse being found upon him, I'm prepared to prove that that's not the boy who took it."

"Well, you can come and give your evidence, can't you? It's no good standing arguing here; the lad had got the purse, and I've got the lad, and that's quite enough for me."

"Where are you going to take him to?"

"Marlborough Street Police Court."

"All right, I'll come round and say what I've got to say. My name's William Standing,—I'm a picture framer; I'll go and tell my governor where I'm off to, and I'll be there as soon as you are."

The man walked away. The policeman proceeded to haul Bertie off with him again. The boy was speechless. He was tired, his feet were sore; the policeman's pace was almost more than he could manage. In consequence, every now and then he received a jerk, which all but pitched him forward on his nose.

"Why don't you leave the boy alone?" inquired a man in the little crowd, which walked alongside in a sort of procession, whose ideas of a policeman's duty were apparently vague. "He ain't done no 'arm to you."

"Why, bless yer, if it wasn't for them little 'uns them policemen would have no one to collar; they daren't lay a finger on a man of your build, old pal."

This remark, from another member of the crowd, produced a laugh. The original speaker was a diminutive specimen of his kind, whom the policeman could have carried in his arms with the greatest of ease.

When they regained Piccadilly they came upon the victim of the robbery. This was a portly, middle-aged female, who was a pleasant combination of mackintoshes and agitation. She was the centre of an interested circle, into whose sympathetic ears she was pouring her tale of woe. The arrival of the policeman with his captive created a diversion.

"Is this the boy?" inquired the constable.

"Have you got my purse?" replied the lady. "It contained thirty-seven pounds, fifteen shillings, and threepence, in two ten pound notes, two fives,— I've got the numbers in my purse,—seven pounds in gold, four of them half-sovereigns, fifteen shillings in silver, and a threepenny bit; and whatever I shall do without it I don't know. I'm the landlady of the 'Rising Sun,' and I was going to pay my wine-merchant's bill, and I said to my daughter only this morning, 'Take all that money loose I didn't ought to do. No, Mary Ann, a cheque it ought to be.' But Mary Ann's that flighty, though she's in her thirties, though twenty-two she tries to pass herself to be—"

The policeman endeavoured to stop the lady's flood of eloquence.

"You can tell us all that when we get to the station. You'll have to come with me to identify the purse and charge the boy."

"I don't want to charge the boy, all I want is to identify the purse. As for the young limb of a boy, I'd like to give him a good banging with my umbrella, that I would!"

The lady shook her umbrella at the boy in a way which caused the crowd to laugh. But there was no laughter left in Bertie.

"We can't have any banging here," said the policeman, who was anxious to get on. "If you take my advice, you'll call a cab and let us all go comfortably together."

"Me go in a cab with a policeman and that there limb of a boy; not if I know it! I've kept the 'Rising Sun' respectable these six-and-twenty years,— sixteen years in my husband's time,—as respectable a man as ever breathed, though cherry brandy was his failing,—and ten long years a widow, and go to prison with a policeman and that there limb of a boy in a cab—"

"Nobody's asked you to go to prison," said the policeman, whose patience was beginning to fade. "I can't stand talking here all day. Now then, boy, best foot forward, march!"

Bertie's poor best foot was blistered, so that the policeman had to assist him, with occasional awkward jerks, to march to jail.

Chapter XV

OUT OF THE FRYING-PAN INTO THE FIRE

There was a meeting in Trafalgar Square that day. Some people thought they had a grievance, and resolved to air it. No matter what the grievance was; the world is very full of them, and too many of them are hard and stern, and old and deep, difficult to be removed. But the authorities had decided that this particular grievance should not be aired in this particular way; they would permit no meeting to be held in Trafalgar Square. The result was, contests with the police. The people with the grievance tried hard to air it; there were ugly rushes, the excitement spread, and in the neighbourhood adjoining there was something very like a riot.

One procession of the people with a grievance making for the Square, had been met by the police and turned aside. Part of the processioners had been turned into Piccadilly, and were being driven along that thoroughfare, helter skelter, just as the procession which escorted Bertie and his captor approached. The policeman saw his danger, and tried to turn aside. It was too late. The fugitives coming tumultuously along, and seeing only a single constable, made a rush in his direction.

In a moment Bertie found himself the centre of a pushing, yelling, struggling crowd, with the policeman holding on to him like grim death. Above the tumult could be distinguished the accents of the landlady of the "Rising Sun."

"I'm the landlady of the 'Rising Sun,' and I've kept the house respectable these six-and-twenty years—ten long years a widow, and sixteen years a respectable married woman—and it's a sin and a shame that a respectable female—"

But the crowd was no respecter of persons; the lady was hustled on one side, where her voice was heard no more. Bertie became conscious that a contest was going on for the possession of himself. The policeman stuck to him with extraordinary tenacity; with equal tenacity the crowd endeavoured to drag him away. Bertie suffered. Without wasting any time in inquiring as to the rights of the case, his new friends did their best to deprive the law of its prey. But they directed their efforts with misguided zeal. If they had left him to his fate, Bertie could only have suffered imprisonment at the worst; now he ran a risk of being drawn and quartered. They apparently did their best to drag his arms and legs out of their sockets; he felt his clothes giving way in all directions. Through all the heat and turmoil he felt that if this was town he preferred the country.

In the unequal strife the constable, unsupported, was vanquished in the end. It was well for Bailey the end came when it did; if he had stuck to his prize much longer the pieces of a boy would have strewed the street. Some one in the crowd struck the constable in the face with a stick. Putting up his hand to ward off a second blow, Bertie was instantly snatched from his grasp. His capture was so unsuspected, that the two zealous friends who were doing their best to tear him limb from limb, recoiling backwards, loosed their hold, and let him fall upon the ground.

"Get up, youngster, and hook it! The peelers will have you again if you don't look sharp; there's a lot of them coming down the street."

A workman stooped over the lad as he lay in the mud and assisted him to rise. He regained his feet, feeling stunned and bewildered. His friendly ally gave him a push, which sent him staggering into the thick of the crowd. It was only just in time to prevent the constable from catching hold of him again. The confusion suddenly became worse confounded.

"The peelers! the peelers!" was the cry.

There was a trampling of hoofs; the crowd parted in all directions, each seeking safety for himself. Half a dozen mounted constables went galloping through.

"Now you cut and run! If you aren't quick about it they'll nail you again as sure as eggs!"

It was the friendly workman urging Bertie to flight. He did not need much urging, but made the best of his way through the crowd, the memory of the policeman's grip still upon him. No one tried to stop him. Every one, including apparently his original captor, was too much engaged in his own affairs. He did not wait to see what became of the landlady of the "Rising Sun," though he seemed to hear her indignant accents above the tumult and the din. As fast as his wearied legs would carry him he tore away.

All that day he had nothing to eat. He saw nothing again of the policeman, nor of the crowd, nor of the lady who had lost her purse with its thirty-seven pounds, fifteen shillings, and a threepenny bit. But he had been in custody; he had signalized his entry into the Land of Golden Dreams by being within an ace of jail; the thought was with him all the day. Every policeman he saw he shrunk away from, and every policeman seemed to follow his shrinking with suspicious eyes. He was in continual expectation of feeling a hand upon his shoulder, and another experience of how it felt to be dragged through the streets.

It never ceased to rain; yet the rain did not come down fast, but always in the same slow, persistent drizzle. It was a cold rain, and the wind, which every now and then became almost tempestuous, was cold. Every one seemed to be in a bad temper; there were sour faces everywhere. The drivers of the various vehicles quarrelled with one another, and cursed and swore. Pedestrians hustled each other into the gutter; each seemed to be persuaded that the other did his best to get into his way.

Bertie had paid three previous visits to London,—this made the fourth. On each of the previous occasions he had been accompanied by his father; this was the first time he had come alone. Many a time that day he wished that he had postponed his personal exploration till a little later on; about the middle of the century after next, he was persuaded, would have been time enough for him.

His first visit had been as one of a family party to see the pantomime. There had been a morning performance; they had left home early in the morning, returning late at night. That day was a red-letter day in Bertie's calendar.

"When I went to see the pantomime," was the words which formed a prelude to many a tale of the wondrous sights which he had seen.

The second time he came up with father alone. The doctor had had some meeting to attend at the hospital at which he had spent his student days, and Bertie bore him company. Afterwards a visit had been paid to Madame Tussaud's and the Zoological Gardens. But the climax of the day had been the dinner at the restaurant in the evening before returning home. Bertie always thought that he had seen life when he looked backwards at that dinner in the after days. Champagne had accompanied that repast, and a band had played.

But the crowning visit had been the third. A certain cousin—feminine—had been a member of the party, and she alone would have canonized the day. They had gone to the exhibition and dined there, and seen the illuminations, and he had told himself that London was a city of delights, a paradise below, fairyland to-day.

This point of view did not occur to him with so much force on this, the occasion of his fourth visit. As he struggled up and down the wet and greasy streets, with his blistered feet and his empty stomach, anything more unlike a city of delights it seemed to him that he had never seen. He was continually getting into everybody's way, always being hustled into the gutter, and once, when an irate elderly gentleman sent him flying backwards to assume a sitting posture in the centre of a heap of mud, everybody laughed. But it was no joke to him. The elderly gentleman was a little sorry when he saw what he had done.

"You oughtn't to get in my way! The police didn't ought to allow boys like you to hang about the streets!"

That was the way he expressed his penitence, and then passed on. Bertie picked himself up at leisure. He was a sorry sight, and when the people saw the spectacle he presented they laughed again.

"If I was you I'd sow seeds in that there mud you've got on you; it'd be as good as 'arf a hacre of ground."

This was the comment of a paper-seller. He resumed his calling, shouting, "Hecho! Fourth hedition! Hecho!" But some one else had a word to say. This was a girl who was selling flowers for button-holes.

"You let me stick these 'ere flowers in that there sile you've just picked up. They'll grow like winkin'!"

All this was hard enough to bear, but the worst was the hunger and thirst. Although it rained all day, his thirst remained unquenched.

Toward evening he found himself in Covent Garden. As he looked shyly round his hopes rose just a little. To begin with, there seemed shelter. If he might only be allowed to stay in this place all night!

On the ground was vegetable refuse, ancient cabbage leaves, odds and ends of garbage which littered the place. If he could only pick up one or two of those cabbage leaves and see how far they would go towards staying his appetite! Surely no one could object to that, since they were placed there only to be thrown away. So he began picking up the cabbage leaves.

"Now then, what are you doing there? None of that now! Clear out of this, or I'll clear you out, and precious quick!"

At the sound of a strident voice Bertie trembled as though he had been guilty of a heinous crime. He dropped the cabbage leaves out of his hands again. A little man, who was apparently some one in authority, had suddenly appeared from behind one of the pillars, and was shouting at Bertie with the full force of his lungs. Like a frightened ewe the hero of yesterday gave a look round and slunk away. He was disappointed of his meal. The ground was evidently holy ground, and the cabbage leaves were evidently sacred cabbage leaves. The disappointment seemed to make his hunger worse. He had scarcely strength enough to slink away. He put his arms around one of the pillars, and, leaning his head against it, cried.

This was what had become of all his golden dreams! Of what stuff are heroes made?

"I say, young one, what's in the wind? Any one trodden on your precious toes? You don't seem so chirpy as some."

Bertie looked up through his tears to see who the speaker was. A little time ago to have been caught crying would have covered him with shame, now all shame of that sort seemed to have gone for ever. He vaguely feared that this was some new Jack-in-office again bidding him move on; but he was wrong.

The speaker was a boy about his own age; but there was something about him which at a very first glance showed that he was different from other boys. He was respectably dressed; the chief peculiarity about his clothing being that it seemed to fit him like his skin. A tighter pair of trousers surely never imprisoned human legs. His waistcoat fitted him without a crease, and it seemed that he had been made for his coat, and not his coat for him. He wore a billycock hat of a particularly knowing pattern, set rakishly upon the side of his head; a stand-up collar made it difficult for him to look anywhere except straight in front of him; and an enormous pin, set in the centre of a gorgeous blue necktie, made his costume quite complete.

Even more remarkable than his costume was his face. It has been said of the famous Lord Chancellor, Lord Thurlow, that no one could be so wise as Lord Thurlow looked; it was almost equally impossible that any one could be so knowing as the expression of his countenance declared this young gentleman to be. It was an unhealthy face, an unpleasant face, with something in it which reminded you of how Methuselah might have appeared in his green old age. It was never still; the eyes seemed to be all over the place at once; it seemed to be continually listening to catch the first sound of something or some one drawing near.

"Down on your luck? What are you piping your eye for? Does that sort of thing suit your constitution? Turn round to the light, and let's have a look what you're like; don't keep hugging that pillar as though it was your ma."

Through all his misery Bertie saw that this young gentleman was centuries older than himself, though they had probably entered the world within the same twelve months. Besides, he was too prostrated to resist, even had he wished, and he allowed the other to drag him into a position in which he might study his features at his leisure.

"I thought so,—directly I caught sight of your back I thought I knew your size. Wasn't you in Sackville Street this morning?"

"In Sackville Street?" repeated Bertie vaguely.

"Yes, in Sackville Street, my bonny boy. Never heard tell of Sackville Street before, I suppose? So I should think by the look of you. Wasn't it you I pitched the old girl's purse to?"

A light was dawning upon Bertie's mind.

"Was it you who stole the purse?"

The other gave a quick look round, as though the question took him by surprise—if anything so self-possessed could be said to be taken by surprise.

"Stow your cackle! Do you want to have me put away? Where do you live when you're at home? You must be a sharp one, though you do look so jolly green! I thought you'd be buckled to a certainty! I never expected to see you walking about as large as life. It gave me quite a start when I saw you hugging that pillar as though you loved it. How did you make tracks?"

Bertie was trying to collect his thoughts. This boy before him was a thief, a miserable hound who tried to escape the consequences of his own misdeeds by putting the odium of his crimes upon the innocent. But Bertie was alone; alone in the great city, hungry, thirsty, tired, wet, and cold. Human companionship was human companionship after all. And this boy looked so much more prosperous than he himself was. Yesterday he would have done great things; to-day he would have welcomed a crust of bread coming even from this thief.

"The policeman wanted to lock me up."

"No! did he though? Funny ones those policemen are! they're always wanting to go locking people up. And did he cop the purse?"

"He took the purse away from me."

"And how come you to be making love to that there pillar, instead of enjoying yourself in a nice warm cell? I suppose you didn't give the policeman one in the nose and knock him down?"

"We met some people in the street, and they made him let me go."

"Did they though? that was kind of them! When policemen was making free with me I wish I was always meeting people in the streets who would make them interfering bobbies let me go. And now, who are you when you're at home? We're having quite a nice little conversation, ain't we, you and I? Glad I met you, quite a treat!" He raised his hat to express his sense of the satisfaction which he felt. "You don't look as though you were raised in these 'ere parts."

Bertie hung his head; he was ashamed: ashamed of many things, but most of all just then of the company he was in. And yet, if he turned this thief adrift, where else should he find a friend? And he was so tired, so hungry, so conscious of his own helplessness.

132

"You very nearly got me locked up this morning," was his answer.

"Well, my noble marquis, wasn't it better for you to be locked up than me? It'll have to come, you know—if not to-morrow the day after."

To Bertie this view of the matter had not occurred before. It had not entered into his calculations that a journey to the Land of Golden Dreams would necessitate the process of locking-up.

"Are you on the cross, or only mouching around?"

This inquiry was Greek to Bertie, and his questioner perceived that he failed to understand.

"You're a fly bloke, that you are! What's your little game? You haven't got a fortune in your pocket, or a marquis for a pa? What do you do to live? I suppose you ain't reckoning to die just yet awhile."

"I wish I could do something, but I can't."

"Oh, you wish you could do something, do you, but unfortunately you can't! Well, you are a trial for the nerves! Have you got any money?"

Bertie hung his head still lower. To be despised by a thief! Was this the result of all his dreams?

"No!"

"Got any friends?"

"I've run away from them."

And here the boy broke down. Turning, and leaning against a pillar, he burst into a passion of tears. The other eyed him for a few moments, whistling beneath his breath.

"That's the time of day, is it? I thought you were something of that kind from the first, I did. What did you run away for?"

Bertie could not have told him to save his life. To have told this thief that he had started on a journey to the Land of Golden Dreams; that he had resolved to emulate the doings of his heroes, Dick Turpin, Crusoe, Jack the Giant-Killer, and Robin Hood! Oh, ye gods! and now to be crying against a post!

"Father living?"

No answer.

"Mother?"

No answer.

How well he knew that he loved his parents now! The mere mention of the word "mother" made him hysterical with woe. To have come within reach of his mother's loving arms, to have been folded to her breast! If he could only come within reach of her again!

The other stood observing him with critical eyes, whistling all the time.

"You seem to have had a considerable lot of water locked up tight. I should think you would have bust if you hadn't had a chance to let it go. What are you a-howling at? Crying for your mammy?"

For answer Bertie turned with a sudden ferocity and struck at him savagely. But the blow was struck at random, and the other had no difficulty in avoiding it by stepping aside.

"Hollo! don't you come that game again, or I'll show you how to use a bunch of fives."

But Bertie showed no further signs of fight. It had only been an almost childish display of passionate spite at the other's coarse allusion to his "mammy"—the mother whom he was now so sure he loved so well. Even the passion of his tears died away into a whimper. He had not strength enough to continue in a passion long.

"Are you hungry?" asked the other.

"I'm starving!"

"Ah, I've been hungry, and more than once, and it isn't nice. I shouldn't be surprised if you found it rather nasty, especially if you aren't used to it. Now, look here; let's have a look at you."

He went close up to Bertie and looked him straight in the face with his keen, restless eyes. Bertie returned the look as well as he could with his tear-stained orbs.

"You look a game 'un, somehow; and you look grit. I suppose it's feeling peckish you don't like. There's a lot of talk about courage what's always the same, but I don't believe there ever was a chap who kept up his pluck upon an empty belly. I've been hungry more than once. Now, look here; if I take you to a crib I know of, and set you up in vittles and a shake-down, will you keep your mouth shut fast?"

"I don't know what you mean."

"Oh, yes, you do; you're not so soft as that. If I act square with you, will you act square with me?"

"I always do act square," said Bertie.

"Very well, then, come along; if you do, then you're the sort for me. I did you a bad turn this morning, now I'll do you a good one to make up."

Chapter XVI

THE CAPTAIN'S ROOM

Trusting himself to his companion's guidance, Bertie went where the other chose to take him. Under ordinary circumstances he would have thought a good many times before he would have allowed himself to be led blindfold he knew not where; but tired, wet, cold, and so hungry, he resigned himself to circumstances. He could not possibly find himself in a worse position than his present one; at least, so it seemed to him. Certainly it had not been part of his plans to be a companion of thieves; but then nothing which had befallen him had been part of his plans.

His companion led him to a court within a stone's throw of Drury Lane, and was just about to turn the corner when something caught his eyes. He walked straight on, taking Bertie with him.

"There's a peeler. I don't want him to see me go down there; it isn't quite what I care for to let them gentry have their eyes upon my family mansion."

What he meant Bertie failed to understand. He saw no one in sight to cause alarm, and indeed it almost seemed that his companion had eyes behind his head, for, as quickly appeared, the policeman was at their back some considerable distance off. They reached the entry to another court, and down this his companion strutted, as though he was anxious all the world should have their eyes upon him. But no sooner was he in than he slunk into a doorway.

"Come in here, my bonny boy, and let the gentleman go past. He's taking a little walk for the benefit of his health, poor chap. They're always taking walks, them peelers are. I wish they'd stop at home; I really do."

A measured tramp, tramp, tramp approached. The thief put his hand over Bertie's mouth as though he were fearful he would make a sound. The policeman reached the entry, paused a moment as if to peer into its depths, and then passed on. When he had gone the thief spoke again.

"Good-bye, dear boy; sorry to lose you, but the best of friends must part. Come along, my rib-stone pippin; you and me'll go home to tea."

Satisfied that the coast was clear, the two ventured out of the doorway, reached the open street again, and this time turned without hesitation into the court which they had passed before. It was unlit by any lamp, and was so narrow that it was not difficult to believe that a man standing on a roof on one

136

side of the way might, if he were an active fellow, spring with a single bound on to the roof on the opposite side. Fortunately it was not long, the whole consisting of apparently not more than twelve or fifteen houses. At the extreme end Bertie's companion stopped.

The place was a *cul-de-sac*. It ended in a dead wall. But on the other side of the wall towered a house of what, in such a neighbourhood, seemed unusual dimensions. The entrance proper was in another street, and the original architect had probably had no intention that an entry should be effected from where they were. In a recess in the wall, so hidden as to be invisible to Bertie in that light, and so placed as to appear to be a door opening into the last house in the court in which they actually stood, was an ancient wooden door, from which the paint had all disappeared owing to the action of time and weather. The two boys stood still for a moment, Bertie dimly wondering what was going to happen next. It seemed to him that he really was an actor in a dream at last—the strangest dream he had ever dreamed. Then the thief whistled a few lines of some uncouth melody in a low but singularly piercing tone. A pause again; then he gave four taps against the ancient wooden door, with a momentary pause between each one. Bertie had heard of mysterious methods of effecting entrances into mysterious houses, and had been charmed with them; but he concluded that they were perhaps better in theory than practice. He would not have liked to have been kept hanging about in the wet such an unconscionable length of time every time he wanted to go home.

At last the door was opened—just as Bertie was beginning to think that the mysterious proceedings would have to be all gone through again.

"Who's there?" inquired a husky voice.

It seemed that after all the whistling and the tapping caution were required.

"All right, mother; it's only me and a friend. Come on, Ikey; cut along inside."

Bertie, thus addressed as "Ikey," was about to "cut along inside," when he found the way barred by the old woman who acted as janitrix. She was a very unpleasant-looking old woman, old and grisly, and very much in want of soap and water: quite unpleasant-looking enough to be called a "hag"—and she smelt of gin. In her hand she carried a guttering tallow candle in a battered old tin candlestick. Hitherto she had held it behind her back, as if to conceal the presence of a light from passers-by. Now she raised it above her head so that its light might fall on Bertie's face. He thought he had never seen a more disagreeable-looking lady.

"Who's the friend?"

"What's that to you? He's a friend of mine, and square; that's quite enough for you. Come along, my pippin."

The answer reminded Bertie of Sam Slater. Even then he wondered if he had not better, after all, trust himself to the tender mercies of the streets; but the other did not allow much time for hesitation. He caught Bailey by the arm, and half led, half dragged him up a flight of steep stone steps. The old woman with the candlestick sent after them what sounded very like a volley of imprecations, while she closed and locked and barred the door.

The thief led the way into a fairly sized room, which was lighted by another tallow candle. The one which the old woman brought with her when she entered made the pair. There was no carpet on the floor, which was extremely dirty; a rickety deal table and four or five rickety chairs formed all the furniture. There was a bright fire burning in an antiquated fireplace, from which the ashes had apparently never been removed for months, and the atmosphere of the room was distinctly close.

"What have you got to eat?" asked the thief, when the old woman reappeared.

"You're always ready enough to eat, but you re not so ready to pay for what you've eaten. You boys is all the same; you'd rob an old woman of her teeth."

The crone tottered to a cupboard in a corner of the room. The allusion to her teeth was not a happy one, for a solitary fang which protruded from her hideous jaws seemed to be all the teeth she still possessed. From the cupboard she produced a couple of chipped plates, a loaf of bread, and a piece of uncooked steak, which probably weighed several pounds. The thief's eyes glistened at sight of it.

"That's the tuck! Cut me off a chunk, and I'll frizzle it in two threes."

The old woman cut off a piece which weighed at least a pound and a half. A frying-pan was produced from some unexpected corner. The young rogue, disencumbering himself of his coat and waistcoat, immediately elected himself to the office of cook. A short dialogue took place between the old woman and himself while the cooking was going on.

"What luck have you had?"

"What's that to you?"

"That means you ain't had none. Ah, Freddy, you ain't what you was. I've known you when you allays came home with your pockets full of pretty things."

"You ain't what you was, neither."

A pause. A savoury smell began to come from the frying-pan. The old woman turned her watery, bloodshot eyes to Bertie.

"Who's your friend?"

"Them who don't ask no questions don't get told no lies."

"What's his lay?"

"His lay's hitting old women in the eye; so now you know."

The old woman shook her head, and mourned the decadence of the times.

"Oh, them boys! them boys! When I was a young gal there weren't none of them boys in them there days! Times is changed."

"And this steak's done! Now then, Ikey, make yourself alive and hand the plates."

Without the interposition of a dish the steak was divided in the frying-pan, placed in two equal portions on the plates, and Bertie and the cook fell to.

Epicures have it that a steak fried is a steak spoiled. Neither of those who ate that one would have agreed to the truth of the statement then. From the way in which they disposed of it, a finer, juicier, or more tender steak was never known. The old woman produced a jug of porter to wash it down. Freddy, as the old woman called the thief, did far more justice to this than Bertie did. With the aid of the dark-coloured liquid the whole pound and a half of meat rapidly disappeared, and with it the better part of a loaf as well.

The old woman sat spectator of the feast.

"There was a time when I could eat like that. It's over now a hundred years ago, but I mind it as though it were yesterday."

"Go on! you're not a hundred years old!"

"I'm a hundred and twenty-two next Tuesday week."

Bertie stared, holding a mouthful of steak suspended on his fork in the air. A hundred and twenty-two! What was his tale of years compared to that? Freddy winked at him.

"Yes, I daresay. You were a hundred and ninety-five yesterday, and sixty-two this morning. It's my belief you're about five and twenty."

"Five and twenty! I daresay I look it, but I ain't. I'm more than that. I always did look a wild young thing."

Freddy roared; anything looking less like five and twenty, or a "wild young thing," could scarcely be conceived. The old woman went placidly on.

"I remember Jacky Sheppard, and Dicky Turpin, and Tommy King; they were all highwaymen in my young days."

"I suppose you were a highwayman's wife?"

"So I was; and they hung him the week after we were married. I went and saw him hung, and I've never seen a better hanging since. No, that I haven't. Times is changed since then."

"But you ain't changed. I wonder you don't marry again, a wild young thing like you."

"I ain't a marrying sort—not now I ain't. I've had ten of them, and that's quite enough for me."

"Lor', no! What is ten?"

"Ten's quite enough for one young woman, and when you've been two hundred and ninety times in prison a woman don't feel much like marrying again. It takes it out of her, it do."

Bertie had ended his meal. The warmth and the food had given the finishing touch to his previous fatigue; his head was already nodding on his breast. He heard the old woman talking as in a dream. Ten husbands! two hundred and ninety times in jail! Were they part of his nightmare, the things which he heard her say?

"Hollo, Ikey, you're blinking! Now then, mother, where are you going to put my pal? Can't you find a place where he can be alone?"

Had Bertie been sufficiently wide awake he would have seen the speaker wink at the old woman.

"There's only the captain's room."

The woman's suggestion seemed to startle Freddy, and to set him thinking.

"The captain's room? Where is the captain?"

"How am I to know where he is or where he ain't? He don't tell me none of his goings on, none of you don't. He says to me he'd be four or five days away. That's all I know about it. Times is changed!"

"Got the key?"

"Of course I've got the key."

"Then hand it over."

The old woman produced a key from a voluminous pocket in her dress.

"Now, Freddy, none of your tricks? He's on the square?"

She pointed the key at Bertie, to show the allusion was to him. The young thief took the key away from her.

"He's as square as you! Come along, Ikey! Mother, you stop there till I come back. I want to have a little talk to you."

Taking up one of the candlesticks, the lad led the way out of the room. Bertie staggered, rather than walked, after him.

The house seemed to be very old-fashioned and very large. There were a curious number of staircases, and passages, and turns and twists, and ins and outs, and ups and downs. As Bertie followed his companion's lead it all seemed to him as though it were part of his dream; as though the house was built in the fashion of a maze, and he were bidden to find his way about it blindfold.

At last he found himself in a room, the door of which he was vaguely conscious his companion had unlocked. Although very far from being luxurious, it was better furnished than the one they had left. There was a piece of carpet on the floor; there were two or three substantial-looking chairs, a horsehair couch, an arm-chair, a table, a chest of drawers with a looking-glass on top, and in the corner an old-fashioned four-poster bed with the curtains drawn all round. The closely-drawn dirty dimity curtains made one wonder if it was occupied already, but Freddy showed that it was not by going to it and drawing the curtains aside.

"There's a bed for you, my bonny boy! The Queen ain't got a better bed than that in Buckingham Palace; and if you have got a marquis for a pa, you ain't seen a better one, I know you ain't. That's the captain's bed, that is, and if he was to know I'd made you free of it he'd have a word to say. But as he's gone to see his grandma, and perhaps won't be back for ever so long, we needn't take no count of what he says."

Tired as he was, Bertie was not by any means so prepossessed by the appearance of the bed as his companion seemed to be. It seemed to him just a trifle dirty, and more than a trifle the worse for wear. The beds at Mecklemburg House were even better, while the beds at home were things of beauty and joys for ever compared to this. But still it was a bed, and a bed is a bed; and especially was a bed a bed to him just then.

Freddy waited while he undressed. He even watched him get between the sheets, and drew the curtains when he was there. Then he went and left Bertie to sleep in peace in the captain's room.

And he slept in peace. Just such a dreamless slumber as he had enjoyed in the Kingston "doss-house," and it lasted at least as long. This young gentleman had over-calculated his strength, and had not supposed he would have been so quickly wearied on his journey to the Land of Golden Dreams.

When he awoke it was some minutes before he collected his thoughts sufficiently to understand his whereabouts. The rapidly-occurring incidents of the last day or two had bewildered a brain which was never very bright at best. Putting out his hand, he parted the curtains which hung about him like so many shrouds, and looked out.

The room was filled with daylight; that is to say, as much filled as it probably ever was. The only window was a small one, and at such a height from the ground that Bertie would have needed to stand upon a chair to reach it even.

Had he desired to imitate his escape from his Kingston hosts he would have found very much more difficulty in climbing from the window of the captain's room. But what interested him more than the peculiar position of the window was something which he saw on the chair beside his bed.

This something was some bread and cheese, a couple of saveloys, and some stout in a jug. On the bread was a little scrap of paper. He took it up, and found that on it was written,—

"Sleep it out, old pal!"

This was short, and to the point. It was written on bad paper in worse writing; but what it meant was, probably, that Freddy, entering with refreshments, had found Bertie wrapt in slumber, and being unwilling to disturb him had left him there to sleep it out. Bertie ate and drank, and lying back again upon the captain's bed prepared to act upon the hint. And he did. He woke once or twice in the course of the day, but each time it was only for a minute or two, and each time he turned round and went to sleep again.

But at last he woke for good—or ill, as it turned out, for he woke to be the victim of a series of adventures which were to nearly cost him his life, and which were to show him, better than anything else possibly could have done, that he had been like the silly little child who plays with fire and burns itself with the element it does not understand. He was a young gentleman who required a considerable amount of teaching before he would consent to write himself down an ass; but he was to get much more than the requisite amount of teaching now.

Exactly the same thing happened as at Kingston. He awoke to hear the sound of voices in the room; and now, as then, the speakers were carrying on a conversation without having the slightest idea that they were being

142

overheard.

At first he could not distinguish the words which were being spoken. He only knew that there was some one speaking. At first he took it for granted that the speakers were the lad who had brought him to the house and the old woman he had nicknamed "Mother." But the delusion only lasted for a moment; he quickly perceived that the voices were voices he had never heard before, and that the speakers were two men. He perceived, too, that the day had apparently gone—he had slept it all away—and that the room was lighted by a lamp.

So unconscious were the speakers of there being a listener that they made no attempt to lower their voices; and one in particular spoke with a strain of intense passion in his tones. His were the words which were the first which Bertie heard.

"Fifty thousand pounds! Fifty thousand pounds! Ha, ha, ha!"

The speaker repeated the words over and over again, bursting into a peal of laughter at the end. Another voice replied—a colder and more measured one. The new speaker spoke with a strong nasal accent. Bertie was not wise enough to know that by his speech he betrayed himself to be that new thing in nationalities, a German American.

"Steady, my friend; fifty thousand pounds in jewels are not fifty thousand pounds in cash, especially when the jewels are such as these."

The other went on unheeding.

"Talk about punting on the Stock Exchange! There are precious few punters on the Stock Exchange who pick up fifty thousand pounds and walk off with it at a single coup."

"And, also, there are very few punters on the Stock Exchange who would run the risk of getting penal servitude for life for doing it."

"Yes, there's that to be considered."

"As you say, there's that to be considered."

"Do you think they'd make it penal servitude for life?"

"I think it extremely probable, with your past history and mine."

"Suppose it came to penal servitude for life, what then?"

"Exactly! That is the question to be asked—'What then?'"

"The Countess of Ferndale's jewels! lying on the table in front of me! and in my time I've run the risk of being sent to prison for a pocket-handkerchief."

"But in that case you did not run the risk, my friend, of penal servitude for life, eh?'

"Rosenheim, what are you driving at? Why do you keep harping upon that string? Do you think they'll nab us?"

"They will have a very good try."

"They have tried before and failed."

"They have also tried before and—not failed."

"Fifty thousand pounds! The finest set of jewels in England! insured for fifty thousand pounds—and that's a lot less than they cost—and we've got the insurance policy and the jewels too! Ha! ha! ha! Should we present the policy?"

"We will be generous and return them that. Or, better still, we will keep the policy in case that anything should happen. Holding it, we might make terms with some one. There have such things been done, eh?"

"Fifty thousand pounds! and they cost perhaps a hundred thousand in their time! Did you ever see such a necklace? Those diamonds remind me of fairy tales which I have read—if I were to put the lamp out they'd light the room."

"Yes; but we will not put the lamp out, for fear some of the jewels should be lost—which would be a pity, eh?"

"Did you ever see anything like those diamonds? See how they are flashing in the lamp-light—now look at them!"

Bertie thought that he might as well look too. He peeped through the curtains of the bed to see what was going on. He felt a not unnatural curiosity, for what he had heard had made him open both his eyes and ears. Fifty thousand pounds! The repetition of this sum had a startling effect.

Chapter XVII

TWO MEN AND A BOY

There was a lamp on the table. The fire was lighted in the grate; the table was drawn close up in front of it. The couch was beside the table, and on it a man reclined full length. The head was turned towards Bertie, so that he only had a back view of the person lying down. He could see that he had brown hair, worn rather long, and that he was smoking a cigar, and that was all he could see.

By the table, standing so that his face was turned towards Bertie, was another man—evidently the impetuous speaker. He was about the middle height, slight, yet sinewy, with coal-black hair cut very short, and a dark olive skin, his face being concealed by neither moustache nor beard. He was holding something in his hands, something which he eyed with ravenous eyes. From his position Bertie was not able to perceive what this something was, but he could see that the table was littered with other articles, and that a roll of paper and two boxes of a peculiar shape lay open on the floor.

The dark man was holding the something in his hands in a variety of positions, so that he might get the full effect from different points of view.

"Did you ever see such stones?"

"They are not bad, considering. Their value consists in their number, my dear friend. Separate stones of better quality can be found."

"How much do you say we shall get for it?"

"That remains to be seen. If you ask me how much it cost I should say, probably, altogether, twenty thousand pounds."

Twenty thousand pounds! The dark man was holding in his hand something which cost twenty thousand pounds. Curiosity was too much for Bertie's discretion. The magnitude of the sum had so startling an effect on his bump of inquisitiveness that before he knew it he was trying his best to see what surprising thing it was which had cost twenty pounds. Half-unconsciously he quitted the security of the bed, and standing in his shirt bare-legged on the floor he strained his eyes to see.

Just then the dark man moved into such a position that the unexpected spectator was yet unable to see what it was he held. It was aggravating, but what followed was rather more aggravating still.

"Fancy wearing a thing like that! I wonder how I should look with twenty thousand pounds worth of diamonds round my neck."

He put his hand up to his neck, clasping round it what seemed to Bertie a line of glittering light. Then he turned, probably with the intention of studying the effect in the looking-glass, and, turning, he saw Bertie.

For a moment there was silence—silence so complete that you could have heard much fainter sounds than the fall of the proverbial pin. The man was apparently thunderstruck, as well he might be. He stared at the figure in the shirt as though it were that of one risen from the dead. As for Bertie, his feet seemed glued to the floor, and his tongue to the roof of his mouth. It suddenly dawned upon him that it would have perhaps been better if he had stayed in bed.

The man was the first to regain his self-possession. It was to be a very long time indeed before Bertie was to be again master of his.

"What the something are you?"

At the sound of his companion's voice, the man on the sofa sprang to his feet as though he had been shot. He gave one quick glance; then, snatching up a revolver which lay upon the table, he fired at the frightened boy.

"Rosenheim!"

At the very moment of pulling the trigger the dark man struck up his arm, so that the bullet was buried in the ceiling. But the effect upon Bertie was just as though it had penetrated his heart—he fell like a log.

"He's only a boy. You've shot him."

"I have not shot him. That I will do in a minute or two."

When Bertie recovered from his swoon the dark man was bending over him. His companion was sitting in a chair regarding him with cold, staring eyes—a long, thin man, with a slight moustache and beard, and a peculiarly cruel cast of countenance.

The dark man was the first to address him.

"So you've come too, have you? Perhaps it's a pity, after all. It'll only prolong your misery. Now stand up, put your hands behind your back, and look me in the face."

Bertie did as he was bid, feeling very weak and tottering on his feet. The dark man was perched on the edge of the table, holding a revolver in his hand. His companion, the long, thin man who sat in the chair, held a revolver too. Bertie felt that his position was not an agreeable one. Of one thing he was conscious, that the table was cleared of its contents, and that the roll of paper and boxes which he had noticed on the floor had disappeared.

The dark man commenced the cross-examination, handling his revolver in a way which was peculiarly unpleasant, as though it were a toy which he was anxious to have a little practice with.

"Look me in the face."

Bertie did as he was bid as best he could, though he found it difficult to meet the keen black eyes.

"He needn't look me in the face, or I'll put five shots inside of him."

This was from the long, thin man. Bertie was careful not to show the slightest symptom of a desire to turn that way. The dark man went on.

"Do you know what truth is? If you don't it'll be a pity, because if you tell me so much as the millionth part of a lie I'll empty my revolver into you where you stand."

As if to emphasize this genial threat the dark man pointed his revolver point-blank at his head.

"I'm on that line. I'll empty mine inside him too."

Bertie was conscious that the long, thin man was following his companion's lead. A couple of revolvers were being pointed at him within three feet of his head. He felt more anxious to tell the truth, even though under difficulties, than he had ever been in all his life.

"What's your name?"

"Bertie Bailey."

"What are you doing here?"

"I—I don't know!"

Bertie very certainly didn't. If he could only have undreamt his dreams about the Land of Golden Dreams how happy had he been.

"Oh, you don't know. Who brought you here?"

"Freddy."

"Freddy? Do you mean Faking Fred?"

"If you please, sir, I—I don't know. The old woman called him Freddy."

"Oh, the old woman had a finger in the pie, had she? I'll have a finger in her pie before I've done, and Freddy's too. So you've been sleeping in my bed?"

"Please, sir, I—I didn't know it was your bed."

"Turn round to me."

As this command came from the long, thin man—he had apparently changed his mind about being looked in the face—Bertie turned with the celerity with which a teetotum turns.

"Where do you live?"

"At Upton, sir."

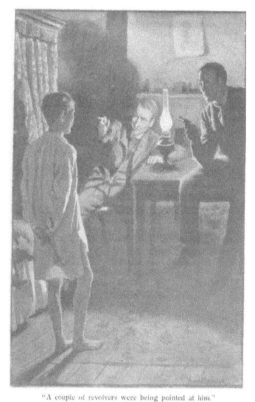

"A couple of revolvers were being pointed at him."
A Hero of Romance]   [Page 238,

A couple of revolvers were being pointed at him."

"Where's that?"

"In Berkshire."

"You're not a thief?"

"No—o, sir."

In his present society Bertie positively felt ashamed to own it. He perhaps felt that these gentlemen might resent it as a slight upon their profession.

"Have you run away from home?"

"Ye—es, sir."

"What for?"

"Fu—fun, sir."

"A good thing to run away for."

Bertie felt that it was a bad thing just then, especially if this sort of thing might be looked upon in the light of fun.

"What's your father?"

"A doctor, sir."

"So you're the son of Dr. Bailey, of Upton, in Berkshire?"

"Ye—es, sir."

"Turn round again!—sharp!"

No one could have turned round sharper than Bertie did then. The dark man took up the questioning.

"How long have you been awake?"

"I—I don't know, sir."

"Did you hear what we were talking about?"

"Ye—es, sir."

"What did you hear?"

"I—I don't know."

"That won't do. Out with it! What did you hear?"

The revolver was brought on a level with Bertie's face. With his eyes apparently doing their best to investigate the contents of the barrel he endeavoured to describe what he had heard.

"I—I heard about the Countess of Ferndale's jewels, and—and about fifty thousand pounds."

"Oh! you did, did you? And what did you hear about the Countess of Ferndale's jewels?"

"I heard that you had—stolen them."

"Is that so? You seem to be gifted with uncommonly good hearing, Master Bailey. What else did you hear? Go on."

"I—I heard that they were insured for fifty thousand pounds, and—and that—that you'd stolen the policy."

"Dear me! What a remarkably fine ear this boy must have! Go on, young man!"

Bertie was painfully conscious that these compliments upon his hearing were not to be taken as they were spoken. He earnestly wished that his hearing had not been quite so good, but with that revolver staring him in the face he felt that perhaps it was better on the whole he should go on. Yet the next confession was made with an effort. He felt that his audience would not receive it well.

"I—I—I heard that if—if you were ta—taken you—you would get pe—penal servitude for life."

There was an ominous silence. The words had had exactly the effect he had intuitively expected. It was the long, thin man who spoke.

"Oh! you heard that if we were caught we should get penal servitude for life? And it didn't occur to you that you might help to catch us, eh?"

"No-o, sir."

"It wouldn't. Now wouldn't it occur to you that such a thing as a reward might perhaps be offered, which it might perhaps be worth your while to handle, eh? That such a trifle as five or ten thousand pounds, in the shape of a reward, might come in useful, eh?"

Bertie did not answer. He could not have answered for his life. The fellow's tone seemed to freeze his blood. The dark man put a question.

"Did you hear any names mentioned?"

"Yes, sir."

"What name did you hear mentioned?"

"I heard you call this gentleman Rosenheim, sir."

In an instant a hand was round his neck, which grasped him as though it were made of steel. There was a sudden twist, and Mr. Rosenheim had flung the lad upon his back. The grasp tightened; he began to choke. If Mr. Rosenheim had been allowed to work his own sweet will it would have been over with him there and then. But the dark man interfered.

"What's the use of killing him?"

The answer was hissed rather than spoken.

"I'll tell you what's the use; it is I who will put him away, not he who will put me away, eh?"

"Leave him alone for a minute; I want to speak to you. It's a nuisance, but I don't think it's so bad as you think. Anyhow, I don't see how we're going to gain anything by killing the boy—at least, not in here."

There was a meaning conveyed in the speaker's last few words which Mr. Rosenheim seemed to understand. They looked at each other for a moment, eye to eye. Then Mr. Rosenheim, standing up, loosed his grasp on Bertie's throat, and the lad was free to breathe again.

"Get up; walk to the end of the room, put your hands behind your back, shut your eyes, and stand with your face to the wall. I'm going to cover you with my revolver, and if you move it'll be for the very last time of asking, for I'll shoot you as dead as mutton. Sharp's the word!"

Sharp was the word. Bewildered, half-stunned, panic-stricken as he was, Bertie had still sense enough to know that he had no alternative but to do as he was bid. The dark man meant what he said, and the youthful admirer of Dick Turpin knew it. The ever-ready revolver covered him as he walked quickly down the room, and took up the ignominious position he was ordered to. Hands behind his back, eyes shut, and his face against the wall! It was worse than standing in the corner at Mecklemburg House Collegiate School, and only little boys had been sent into the corner there.

How long he remained standing there he never knew. It seemed to him hours. But time goes slowly when we stand with our hands behind, eyes shut, face to the wall, and know that a revolver is taking deliberate aim at us behind our backs. A minute becomes an hour, and we feel that old age will overtake us prematurely if we stand there long. They say that when a man is drowning his whole life passes in a moment before his eyes. As Bailey stood with his face against the wall he felt something of that feeling too, and if ever there was a veritable Land of Golden Dreams his home at Upton was that land then. If he could only stand again within the shadow of his mother's door, ah, what a different young gentleman he would be!

Certainly, Mr. Rosenheim and his friend took their time. What they said Bertie could not hear, strain his ears how he might. The sound of their subdued whispering added to the terror of the situation. What might they not be resolving? For all he knew, they might be both examining their revolvers with a view of taking alternate pops at him. The idea was torture. As the moments passed and still no sign was made his imagination entered into details. There was a movement behind him. He fancied they were taking their positions. Silence again. He waited for the shooting to begin. He wondered where the first shot would hit him. Somewhere, he fancied, about the region of the left knee. That would probably bring him to the ground, and the second and third shots would hit him where he fell—probably in the side. The fourth and fifth shots would miss, but the sixth would carry away his nose, while the seventh would finish his career. Promiscuous shooting would ensue, the details of which would have no interest for him, but for some occult reason he decided that they would not cease firing until they had put inside him about a couple of pounds of lead.

In the midst of these agreeable speculations it was a relief to hear the dark man's voice.

"Turn round!"

Bertie turned round, with surprising velocity.

"Where are your clothes?"

"I think they're on the bed, sir."

"Put them on! Sharp's the word!"

Sharp always was the word. Bertie had done some quick things in dressing before to-day, but never anything quite so quick as that. Mr. Rosenheim was sitting in the arm-chair, still fondling his revolver, eyeing Bertie with a most uncomfortable pair of eyes. When Bertie found that in his haste he was putting on his trousers hind side foremost Mr. Rosenheim gave a start. Bertie gave one too, a cold shiver went down his back, and the time in which he reversed the garment and got inside his breeches was perhaps the best on record.

The dark man meanwhile was brushing his hat, putting on his overcoat, and apparently preparing himself for a journey. There was a Gladstone bag on the table. Into this he put several articles which he took from the chest of drawers. Bertie had completed his own costume for some little time before either spoke.

It was Mr. Rosenheim who addressed him first.

"Come here!"

Bertie went with remarkable celerity. "For a doctor's son, my friend, you are not too well dressed, eh?"

Bertie hung his head; he was conscious of the defects in his attire. The dark man flung him a clothes-brush.

"Brush yourself, and make yourself presentable. There's a jug and basin behind that curtain; wash yourself and brush your hair."

Bertie did as he was bid; never had he been so docile.

It was the most uncomfortable toilet he had ever made. When he had carefully soaped his face all over, and was about to wash it off again, there was a report. A shot whistled through the air and buried itself in the wall about a foot above his head. He dropped as though it had struck him, and all but repeated his former swoon.

"You can get up, my friend. It is only a little practice I am having."

Bertie got up, but the pleasure of that wash was destroyed for him. Mr. Rosenheim's ideas of revolver practice were so peculiar that he was in momentary terror of his aiming at an imaginary bull's-eye in the centre of his back.

"How long are you going to be? Come here and let me have a look at you."

Though only half-dried, the soap-suds still remaining in the corners of his eyes, Bertie obeyed the dark man's order and stood in front of him. That gentleman still held the too-familiar revolver in his hand. It had long been the secret longing of Bertie's soul to possess one of his own; henceforward he would hate the sight of the too-agile arm for evermore.

"You don't look like a doctor's son. Own up you

lied." "I—I didn't, sir."

"A pretty sort of doctor's son you look! Has your father any money?"

A wild idea entered Bertie's brain. He remembered how Mr. and Mrs. Jenkins had risen to the bait.

"Ye—yes, sir; he's very rich. He'd give a thousand pounds to get me back again."

But this time the bait failed, and signally.

"Oh, he would, would he? Then he must be about the most remarkable fool of a father I ever came across. Don't you try to stuff your lies down my throat, my joker, because I'm a liar myself, and know the smell. You listen to me. You'd better; because if you don't listen to every word, and stick it inside your head, it'll be a case of shooting, though I'm hung for you five minutes after. Do you hear?"

"Ye—yes, sir."

"My name's Captain Loftus. Do you hear that?"

"Ye—yes, sir."

"And I'm your uncle—your Uncle Tom. Do you hear that? I'm your Uncle Tom."

"Ye—yes, sir."

"Don't say 'sir,' say 'Uncle Tom.'" "Ye—

yes, Un—Uncle Tom."

"And don't you stutter and stammer; there's no stuttering and stammering about this."

"This" was the revolver which "Uncle Tom" pointed in his playful way at his nephew.

"And you've been a bad boy, and you've run away from your poor mother, and I'm going to take you back again. You understand?"

"Ye—yes, sir—I mean, Uncle Tom."

"Mind you do mean 'Uncle Tom,' and don't let us have any fooling about it. Do you hear? Don't let's have any fooling about it."

"No—o, Uncle Tom."

How devoutly he hoped that what his "uncle" said was true, and that he was going to be taken back to his mother. But the hope was shattered by the words which followed.

"Now just you listen to me. I've got half a dozen more words to say, and they're the pick of the lot. I'm going to take you with me. You'll be all right so long as you keep your mouth shut; but if you speak a word without permission from me, or if you hint anyhow at the pleasant little conversation we've had here, I'll shoot you on the spot. You see, I'm going to put my revolver into the inside pocket of my coat; it will be always there, and always ready for you, and mind you don't forget it."

Bertie was not likely to forget it. He watched the captain placing the weapon in a convenient inner pocket of his overcoat with an interest too deep for words. Mr. Rosenheim added an agreeable little remark of his own.

"You understand, my friend? You are to dismiss from your mind any little ideas you may have had about the Countess of Ferndale's jewels, or your uncle, Captain Tom Loftus, will practise a little revolver shooting upon you, eh, my friend?"

And Mr. Rosenheim covered the lad with his own revolver. There was such an absolutely diabolical grin upon the gentleman's face that Bertie felt as though his blood had congealed in his veins. The revolver might go off at any moment, and this time it would be a case of hitting. Bertie was persuaded that one more of Mr. Rosenheim's little practice shots would be quite enough for him.

The change from Mr. Rosenheim to Captain Loftus was actually a relief.

"Are you ready?"

"Ye—yes, sir!"

"*Sir?*"

The "sir" was shouted in a voice of thunder, and the captain's hand moved towards the inner pocket of his coat.

"Un—Uncle Tom, I mean."

"And you better mean it too, and say it, or you'll never say another word. Put your hat on. Catch hold of that Gladstone."

Bertie put his hat on, and took the bag. The captain turned to Mr. Rosenheim.

"Good-bye."

"Good-bye, my friend; I wish you a pleasant journey, and your nephew too."

The captain put his own hat on, took Bertie's hand, led him out of the room, and almost before the lad knew it they were standing in the street. Bertie thanked his stars that at least Mr. Rosenheim was left behind.

Chapter XVIII

THE BOAT-TRAIN

They did not leave the house by the same mysterious door by which Freddy had entered, but by one which brought them at once into a busy street. Vehicles were passing to and fro, and they had not gone many steps before the captain—to give him the title which he had not improbably himself affixed to his name—called a hansom. Bertie got in. The captain directed the driver where to drive in an undertone, seated himself beside his "nephew," and they were off.

During the drive not a word was spoken. Where they were going Bertie had not the faintest notion; he felt pretty certain that he was not really being taken home. His head was in a whirl; he was in such awe of his companion that he scarcely dared to move, far less to use his eyes in an endeavour to see where they were going. The cab almost immediately turned into a busy thoroughfare. The hubbub of the traffic and the confusion of the crowded streets completed the lad's bewilderment, making it seem to him as though they were journeying through pandemonium. The busy thoroughfare into which the cabman turned was, in fact, the Strand—the Strand at what is not the least busy hour of the day, when the people are crowding into the theatres. The cabman took another turn into comparative quiet, and in another minute they were whirling over Waterloo Bridge, along Waterloo Bridge Road, into the huge terminus of the South-Western Railway. A porter came forward to help them to alight, but the captain, dismissing him, took his bag with one hand, and taking Bertie's own hand in the other, stepped on to the platform of the station.

He had only taken a few steps when, pulling up, he spoke to Bailey in low, quick, significant tones.

"Look here, my lad; I don't want to haul you about as though I'd got you in custody, and I don't mean to let you get out of my sight. I'm going to loose your hand, and let you walk alone. Carry this bag, and stick as close to me as wax, or—"

A significant tap against the pocket which contained the revolver served to complete the sentence. Bertie needed no explanation in words; the action was as full of meaning as any eloquence of speech could possibly have been.

The hansom had put them down at the departure platform of the main-line trains. The captain looked at the station clock as they came in, and Bertie, following the direction of the other's eye, saw that it was a quarter-past nine. The station was full of people; porters and passengers were hurrying hither and thither, mountains of baggage were passing to and fro.

The captain turned into the booking-office, Bertie sticking close to his side. Some wild idea of making a dash for freedom did enter his mind, but to be dismissed as soon as it entered. What could he do? He was fully persuaded that if he were to make the slightest sign of attempting to escape, his companion would shoot him on the spot. But even if he did not proceed to quite such extreme lengths, what then? To have attempted to take to actual flight, and to have run for it, would have been absurd. He would have been caught in an instant. His only hope lay in an appeal to those around him. But what sort of appeal could he have made? If he had suddenly shouted, "This man has stolen the Countess of Ferndale's jewels, worth fifty thousand pounds!" no doubt he would have created a sensation. But the revolver! Bertie was quite persuaded that before he would have had time to have made his assertion good the captain would have put his threat into execution, and killed him like a cat, even though, to use that gentleman's own words, he had had to hang for it five minutes afterwards.

No; it seemed to him that the only course open to him was to obey the captain's instructions.

There was a crowd round the ticket-office, at sight of which the captain put the lad in front of him, and his hand upon his shoulder, holding him tight by means of the free use of an uncomfortable amount of pressure. Under these circumstances he could scarcely ask for tickets without the lad hearing what it was he asked for—as in fact he did.

"Two first for Jersey."

Two first-class tickets for Jersey! The tickets were stamped and paid for, and they were out of the crowd again. It was some satisfaction to know where it was they were going, but not much. He was too evidently not being taken home again. Jersey and Upton were a good many miles apart.

The captain went up and down the train with the apparent intention of discovering a compartment which they might have for themselves. But if that was his intention he sought in vain. The tourist season had apparently set in early, and on this particular night the train was crowded. They finally found seats in a compartment in which there were already two passengers, and into which there quickly came two more. It was a smoking carriage; and as the other passengers were already smoking, and the captain lit a cigar as soon as he entered, the atmosphere soon became nice and fresh for Bertie. Five smoking passengers in a first-class compartment do not make things exactly pleasant for a non-smoking sixth. The captain took a corner seat; Bertie sat on the middle seat next to him, right in the centre of the smoke.

They started. All the passengers, with the exception of the captain and Bertie, had books or papers. For a time silence reigned. The passengers read, the captain thought, the lad lamented. If the train had only been speeding towards Slough instead of Jersey! It may be mentioned that at this point of the expedition Bertie was not even aware where Jersey was, and was not even conscious that to reach it from London one had to cross the sea.

As they passed Woking the silence was broken for a moment. A tall, thin, severe-looking gentleman, with side whiskers, and a sealskin cap tied over his ears, having finished with the *Globe*, handed it to the captain.

"Have you seen the *Globe*?"

"Thank you, I haven't."

The captain took it, and began to read. Almost without intending it Bertie watched him. For some reason, though he could scarcely have told what it was, for the reader gave no outward signs of anything of the kind, he was persuaded that the paper contained something which the captain found of startling interest. He saw the captain stare with peculiar fixedness at one paragraph, never taking his eyes off it for at least five minutes. He even thought that the captain's lips were twitching, that the captain's face grew pale. As if perceiving the inspection and resenting it, he drew the paper closer to him, so that it concealed his countenance.

As they were nearing Aldershot and Farnham a little conversation was commenced which had a peculiar interest for Bertie, if for no one else in the compartment.

In the opposite corner, at the other end of the carriage, was seated a stout old gentleman, with a very red face and very white hair. He wore a gorgeous smoking-cap, which was stuck at the back of his head, and there was something about his appearance and demeanour which impressed the beholder with the fact that this was a gentleman of strong opinions.

In front of him was a thin young gentleman with a pale face, who puffed at a big meerschaum pipe as though he did not exactly like it. He was reading a novel with a yellow back, which all the world could perceive was *The Adventures of Harry Lorrequer*. The old gentleman had been reading the *Evening Standard* through a pair of gold glasses of the most imposing size and pattern.

He had apparently finished with his paper, for he lowered it and stared through his glasses at the thin young man in front of him. The thin young man did not seem to be made the more comfortable by his gaze.

"Have you seen about the Countess of Ferndale's jewels?"

This was said in loud, magisterial tones, which commanded the attention of the whole compartment. The young man seemed startled. Bertie was startled; he almost thought he saw the *Globe* tremble in the captain's hands.

"I beg your pardon?"

"Have you seen about the Countess of Ferndale's jewels?"

This was said in tones rather louder and more magisterial than at first.

"No! No! I haven't!"

"Then, sir, I say it's a disgrace to the country."

Whether it was a disgrace to the country that the thin young man had not heard about the Countess of Ferndale's jewels was not quite clear. The thin young man seemed to think it was, for he turned pink. However, the old gentleman went on,—

"Here's a noble lady, the wife of one of the greatest English peers, returning from personal attendance upon her sovereign, bearing with her jewels of almost priceless value, and they disappear from underneath her nose. I say it's a disgrace to the country, sir!"

The thin young man seemed relieved. It was evidently not his want of knowledge which was a disgrace to the country, but the disappearance of the lady's jewels. Bertie pricked up his ears; the captain gave no sign of having heard.

The young man ventured on a question.

"How's that? Have they been stolen?"

"How's that, sir! Stolen, sir! I should think they have been stolen!"

The words were spoken with almost volcanic force. All the carriage began to take an interest in what was being said—excepting always "Uncle Tom."

The old gentleman grasped his paper with his right hand, and emphasized his words with the first finger of his left.

"At half-past two this afternoon the Countess of Ferndale, who has been in attendance at Windsor Castle, started from Windsor to London. Windsor, sir, is at a distance of twenty-two miles from town—twenty-two miles; no more. The traffic between that place and London, sir, is extremely large; and yet, travelling on that short strip of railway, in one of Her Majesty's own state coaches—"

"I don't think it was in one of the Queen's own coaches she was travelling."

"No; it wasn't."

The first interruption came from the severe-looking gentleman who had lent the Captain the *Globe*; the second from a placid-looking gentleman with black whiskers, who sat beside him in front of Bertie.

"Well, sir, and what difference does that make?"

"None at all, perhaps, to the main issue," the severe gentleman allowed. "It's only a statement of fact."

"Well, sir, supposing it is a statement of fact, which, as at present advised, I am not prepared to allow, I suppose I may take it for granted that she was travelling in a compartment which was exclusively reserved for her own use?"

"That, I believe, was the case."

"Well, sir, travelling on that short strip of railway, in a compartment exclusively reserved for her own use, what happens in this England of the nineteenth century? It is incredible! monstrous! She had with her certain family jewels of almost priceless value. She had been wearing them in Her Majesty's own presence. They were in the charge of certain officers of her household; and yet, when she comes to the end of that journey of two and twenty miles, they were gone, sir!—gone! vanished into air!"

"No! If they were stolen, he must have been a jolly clever thief," observed the thin young man.

"A jolly clever thief!" said, or rather roared the stout old gentleman. "You speak of the author of such an outrage as a jolly clever thief. If I had the miscreant within reach of my hand"—the stout old gentleman stretched out his hand, and the thin young man shrank out of the way—"I should consider myself justified in striking him down, and trampling the life out of his wretched carcass. I should consider the doer of such an act deserved well of his country, sir!"

Bertie felt a cold shiver go down his back. He pictured the stout old gentleman striking him down, and trampling the life out of his wretched carcass. At that moment he almost felt as though he had been guilty of the crime; he almost expected the stout old gentleman to read his guilt upon his countenance, and conclude the business there and then. As for the captain— the least that Bertie expected him to do was to open the door and, without waiting for such a small detail as the stopping of the train, disappear into the night. What he actually did was to return the *Globe*, with a courteous bow, to the severe-looking gentleman, carefully cross his knees, and light a fresh cigar. Then he listened to what was being said with an air of placid interest.

"What was the value of the jewels?" inquired the gentleman with the black whiskers.

"Priceless! priceless! How can you value jewels which have been in the possession of a noble family for generations? which are family heirlooms?"

"I suppose they must be pretty well known, in which case the thieves will find considerable difficulty in getting rid of their spoil."

"Getting rid of their spoil! Is it conceivable that such villains are to be allowed to get rid of their spoil, to sell it, and fatten on the proceeds?"

"Very conceivable, indeed, unless something is done to stop them."

The stout old gentleman was so affected by the idea of the countess's jewels being brought into the market in such an ignoble way that words failed him, and he gasped for breath.

During all this time Bertie's sensations were indescribable. He felt as though he were under the power of some hideous spell. He would have given anything to have been able to spring up and denounce the miscreant who had wrought this crime. There would have been something worthy of a hero in that; but he could not do it, he was spellbound. Perhaps the consciousness of the revolver which was in the captain's pocket had something to do with his state of mind; but it was not only that, he was paralysed by the position itself —by the knowledge that his own act had made him the companion of such a rogue.

Just at the moment the captain raised his hand, as if by chance, and tapped the inner pocket of his coat. Slight though the action was, Bertie saw it, and he shuddered. But there was worse to follow.

The remark was made by the severe-looking gentleman. .

"What strikes me is, how was the theft performed? Those in charge of the box swear that it was never out of their sight. When they started the jewels were in it; when they reached their journey's end they were gone. They couldn't have been spirited away."

"The boxes were changed."

Bertie felt that his heart had ceased to beat. The words were spoken by "Uncle Tom."

It was the first time he had opened his lips. The eyes of all in the carriage were fixed upon him. He was seated, apparently quite at his ease, a cigar in his mouth, one hand upon his knee, and, as he spoke, with the other he undid the top button of his overcoat.

"How could they be changed? Those in charge state that they never lost sight of the particular box in which the jewels were."

The captain took his cigar out of his mouth, and puffed out a wreath of smoke.

"I have a theory of my own upon the subject."

"And I say it is monstrous! preposterous! incredible! Do you mean to tell me such a trick as that could have been played in the light of day?"

This was from the stout old gentleman.

"Apparently it was done in the light of day, however it was done. I have only suggested a theory. Of course you are at liberty to accept it or reject it, as you please."

"I do reject it entirely! absolutely! I am sixty-seven next June, and I know perfectly well that no such trick would be played on me."

"You are, probably, a person of peculiar acumen."

But the stout old gentleman was not to be flattered.

"As you have a theory of how the robbery was performed, perhaps you have a theory of how the robbers might be caught."

"I have one or two theories. I could go further and say that, if it were made worth my while, I would engage to find the thieves."

"Made worth your while, sir! Isn't it worth every honest man's while to find a thief?"

"Not necessarily. Take your own case. Would you be prepared to find the thieves?"

"If I knew where they were."

"Precisely; that is just the point. What you mean is, that if they were found you would give them into custody, but you have to find them first. People don't go thief-hunting from motives of pure philanthropy; even a policeman requires you to make it worth his while."

"May I ask if you are an amateur detective?" inquired the severe-looking gentleman.

"I shouldn't call myself quite that," said "Uncle Tom."

"But you have evidently had considerable experience in dealing with crime?"

"It has been the study of my life," said "Uncle Tom."

"I suppose that it is a very interesting study?"

"Very interesting indeed."

"If it is not an impertinent question, may I ask whether it has been your own experience that such a study improves the moral nature of a man?"

"Quite the reverse," said "Uncle Tom."

"You are frank."

"What is life unless you are?" asked "Uncle Tom."

The captain laughed; but Bertie was in agony The train began to slow.

"I think this is Southampton," said the thin young man.

And it was.

Chapter XIX

TO JERSEY WITH A THIEF

The night's boat was the *Ella*. When the train drew to a standstill and the passengers got out Bertie supposed that their journey was at an end. His ideas as to the whereabouts of Jersey were very vague indeed. He was surprised, therefore, when the captain, taking his hand, led him along the gangway to the boat. The stars were shining brightly overhead, but midnight never is quite as light as noon, and in the uncertain light he could neither see nor understand where it was that they were going.

The captain led him to the hurricane deck, and then he paused. Then he led Bertie to a seat.

"This will be your bed to-night. I don't choose to go into the cabin, and I don't choose that you shall go without me."

Bertie sat down and wondered. Dark figures were passing to and fro; there were the lights on the shore; he could feel the throbbing of the engines; there was the unclouded sky above; he still was in a dream. Unfortunately the figure of the captain standing near turned the dream into a nightmare.

Most of the passengers went at once into their cabins. No one came near them.

"Look up at me."

Bertie looked up. The captain, standing, looked down at him.

"Do you think I didn't see you in the train? Do you think I didn't see you wanting to open your mouth and blab before all those fools? It would have been capital fun for you, now, wouldn't it?"

Bertie shivered. The captain's ideas of fun were singular. Bertie would have almost given his life to have done what the rascal hinted at, but he would have done it in his extremity of agony and with no idea of fun. It would have taken a burden off his mind which seemed almost greater than he could bear; it threatened to drive him mad. But to have played the part suggested would have needed a touch of the heroic—a courage, a strength which Bertie had not got.

The captain went on.

"I had half a mind to have shot you then. If you had winked your eye I think I should have done the trick. I have not quite made up my mind what I shall do with you yet. We shall soon be out at sea. Boys easily fall overboard at night. I shouldn't be surprised if you fall overboard—by accident, you understand."

The captain smiled; but Bertie's heart stood still.

"Now lie down upon that seat, put your head upon that bag, and don't you move. I shan't go out of revolver range, you may rest assured."

Bertie lay down upon the seat. The captain began pacing to and fro. Every second or two he passed the recumbent boy. Once Bertie could see that he was examining the lock of the revolver which he was holding in his hand. He shut his eyes, trying to keep the sight away.

What an unsatisfactory difference often exists between theory and practice! If there was one point in which he had been quite sure it was his courage. To use his own words, he had pluck enough for anything. To "funk" a thing, no matter what; to show the white feather under any set of conditions which could be possibly conceived—these things were to him impossible.

In such literature as he was acquainted with, the boy heroes were always heroes with a vengeance. They were gifted beings whose nerve was never known to fail. They fought, with a complete unconsciousness of there being anything unusual in such a line of conduct, against the most amazing odds. They generally conquered; but if they failed their nerves were still unshaken, and they would disengage themselves with perfect coolness from the most astounding complication of disasters. They never hesitated to take life or to risk it; blood was freely shed; they thought nothing of receiving several shots in the body and a sword-cut at the back of the head.

As for Dick Turpin, and Robin Hood, and Robinson Crusoe, and Jack the Giant-Killer—all the world knows that they went through adventures which makes the hair stand up on end only to read of, and through them all they never winced. Bertie was modestly conscious that these gentlemen were perhaps a little above his reach—just a little, perhaps; but what the aforementioned boys had done he had thought that he himself could do.

Yet here he was, lying upon a seat and shutting his eyes to prevent him from seeing a revolver. Why, one of those heroic boys would have faced the whole six shots and never trembled!

The steamer started, and so did Bertie. Taken by surprise by the sudden movement, he raised himself a little on the seat.

"Keep still!"

The captain's voice came cool and clear. Bertie returned to his former position, not pausing to consider what his heroes would have done.

"If you want to move you must first ask my permission; but don't you move without it, my young friend."

Bertie offered no remonstrance. The seat was not a comfortable one to lie upon. It was one of those which are found in steamers, formed of rails, with a space between each rail. Possibly when they reached the open sea it would be less comfortable still. But Bertie lay quite quiet, and never said a word. It was not exactly what his heroes would have done. They would have faced the villain, and dared him to do his worst; and when he had done his worst, and sent six shots inside them, with a single bound they would have grasped him by the throat, and with a laugh of triumph have flung him head foremost into the gurgling sea.

But Bertie did not do that.

So long as they remained in the river one or two of the passengers still continued to move about the decks. The night was so glorious that they probably thought it a pity to confine themselves in the stifling cabins. But by degrees, one after the other, they disappeared, until finally the decks were left in possession of the captain and Bertie, and those whose duty it was to keep watch at night.

Although they had passed Hurst Castle and reached the open sea, the weather was so calm that hardly any difference was perceptible in the motion of the vessel. Bertie still lay on the seat, looking at the stars.

He had no inclination to sleep, and even had he had such inclination, not improbably the neighbourhood of "Uncle Tom" and his revolver would have banished slumber from his eyes.

He was not a sentimental boy. Sentimental boys are oftener found in books than life. But even unsentimental boys are accessible to sentiment at times. He was not a religious boy. Simple candour compels the statement that the average boy is not religious. But that night, lying on the deck, looking up at that wondrous canopy of stars, conscious of what had brought him there, aware of his danger, ignorant of the fate which was in store for him, knowing that for all he could tell just ahead of him lay instant death, he would have been more or less than boy if his thoughts had not strayed to unwonted themes.

Through God's beautiful world, across His wondrous sea—the companion of a thief. Bertie's thoughts travelled homewards. A sudden flood of memories swept over him.

All at once the captain paused in front of him.

"Shall I throw you overboard?"

There was a glitter in his eyes. A faint smile played about his lips. Bertie was not inclined to smile. His tongue clave to the roof of his mouth.

"I have been asking myself the question, Why should I not? I shall have to dispose of you in one way or other in the end; why not by drowning now? One plunge and all is over."

This sort of conversation made Bertie believe in the possibility of one's hair standing straight up on end. He felt persuaded that none of his heroes had ever been spoken to like this; nothing made of flesh and blood could listen to such observations and remain unmoved, especially with the moonlit waters disappearing into the night on every side. What crimes would they not conceal?

"It is this way. It is you, or—I. In the railway train you would have proclaimed me had you dared. You did not dare; sooner or later, perhaps, you will dare more. Why should I wait for your courage to return? We are alone; the sea tells no tales. Boys will lean overboard: what more natural than that you should fall in? It is distressing to lose one's nephew, especially so dear a one; but what is life but a great battle-field which is covered with the slain? Sit up, my boy, and let us talk together."

Bertie sat up, not because he wished it, but because he could not help it. He had lost all control over his own movements. This man seemed to him to be some supernatural being against whom it was vain to attempt to struggle.

There was no one by to listen to the somewhat curious conversation which occurred between these two.

"So you have run away? I think you said you ran away for fun. You have evidently a turn for humour. Does this sort of thing enter into your ideas of fun—this little trip of ours?"

It emphatically did not. Bertie stammered out a negative.

"No—o!"

"You say your father is rich, you have a good home. Were you not happy there?"

"Ye—es!"

"Seriously, then, what did you propose to yourself to do when you ran away?"

"I—I don't know."

"Did you propose to yourself a life like mine?"

Bertie shuddered. He shrank away from the man in front of him with an air of invincible repugnance.

"Answer me! Look me in the face and answer me. I have a taste for learning the opinions of my fellow-men, and you are something original in boys. Tell me, what is your candid opinion of myself? What do you think of me?"

Bertie looked up as he was bidden. There was in his face something of his old bull-dog look. Something of his old courage had come back again, and on his countenance was the answer ready written. But the captain meant to have the answer in plain words.

"Speak! you're not moonstruck, are you? Tell me what you think of me?"

"You'll kill me if I do."

The words came out heavily, as though he had to rid himself of an overpowering weight before he could get them out. There was a momentary pause; then the captain laughed.

"I shall kill you anyhow. What difference will it make? Tell me what you think of me."

"You are a coward and a thief!"

The words were spoken; and in speaking them perhaps Bertie came nearer to what is called a hero than ever in all his life before. But their effect upon the captain was not agreeable. Those who play at bowls must expect rubbers, and those who insist upon receiving an answer which they know can scarcely be agreeable should make the best of it when it comes. But the captain did not seem to see it.

Directly he had spoken Bertie saw that he had put his foot in it. Instinctively he slipped his hands between the rails of the seat and held on tight. Only just in time, for the captain, stooping forward, tried to lift him in his arms.

"Leave go, you young brute!"

Bertie did leave go, but only to throw his arms about the captain's neck. Instantly the captain stood up straight, holding Bertie in his arms, staggering beneath his weight, for the convulsive clutch of the lad's arms about his neck encumbered him.

"If you don't take your arms away I'll kill you!"

But Bertie only clutched the tighter.

"Let me go! let me go!" he screamed with the full strength of his lungs.

The effect was startling. In the prevailing silence the boy's voice was heard far out across the sea. Taken aback by such a show of resistance where none had before been offered, the captain promptly replaced the lad upon the seat.

"What's the matter with you? It was only a joke."

Bertie unclasped his arms. The expression of his face showed that it had been no joke to him. He looked like one who was not even yet quite sure that he had escaped from death.

The man at the helm was unable to see the seat on which they sat. The forward watch had been on the other side the ship. This man now advanced.

"What's the matter there?"

The captain met him with his most placid air.

"Did you hear my nephew's voice? He had no idea he spoke so loud; he was forgetting where we were."

The man advanced still closer.

"What's the matter with you, boy?"

Quite unconsciously the captain unbuttoned his overcoat, and his hand strayed to the pocket at the top.

"No—nothing," stammered Bertie.

"Nothing! I don't know what you call nothing! I should think you was being murdered, hollering out like that. Why don't you go down to the cabin and go to sleep?"

The captain drew the man aside.

"My nephew is a little excitable at times," he said, and tapped his forehead. "He is best away from the cabin. He is better alone up here in the fresh air with me."

The man, a weather-beaten sailor, with an unkempt grey beard, looked him straight in the face.

"Do you mean he's cracked?"

"Well, we don't call it by that name. He's excitable—not quite himself at times. You had better pay no heed to him; he has one of his fits on him to-night—the journey has excited him."

"Poor young feller!"

And the sailor turned to look at the boy. The captain slipped something into his hand. The man touched his hat and went away, looking at the piece of money as he went. And the man and the boy were left alone again.

Bertie, on the seat, clutched the rails as he had done before. The captain, standing in front, looked down at him.

"There's more in you than meets the eye; though, considering you pretend to have a turn for humour, one would have thought you would have been quicker to understand a joke. I say nothing of the noise you made, but you were wise not to answer that fellow's impertinent question. Your presence of mind saved you from accidental contact with the waters, but nothing could have saved you from my six-shooter. You can lie down again. You need have no fear of another accident; your screeching has made that fellow, and probably his comrades, too inquisitive to make it worth one's while to venture that. But when it comes to the question of letting your tongue wag too freely, nothing can save you from my revolver—mark that. It will be then a case of you or I. If you have made up your mind to spoil me, I will spoil you, my little friend. I say you can lie down."

Bertie lay down; and again the captain resumed his pacing to and fro, keeping watch, as it were, over his young prisoner.

The boy fell asleep. The reaction which followed the short sharp struggle beguiled him, and he slept. And oddly enough he slept the sleep of peace. And more than once the captain, pausing in his solitary vigil, bent over the sleeping boy, and looked down at him.

"The young beggar's actually smiling."

And in fact a smile did flit across the sleeper's face. Perhaps he was dreaming of his mother.

"Ran away for fun, did he? Yet the youngster isn't quite a fool. Pity it should be a case of he or I, but self-preservation is Nature's first law! That was a headline in my copy-books unless I greatly err."

The captain lit a fresh cigar, and continued his patrol. What did he think of? A hopeless past and a hopeless future? God forgive him! for such as he there is no forgiveness to be had from men. That self-preservation, which is Nature's first law, is a law which cuts both ways. Honest men must destroy the Captain Loftuses, or they will be themselves destroyed.

The morning dawned; the day returned to the world. Still the boy slept on. At last the captain woke him. He got up, as if bewildered, and rubbed his eyes.

"Well, nephew mine, are you going to sleep for ever? If so, I'm sorry that I woke you. Jump up and come with me."

His "uncle" led the way into the cabin. They were preparing breakfast; the passengers were falling to. The night had been so tranquil that not one had suffered from sea-sickness, and appetite had come with the morning. A trained eye, looking at the fleecy clouds which were peeping over the horizon, would have prophesied a change, and that rough weather was at hand. But the day had dawned in splendour, and so far the morning was as tranquil as the night had been. So those passengers who were going through to Jersey sat down with light hearts to breakfast.

The captain and Bertie joined them. That his "uncle" had no present intention of starving him was plain, for he was allowed a hearty meal of whatever took his fancy.

And while they were at breakfast the *Ella* was brought up alongside the jetty, St. Peter's Port, Guernsey.

Chapter XX

EXIT CAPTAIN TOM

When they returned to the deck the boat was preparing to continue her journey. The fruit vendors—and with what delicious fruit the Guernsey men board the Jersey boats!—were preparing to take their leave, and those passengers who had gone to stretch their legs with a saunter on the jetty were returning to the steamer.

The rest of the voyage was uneventful. Jersey is not very far away from Guernsey, and for a considerable part of the distance the passengers were in sight of land. The breeze began to freshen, and as they steamed round Jersey towards St. Heliers it began to dawn upon not a few that enough of this sort of thing was as good as a feast. There is such a very striking difference between steaming over a tranquil sea and being tossed and tumbled among boisterous waves. It was fortunate they were so near their journey's end. Several of the travellers were congratulating themselves that, when they reached dry land, they would be able to boast that they had voyaged from Southampton to Jersey without experiencing a single qualm. Had the journey been prolonged much further, that boast would have been cruelly knocked on the head. When they drew up beside the pier at St. Heliers, coming events, as it were, had already cast their shadows before. They were saved just in the nick of time.

Bertie and the captain were among the first on shore; and, not unnaturally, the young gentleman supposed that their journeying was at an end. But he was wrong.

"Step out! We have no time to lose! We have to catch another boat, which is due to start."

Bertie stepped out. He wondered if the other boat was to take them back to England. Did the captain mean to pass the rest of his life in voyaging to and fro?

The disappointed flymen, to whom the arrival of the mail-boat is the great event of the St. Heliers day, let them pass. The hotel and boarding-house touters touted, so far as they were concerned, in vain. The captain gave no heed to their solicitations. He evidently knew his way about, for he walked quickly down the jetty, turned unhesitatingly to the left when he reached the bottom, crossed the harbour, and down the jetty again upon the other side. About half-way down was a fussy little steamer which was making ready to start.

"Here you are! Jump on board!"

If Bertie did not exactly jump, he at any rate got on board.

What the boat was Bertie knew not, nor whither it was going. Compared to the *Ella*, which they had just quitted, it was so small a craft that he scarcely thought it could be going back the way the mail had come.

As a matter of fact it was not.

Two or three times a week a fussy little steamer passes to and fro between Jersey and France. The two French ports at which it touches are St. Malo and St. Brieuc. One journey it takes to St. Malo, the next to St. Brieuc. On this occasion it was about to voyage to St. Brieuc.

St. Brieuc, as some people may not know, is the chief town of the department of Cotes-du-Nord, in Brittany—about as unpretending a chief town as one could find. That Captain Loftus had some preconceived end in view, and had not started on a wild-goose chase, not, as might have at first appeared, going hither and thither as his fancy swayed him, seemed plain.

A more roundabout route to France he could scarcely have chosen. Had he simply desired to reach the Continent, fast steamers which passed from Southampton to Havre in little less than half the time which the journey had already occupied, were at his disposal. Very many people, some of them constant travellers, are ignorant of the fact that a little steamer is constantly plying between Jersey and Brittany. It is dependent on the tides for its time of departure. Only in the local papers are the hours advertised. Captain Loftus must have been pretty well posted on the matter to have been aware that on this particular day the little steamer, *La Commerce*, would be starting for St. Brieuc about the time the mail-boat entered Jersey.

He must have had some particular object in making for that remote corner of Breton France. No sooner did the boat enter the little harbour than he made a dash for the railway station.

Bertie seemed to have passed into another world. He had not the faintest notion where he was. He was not even sure that they had reached Jersey. He heard strange tongues sounding in his ears; saw strange costumes before his eyes. In his then state of bewilderment he would have been quite ready to believe anybody who might have chosen to tell him that he had arrived in Timbuctoo.

Some light was thrown upon the subject when they reached the station. The captain took some money out of his pocket and held it out to Bertie.

"Go and ask for the tickets," he said.

Bertie stared. If he had been told to go and ask the man in the moon for a lock of his hair he could not have been more puzzled.

"Do you hear what I say? Go and ask for the tickets."

"Tickets? Where for?"

The captain hesitated a moment, then said:

"Two first-class tickets for Constantinople."

He handed Bertie some silver coins.

"Two first-class tickets for Constantinople."

Bertie stammeringly repeated the words. Could the captain be in earnest?

"I want to catch the train; look alive, or—"

The captain touched the pocket where the revolver was.

Bertie doubtfully advanced to the booking office, gazing behind him as he went to make quite sure that the captain had meant what he said. There was an old lady taking tickets, so he waited his turn.

"Two first-class tickets for Constantinople."

"*Comment?*"

He stared at the booking-clerk, and the booking-clerk stared at him, each in complete ignorance of what the other meant.

"Do you mean to say you can't speak French?"

The captain came to the rescue, speaking so gently that his words were only audible to Bertie's ears.

"No—o."

"Do you mean to say you don't know enough to be able to ask for two first-class tickets for Constantinople?"

"No—o."

"How much French do you know?" "No—

one."

The captain evidently knew a great deal, for he immediately addressed the booking-clerk in fluent French—French which that official understood, for two tickets were at once forthcoming. But whether they were for Constantinople, or for Jericho, or for Kamtchatka, was more than the boy could tell. He was in the pleasant position of not being able to understand a word that was said; of being without the faintest notion where he was, and of not having the least idea where he was going to.

It may be mentioned, however, that the captain had not asked for tickets for Constantinople—which at St. Brieuc he would have experienced some difficulty in getting—but for Brest.

They had not long to wait before the through train from Paris entered the station. They got into a first-class carriage, which they had for themselves, and in due time they were off.

The state of Bertie's mind was easier imagined than described. He had been in a dream since he had started on his journey to the Land of Golden Dreams; and dreams have a tendency to become more and more incoherent.

His adventures up to the time of leaving London had been strange enough, but he had at least known in what part of the world he was. Now he was not possessed of even that rudimentary knowledge. The continued travelling towards an unknown destination, the unresting onward rush, as though the captain meant, like the brook, to "go on for ever"—and this in the case of a boy who had never travelled more than twenty miles from home in his life—had in itself been enough to confuse him; but the sudden discovery that he was in an unknown country, in which they spoke an unknown tongue, put the climax to his mental muddle. Had the captain, revolver in hand, then and there insisted on his informing him which part of his body as a rule was uppermost, he would have been wholly at a loss to state whether it was on his head or heels he was accustomed to stand.

Something strange, too, about the railway carriage, about the country through which they passed, about the people and the very houses he saw through the carriage window made his muddle more.

The names of the roadside stations at which they stopped, which were shouted out with stentorian lungs, were such oddities. They came to one where the word "Guingamp" was painted in huge letters on a large white board. Guingamp! What was the pronunciation of such a word as that? And fancy living at a town with such a name! He was not aware that, like a conjurer's trick, it was only a question of knowing how it was done, and Guingamp would come as glibly to his tongue as Slough or Upton.

And then Belle-Isle-en-Terre and Plouigneau—what names! The educational system which flourished at Mecklemburg House had tended to make French an even stranger tongue than it need have done. He saw the letters on the boards, but he could no more pronounce the words which they were supposed to form than he could fly.

Throughout the long journey—and it is a long journey from St. Brieuc to

Brest—not a word had been exchanged. The captain had scarcely moved. He had stretched his legs out on the seat, and had taken up the easiest position which was attainable under the circumstances; but he had not closed his eyes. Bertie wondered if he never slept; if those fierce black eyes remained always on the watch.

The captain looked straight in front of him; and, although he seemed to pay no heed to what the boy was doing, Bertie was conscious that he never moved without the captain knowing it. What a life this man must lead, to be ever on the watch; to be ever fearful that the time of the avenger had come at last; that the prison gates were about to close on him, and, perhaps, this time for ever.

"Uncle Tom" seemed to be as much at home in Brest as he had been everywhere. The station was filled with the usual crowd. Porters advanced to offer their services to carry the Gladstone bag and place it on a cab, outside the cabmen hailed them in the hope of a fare; but the captain, paying no heed to any of them, marched quickly on.

Were they at their journey's end? Bertie wondered. Was this Constantinople, or had they another stage to go? If not Constantinople, and he had a vague idea that Constantinople could not be reached quite so quickly as they had come—what place was it?

What struck him chiefly as they passed into the town was the number of men in uniform there seemed to be about. Every third person they met seemed to wear a uniform. He supposed they were soldiers, though he had never seen soldiers dressed like these before; and then what a number of them there were! Geography is not a strong point of the English education system, and he had never been taught at Mecklemburg House that Brest was to France much more than Portsmouth is to England, and that its population consists of four classes, soldiers, sailors, dockyard labourers—looking at all those, of whatever grade, who labour in the dockyard in the light of labourers—and, a long way behind the other three, civilians: "civilians" being a generic name for that—regarded from a Brest point of view—absolutely insignificant class who have no direct connection with war or making ready for war.

On their arrival the day was well advanced, and as they went down the Rue de Siam they met the men returning from the yards. Bertie had never seen such a sight before, not even in the course of his present adventures. The Rue de Siam runs down the hill. The dockyards are at the foot. From where they stood, as far as the eye could reach, advanced a dense mass of dirt-grimed men. They were the Government employés, employed by France to make engines and ships of war, and as the seemingly never-ending stream went past he actually moved closer to the captain with a vague idea that he might— think of it, ye heroes!—need *his* protection; for it seemed to the lad that, taken in the mass, he had never seen a more repulsive-looking set of gentlemen even in his dreams.

The captain went straight down to the bridge; then he paused, seeming to hesitate a moment, then turned to the right, striking into what seemed very much like a nest of rookeries. They came to an ancient, disreputable-looking inn. This they entered; and as they did so Bertie's memory suddenly travelled back to the Kingston inn, into which he had been enticed by the Original Badger. The two houses were about on a par.

Apparently the establishment was not accustomed to receive guests of their distinguished appearance—though Bertie was shabby enough—for the aged crone who received them was evidently bent double by her sense of the honour which was paid to the house.

She and the captain carried on a voluble conversation, though, for all that Bertie understood of what they said, they might as well have held their peace. He remained standing in the centre of the brick floor, shuffling from foot to foot, feeling and looking as much out of place as though he had been suddenly dropped into the middle of China. Gabble, gabble went the old crone's tongue, wiggle-waggle went her picturesque white cap—the only picturesque thing there was about her—up and down went her arms and hands. She was the personification of volubility, but unfortunately she might have been dumb for any meaning which her words conveyed to Bertie.

Yet, incomprehensible as her speech might be and was, he could not rid himself of an impression, derived from her manner to the captain, and the captain's manner to her, that they two had met before, and that, in fact, they knew each other very well indeed. But neither then nor at any other time did he get beyond impression.

Certainly her after-conduct was not of a kind to show that, even if she knew the gentleman, she had much faith in his integrity, unless, as was possible, the understanding between the two was of a very deep and subtle kind indeed.

She showed the new arrivals up a flight of rickety stairs, into a room in which there were two beds of a somewhat better sort than might have been expected. Some attempt had also been made to fit the room up after the French fashion, so that it might serve as sitting-room as well as bedroom. There was a table in the centre, and the apartment also contained two or three rush-bottomed chairs.

The old crone, having shown them in, said something to the captain and disappeared. The man and the boy were left alone. They had not spoken to each other since they had left St. Brieuc, and there was not much spoken now.

"You can take your hat off and sit down. We shall sleep here to-night."

So at any rate they had reached a temporary resting-place at last; their journey was not to be quite unceasing. It was only the night before they had left London, but it seemed to Bertie that it was a year ago.

He did as he was bid—took his hat off and sat on a chair. The captain sat down also, seating himself on one chair and putting his feet upon another. Not a word was spoken; they simply sat and waited, perhaps twenty minutes.

Bertie wondered what they were waiting for, but the reappearance of the crone with a coarse white tablecloth shed light upon the matter. They had been waiting while a meal was being prepared.

The prospect revived his spirits. He had not tasted food since they had left the *Ella*, and his appetite was always hale and hearty. But he was thrown into the deepest agitation by a remark which the crone addressed to him. He had not the faintest notion what it was she said; but the mere fact of being addressed in a foreign and therefore unknown tongue made him feel quite ill.

The captain did not improve the matter.

"Why don't you answer the woman?"

"I don't know what she says."

"Are you acting, or is it real?"

Bertie only wished that he had been acting, and that his ignorance had not been real. At Mecklemburg House the idea of learning French had seemed to him absurd, an altogether frivolous waste of time. What would he not have given then—and still more, what would he not have given a little later on—to have made better use of his opportunities when he had them? Circumstances alter cases.

The captain looked at him for a moment or two with his fierce black eyes; then he said something to the old woman which made her laugh. Not a pleasant laugh by any means, and it did not add to Bertie's sense of comfort that such a laugh was being laughed at him.

"Sit up to the table!"

The old woman had laid the table, and had then disappeared to fetch the food to put before her guests. Bertie sat up. The meal appeared. Not by any means a bad one—better, like the room itself, than might have been expected.

When they had finished, and the old crone had cleared the things away, the captain stood up and lighted a cigar.

"Now, my lad, you'd better tumble into bed. I've a strong belief in the virtue of early hours. There's nothing like sleep for boys, even for those with a turn for humour."

Bertie had not himself a taste for early hours as a rule—it may be even questioned if the captain had—but he was ready enough for bed just then, and he had scarcely got between the sheets before he was asleep. But what surprised him was to see the captain prepare himself for bed as well. Bertie had one bed, the captain the other. The lights were put out; and at an unusually early hour silence reigned.

Perhaps the journey had fatigued the man as much as the boy. It is beyond question that the captain was asleep almost as soon as Bertie was.

But he did not sleep quite so long.

While it was yet dark he got up, and, having lit a candle, looked at his watch. Then he dressed very quietly, making not the slightest noise. He took his revolver from underneath his pillow, and replaced it in the top pocket of his overcoat. He also took from underneath his pillow a leathern case. He opened it. It contained a necklace of wondrous beauty, formed of diamonds of uncommon brilliancy and size. His great black eyes sparkled at the precious stones, and the precious stones sparkled back at him.

It was that necklace which had once belonged to the Countess of Ferndale, and which, according to Mr. Rosenheim, had cost more than twenty thousand pounds. The captain reclosed the leathern case, and put it in the same pocket which contained his revolver.

Then, being fully dressed, even to his hat and boots, he crossed the room and looked at Bertie. The boy was fast asleep.

"The young beggar's smiling again."

The young beggar was; perhaps he was again dreaming of his mother.

The captain took his Gladstone bag and crept on tiptoe down the stairs. Curiously enough the front door was unbarred, so that it was not long before he was standing in the street. Then, having lighted, not a cigar this time, but a pipe, he started at a pace considerably over four miles an hour, straight off through the country lanes, to Landerneau. He must have had a complete knowledge of the country to have performed that feat, for Landerneau is at a distance of not less than fifteen miles from Brest; and in spite of the darkness which prevailed, at any rate when he started, he turned aside from the high road, and selected those by-paths which only a native of the country as a rule knows well.

Landerneau is a junction on the line which runs to Nantes. He caught the first train to that great seaport, and that afternoon he boarded, at St. Nazaire, a steamer which was bound for the United States of America, and by night he was far away on the high seas.

Henceforward he disappears from the pages of this story. He had laid his plans well. He had destroyed the trail, and the only witness of his crime whom he had any cause to fear he had left penniless in the most rabid town in France, where any Englishman who is penniless, and unable to speak any language but his own, was not likely to receive much consideration from the inhabitants.

Chapter XXI

THE DISADVANTAGES OF NOT BEING ABLE TO SPEAK FRENCH

In the meantime Bertie slept, perhaps still continuing to dream of his mother. When he woke he thought the captain was still taking his rest. He remained for a time motionless in bed. But it began to dawn upon him that the room was very quiet, that there was no sound even of gentle breathing. If the captain slept, he slept with uncommon soundness.

So he sat up to see if the captain really was asleep, and saw that the opposite bed was empty. Still the truth did not at once occur to him. It was quite possible that the captain had not chosen to wait till his companion awoke before he himself got up.

For the better part of an hour Bertie lay and wondered. By degrees he could not but perceive that the captain's absence was peculiar. Considering the close watch and ward which he had kept upon the lad, it was surprising that he should leave him so long to the enjoyment of his own society.

An idea occurred to Bertie. Supposing the captain was guarding him even in his absence? Then the door would be locked. He got up to see. No; he had only to turn the handle, and the door was open. What could it mean? Bertie returned to his bed to ponder.

Another half-hour passed, and still no signs of the captain. Bertie would have liked to get up, but did not dare. Supposing when the captain returned he chose to be indignant because the lad had taken upon himself to move without his advice?

There came a tapping at the door. Was it the captain? He would scarcely knock at the door to ask if he might be allowed to enter. The tapping again.

"Come in," cried Bertie.

Still the tapping continued. Then some one spoke in French. It was the old crone's voice.

"M'sieu veut se lever? C'est midi!"

Not in the least understanding what was said, Bertie cried again, "Come in!"

The door was opened a few inches, and the old crone looked in. She stared at Bertie sitting up in bed, and Bertie stared at her.

"M'sieu, vot' oncle! Il dort?"

"I don't know what you mean," said Bertie.

They were in the agreeable position of not having either of them the faintest conception of what the other said. She came further into the room and looked about her. Then she saw that the captain's bed was empty.

"Vot' oncle! Où est-il donc?"

Bertie stared, as though by dint of staring he could get at what she meant. The Mecklemburg House curriculum had included French, but not the sort of French which the old lady talked. "Mon père" and "ma mère," that was about the extent of Bertie's knowledge of foreign tongues; and even those simple words he would not have recognised coming from the peculiarly voluble lips of this ancient dame.

While he was still endeavouring to understand, from the expression of her face, what it was she said, all at once she began to scold him. Of course he had still not the slightest knowledge as to what were the actual words she used; but her voice, her gestures, and the expression of her countenance needed no interpreter. Never very much to look at, she suddenly became as though possessed with an evil spirit, seeming to rain down anathemas on his non-understanding head with all the virulence of the legendary witch of old.

What was the matter Bertie had not the least conception, but that something was the matter was plain enough. Her shrill voice rose to a piercing screech. She seemed half choked with the velocity of her speech. Her wrinkled face assumed a dozen different hideous shapes. She shook her yellow claws as though she would have liked to have attacked him then and there.

Suddenly she went to the door and called to some one down below. A man in sabots came stamping up the stairs. He was a great hulking fellow in a blouse and a great wide-brimmed felt hat. He listened to what the woman said, or rather screamed, looking at Bertie all the time from under his overhanging brows. Then he took up the lad's clothes which lay upon the bed, and very coolly turned out all the pockets. Finding nothing in the shape of money to reward his search, he put them down again and glowered at Bertie.

Some perception of the truth began to dawn upon the lad. Could the captain have gone—absconded, in fact—and forgotten to pay his bill? From the proceedings of the man and woman in front of him it would seem he had. The man had apparently searched the youngster's pockets in quest of money to pay what the captain owed, and searched in vain.

All at once he caught Bertie by the shoulders and lifted him bodily on to the floor. Then he pointed to his clothing, saying something at the same time. Bertie did not understand what he said, but the meaning of his gesture was plain enough.

Bertie was to put on his clothes and dress. So Bertie dressed. All the time the woman kept up a series of exclamations. More than once it was all that the man could do to prevent her laying hands upon the boy. He himself stood looking grimly on, every now and then seeming to grunt out a recommendation to the woman to restrain her indignation.

When the boy was dressed he unceremoniously took him by the collar of the coat and marched him from the room. The old crone brought up the rear, shrieking out reproaches as they went.

In this way they climbed down the rickety stairs, Bertie first—a most uncomfortable first; the man next, holding his coat collar, giving him little monitory jerks, in the way the policeman had done down Piccadilly; the woman last, raining abuse upon the unfortunate youngster's head. This was another stage on the journey to the Land of Golden Dreams.

Across the room below to the front door. There was a temporary pause. The old crone gave the boy two sounding smacks, one on each side of the head, given with surprising vigour considering her apparent age. Then the man raised his foot, sabot and all, and kicked the young gentleman into the street!

Then Bertie felt sure that the captain had forgotten to pay his bill.

He stood for a moment in the narrow street, not unnaturally surprised at this peremptory method of bidding a guest farewell. But it would have been quite as well if he had stood a little less upon the order of his going; for the crone, taking advantage of his momentary pause, caught off her slipper and flung it at his head. This, too, was delivered with vigour worthy of a younger arm, and as it struck Bertie fairly on the cheek he received the full benefit of the lady's strength. The other slipper followed, but that Bertie just dodged in time. Still, he thought that under the circumstances, perhaps, he had better go. So he went.

But not unaccompanied.

A couple of urchins had witnessed his unceremonious exit, and they had also seen the slippers aimed. The whole proceeding seemed to strike them in a much more humorous light than it did Bertie, and to mark their enjoyment of the fun they danced about and shrieked with laughter.

As Bertie began to slink away the man said to them something which seemed to make them prick up their ears. They followed Bertie, pointing with their fingers.

"V'là un Anglais! C'est un larron! au voleur! au voleur!"

What it was they shrieked in their shrill voices Bertie had not the least idea, but he knew it was unpleasant to be pointed and shouted at, for their words were caught up by other urchins of their class, and soon he had a force of ragamuffins shrieking close at his heels.

"V'là un Anglais! un Anglais! C'est un lar—r—ron!"

The stress which they laid upon the *larron* was ear-splitting.

As he went, his following gathered force. They were a ragged regiment. Some hatless, some shoeless, all stockingless; for even those who wore sabots showed an inch or two of naked flesh between the ends of their breeches and the tops of their wooden shoes.

As Bertie found his way into the better portions of the town the procession created a sensation. Shopkeepers came to their doors to stare, the loungers in the cafés stood to look. Some of the foot-passengers joined the rapidly-swelling crowd.

The boy with his sullen face passed on, his lips compressed, his eyes with their dogged look. What the hubbub was about, why they followed him, what it was they kept on shouting, he did not understand. He knew that the captain had left him, and left him penniless. What he was himself to do, or where he was going, he had not the least idea. He only knew that the crowd was hunting him on.

There was not one friendly face among those around him—not one who could understand. The boys seemed like demons, shrieking, dancing, giving him occasional shoves. Separately he would have tackled any one of them, for they could not despise him for being English more heartily than he despised them for being French. But what could he do against that lot?—a host, too, which was being reinforced by men. For the cry "Un Anglais!" seemed to be infectious, and citizens of the grimier and more popular type began to swell the throng and shriek "Un Anglais!" with the boys.

One man, a very dirty and evil-looking gentleman, laying his two hands on Bertie's shoulders, started running, and began pushing him on in front of him. This added to the sport. The cavalcade broke into a trot. The shrieks became more vigorous. Suddenly Bertie, being pushed too vigorously from behind, and perhaps a little bewildered by the din, lost his footing and fell forward on his face. The man, taken unawares, fell down on top of him. The crowd shrieked with laughter.

A functionary interfered, in the shape of a *sergent de ville*. He wanted to know what the disturbance was about. Two or three dozen people, who knew absolutely nothing at all about it, began explaining all at once. They did not render the matter clearer. Nor did the man who had pushed Bertie over. He was indignant; not because he had pushed Bertie over, but because he had fallen on him afterwards. He evidently considered himself outraged because Bertie had not managed to enjoy a monopoly of tumbling down.

The policeman, not much enlightened by the explanations which were poured upon him, marched Bertie off to the *bureau de police*. They manage things differently in France, and the difference is about as much marked in a police station as anywhere else. Bertie found himself confronted by an official who pelted him with questions he did not understand, and who was equally at a loss to understand the observations he made in reply. Then he found himself locked up. It is probable that while he was held in durance vile an attempt was made to discover an interpreter; it would appear from what followed that if such an attempt were made, it was made in vain.

The afternoon passed away. Still the boy was left to enjoy his own society. He had plenty of leisure to think; to wonder what was going to happen to him —what was the next page which was to be unfolded in the history of his adventures. He had leisure to learn that he was getting hungry. But no one brought him anything to eat.

At last, just as he was beginning to think that he surely was forgotten, an official appeared, who, without a word, took him by the collar of his coat—he had been taken a good many times by the collar of his coat of late—led him straight out of the station-house, through some by-streets to the outskirts of the town.

Then, when he had taken him some little distance outside the walls, and a long country road stretched away in front, he released the lad's collar, and with a very expressive gesture, which even Bertie was not at a loss to understand, he bade him take himself away.

And Bertie took himself away, walking smartly off in the direction in which the sergeant pointed—away from the town. The policeman watched him for some time, standing with his hands in his pockets; and then, when a curve in the road took the lad out of sight, he returned within the walls.

It was already evening. The uncertain weather which had prevailed during the last few days still proved its uncertainty. The day had been fine, the evening was clouded. The wind was high, and, blowing from the north-west, blew the clouds tumultuously in scurrying masses across the sky.

The country was bare, nearly treeless. It was very flat. The scant fields of

Finistère offered no protection from the weather, and but little pleasure to the eye. It was a bleak, almost barren country, with but little natural vegetation— harsh, stony, and inhospitable.

Along the wind-swept road he steadily trudged. He knew not whither he was going, not even whence he came. He was a stranger in a strange land. The captain had asked him whether he spoke French; he supposed, therefore, that this land was France. But the captain had confused him—bidden him ask for tickets for Constantinople. Even Bertie's scanty geographical knowledge told him that Constantinople was not France. On the other hand, the same scant store suggested that it needed a longer flight than they had taken to bring him into Turkey.

A very slight knowledge of French would have enabled him to solve the question. If he had only been able to ask, Where am I? The person asked might have taken him to be an English lunatic in a juvenile stage of his existence, but would probably have replied. Unfortunately this knowledge was wanting. If sometimes a little knowledge is a dangerous thing, it is also, and not seldom, very much the other way.

Nearly all that night Bertie went wandering on. The darkness gathered. The wind seemed to whistle more loudly when the darkness came, but there was no escape from it for him. Seen in the light of clustering shadows the country seemed but scantily peopled. He scarcely met a soul. A few peasants, a cart or two—these were the only moving things he saw. And when the darkness deepened he seemed to be alone in all the world.

A house or two he passed, even some villages, in which there were no signs of life except an occasional light gleaming through a wayside window. He made no attempt to ask for food, or drink, or shelter. How could he have asked? As he went further and further from the town he began to come among the Breton aborigines; and in Brittany, as in Wales, you find whole hamlets in which scarcely one of the inhabitants has a comprehensible knowledge of the language of the country which claims them as her children. Even French would have been of problematic service in the parts into which he had found, or rather lost his way, and he was not even aware that there was a place called Brittany, and a tongue called Breton. He was a stranger in a strange land indeed!

It was a horrible night, that first one he spent wandering among the wilds of Finistère. After he had gone on and on and on, and never seemed to come to anything, and the winds shrieked louder, and he was hungry and thirsty and weary and worn, and there was nothing but blackness all around and the terror-stricken clouds whirling above his head, somewhere about midnight he thought it was time he should find some shelter and rest.

So he clambered over a stone wall which bound the road on either side, and on the other side of this stone wall he ventured to lie down. It was not comfortable lying; there was no grass, there were thistles, nettles, weeds, and stones—plenty of stones. On this bed he tried to take some rest, trusting to the wall to shelter him.

In vain. It requires education to become accustomed to a bed of stones. All things come by custom, but those who are used to sheets find stony soil disagreeable ground. Bertie gave it up. The wind seemed to come through the chinks in the wall with even greater bitterness than if there had been no wall at all. The stones were torture. There was nothing on which he could lay his head. So he got up and struck across the field, seeking for a sheltered place in which to lie. For another hour or so he wandered on, now sitting down for a moment or two, now kneeling, and feeling about with his hand for comfortable ground. In an open country, on a dark and windy night, it is weary searching for one's bed, especially in a country where stones are more plentiful than grass.

In his fruitless wanderings, confused by the darkness and the strangeness of the place, Bertie went over the same ground more than once. Without knowing it, meaning to go forwards, he went back. When he suspected that this was the case, his helplessness came home to him more forcibly than it had done before. What was he to do if he could not tell the way he had come from the way he was going?

At last he blundered on some trees. He welcomed them as though they had been friends. He sat down at the foot of one, and found that the ground was coated by what was either moss or grass. Compared to his bed of stones it was like a bed of eider-down. It was quite a big tree, and he found that he could so lean against it that it would serve as a very tolerable barrier against the wind at his back.

At the foot of this tree he sat down, and pillowing his head against the trunk he sought for sleep. But sleep was coy, and would not come on being wooed. The utter solitude of his position kept him wakeful. Robinson Crusoe's desolation was scarcely more complete; his helplessness was not so great. It came upon Bertie, as it came upon Crusoe in his lonely island, that he was wholly in the hands of God. The teachings which he had been taught at his mother's knee, and which seemed to go into one ear and out of the other, proved to be the bread which is cast upon the waters, returning after many days. He remembered with startling vividness how his mother had told him that God holds us all in the hollow of His hand: he understood the meaning of that saying now.

He was so sleepy, so tired out and out, that from very weariness he forgot that he was hungry and athirst. Yet, in some strange fantastic way, the thought, despite his weariness, prevented him from sleeping—that the winds which whistled through the night were the winds of God. The winds of God! And it seemed to him that all things were of God, the darkness and the solitude, and the mysterious place. Who shall judge him? Who shall say that it was only because he was in trouble that he had such thoughts? It is something even if in times of trouble we think of God. "God is a very present help in times of trouble," has been written on some page of some old book.

Bertie was so curiously impressed by a sense of the presence of the Almighty God that he did what he had not done for a very long time—he got up, and kneeling at the foot of the friendly tree, he prayed. And it is not altogether beyond the range of possibility that, when he again sought rest, it was because of his prayer that God sent sleep unto his eyes.

Chapter XXII

THE END OF THE JOURNEY

Throughout the day which followed, and throughout the night, and throughout the succeeding days and nights, Bertie wandered among the wilds of Finistère, and among its lanes and villages. How he lived he himself could have scarcely told. The misfortunes which had befallen him since he had set out on his journey to the Land of Golden Dreams had told upon him. He became ill in body and in mind. He needed rest and care, good food and careful nursing. What he got was no food, or scarcely any, strange skies to shelter him, a strange land to serve him as his bed.

It was fortunate that summer was at hand. Had it been winter he would have lain down at night, and in the morning they would have found him dead. But he was at least spared excessive cold. The winds were not invariably genial. The occasional rain was not at all times welcome—to him at least, whatever it might have been to the thirsty earth—but there was no frost. If frost had come he would certainly have died.

What he ate he scarcely knew. Throughout the whole of his wanderings he never received food from any human being. He found his breakfast, dinner, tea, and supper in the fields and on the hedges. A patch of turnips was a godsend. There was one field in particular in which grew both swedes and turnips. It was within a stone's-throw of a village; to reach it from the road you had to scramble down a bank. To this he returned again and again. He began to look upon it almost as his own.

Once, towards evening, the farmer saw him getting his supper. The farmer saw the lad before the lad saw him. He stole upon him unawares, bent upon capturing the thief. He had almost achieved his purpose, and was within half a dozen yards of the miscreant, when, not looking where he was going in his anxiety to keep his eyes upon the pilferer, he caught his sabot in a hole, and came down upon his knees. As he came he gave vent to a deep Breton execration.

Startled, Bertie looked behind and saw the foe. He was off like the wind. When the farmer had regained, if not his temper, at least his perpendicular, he saw, fifty yards ahead, a wild-looking, ragged figure tearing for his life. The Breton was not built for speed. He perceived that he might as well attempt to rival the swallow in its flight as outrun the boy. So he contented himself with shaking his fists and shouting curses after the robber of his turnip field.

Never washing, never taking his clothes from his back nor his shoes from his feet, in appearance Bertie soon presented a figure which would have discredited a scarecrow. Scrambling through hedges, constant walking over stony ways, beds on dampish soil—these things told upon his garments; they soon began to drop away from him in shreds. His face went well with his clothing. Very white and drawn, very thin and dirty, his ravenous eyes looked out from under a tangled shock of hair. One night he had been startled in his sleep, as he often was, and he had sprung up, as a wild creature springs, and run for his life, not waiting to inquire what it was that had startled him, whether it was the snapping of a twig or the movement of a rabbit or a bird. In his haste he left his hat behind him, and as he never returned to get it, afterwards he went with his head uncovered.

It began to be rumoured about those parts that some strange thing had taken up its residence in the surrounding country. The Breton peasants and small farmers are ignorant, credulous, superstitious. The slightest incident of an unusual character they magnify into a mystery.

It was told in the hamlets that some wild creature had made its appearance in their neighbourhood. Some said it was a boy, some said it was a man, some said it was a woman; some said it was neither one thing nor the other, but a monster which had taken human shape.

Bertie lent an air of veracity to the different versions by his own proceedings. He was not in his own right mind. Had care been taken, and friends been near, all might have been well; as it was, fever was taking more and more possession of his brain. He shunned his fellow-creatures. At the sight of a little child he would take to his heels and run. He saw an enemy in every bush, in every tree; in a man or a woman he saw his worst enemy of all.

In consequence the tales gained ground and grew. A lout, returning from his labour in the fields, saw on a distant slope in the gathering twilight a wild-looking figure, who, at sight of him, turned and ran like the wind. The lout ran too. The tale did not lose by being told. Bertie was magnified into a giant, his speed into speed of the swiftest bird. The lout declared that he uttered mysterious sounds as he ran. He became a mysterious personage altogether— and a horrible one.

Others saw this thing of evil, for that it was a thing of evil all were agreed. The farmer who saw him in his turnip field had a wondrous tale to tell.

He had not tripped through his own stupidity and clumsiness. On the contrary, it was all owing to the influence of the evil eye. Bertie, being a thing of evil, had seen him—as things of evil have doubtless the power of doing— although his approach was made from the rear; and, seeing him, had glanced at him with his evil eye through the back of his head, as things possessing that fatal gift have, we may take it for granted, the power of doing. Nay, who shall decide that the evil eye is not itself located in the back of the head?

Anyhow, under its influence the farmer tripped. This became clearer to his mind the more he thought of it, and, it may be also added, the farther off the accident became. The next morning he remembered that he had been conscious of a mysterious something in his joints as he approached the turnip stealer—a something not to be described, but altogether mysterious and horrible. In the afternoon he declared that he had not followed the plunderer because he had been rooted to the ground, he knew not how nor why—rooted in the manner of his own turnips, which he had seen disappearing from underneath his eyes.

That night the tale grew still more horrible. He had a couple of glasses of brandy, at two sous a glass, with a select circle of his friends, and under the influence of conviviality the farmer made his neighbours' hair stand on end. He went to bed with the belief impressed firmly on his mind that he had encountered Old Nick in person, engaged in the nefarious and characteristic action of stealing turnips from his turnip field.

Thus it came about that while Bertie avoided aboriginals, the aboriginals were equally careful in avoiding him. One day some one heard him speak. That was the climax. The tongue he spoke was neither Breton nor French. Delirium was overtaking the lad, and under its influence he was beginning to spout all sorts of nonsense in his feverish wanderings here and there.

The aboriginal in question had seen him running across the field and shouting as he ran. He declared, probably with truth, that never had he heard the like before. It was undoubtedly the language which was in common use among things of evil. This conclusion was not flattering to English-speaking people, but there are occasions on which ignorance is not bliss, and it is not folly to be wise. Being a Breton peasant of average education, this aboriginal decided that Bertie's English was the language in common use among things of evil.

That settled the question. There are possibly Beings—Beings in this case should be written with a capital letter—of indifferent, and worse than indifferent character, who have at least some elementary acquaintance with the Breton tongue. Let so much be granted. But it cannot be doubted—at any rate no one did doubt it—that the fact of this stranger speaking in a strange tongue made it as plain as a pike-staff that he was the sort of character which is better left alone.

So, as a rule, they left him alone in the severest manner.

Of course this could not endure for ever. Bertie was approaching the Land of Golden Dreams in a sense of which he had not dreamed even in his wildest dreams. One cannot subsist on roots alone. Nor can a young gentleman, used to cosy beds and well-warmed rooms and regular meals, exist for long on such a diet, under ever-changing skies, in an inhospitable country, in the open air. Bertie was worn to a shadow. He was wasted not only physically, but mentally and morally. He was a ghost of what he once had been, enfeebled in mind and body.

If something did not happen soon to change his course of living, he would soon bring his journeying to an untimely end, and reach the Land of Dreams indeed.

Something did happen, but it was not by any means the sort of thing which was required.

One day a great hunt took place in that district. It was first-rate sport. They occasionally hunt wolves, and even wild boars in Finistère, but this time what was hunted was a boy. And the boy was Bertie.

The mayor of St. Thégonnec was a wise man. All mayors are of necessity, and from the nature of their office, wise, especially the mayors of rural France; and this mayor was the wisest of wise mayors. He was a miller by trade, honest as millers go, and as pig-headed a rustic as was ever found in Finistère. His name was Baudry—Jean Baudry.

It was reported to M. Baudry by his colleague, the mayor of the commune of Plouigneau, which lies on the other side of Morlaix, that there was a Being —with a capital B—which had come no one knew from whence, and which was plundering the fields in a way calculated to make the blood of all honest men turn cold—or hot, as might accord best with the natural disposition of the blood of the man in question.

The mayor of St. Thégonnec had told this story to the mayor of Morlaix; and the mayor of Morlaix, being the mayor of the *arrondissement*, had thought it an excellent opportunity to snub the mayor of a mere commune, and had snubbed the mayor of St. Thégonnec accordingly; who, coming fresh from the snubbing, had encountered his colleague in the market-place, and then and there told his wrongs.

The two worthies agreed that, at the first opportunity, they would lay violent hands upon this plunderer of the fields of honest men, and make him wish that he had left such fields alone.

Such an opportunity, or what looked like such an one, was not long in offering itself to M. Baudry.

One afternoon he was engaged in his occupation of grinding flour, standing in an atmosphere which would have rendered life disagreeable, if not altogether unsupportable, to any one but a miller, when Robert, Madame Perchon's eldest born, put his head inside the open door of the mill.

"This creature, M. le Maire; this creature!"

Robert Perchon was an undersized youth of some twenty years of age, who had escaped military service not only as being the eldest son of a widow, but as being in possession of an unrivalled squint, which would have excluded him in any case, and which would have rendered it really difficult for a drill sergeant to have ascertained to his own satisfaction whether, at any given moment, the recruit had his "eyes front" or behind.

"Ah, at last! Where is this vagabond? We will settle his business in a trice!"

Having shouted instructions to his assistant to keep his eyes upon the stones, M. le Maire came forth.

"He is in the buck-wheat field! I was going to the little field by the river, when, behold! what should I see in the buck-wheat field, lying close to the hedge, and yet among the wheat, what but this creature, fast asleep! It is so, I give you my word. At this time of day, when all honest people are at work, in the middle of my field there was this creature, fast asleep. I knew him at once, although I have not seen the wretch before; but I have heard him described, and there is indeed something absolutely diabolical in his aspect even as he lies among my buck-wheat fast asleep!"

"You did not wake him?"

"Ah, no! Why should I wake him? Who knows what injury the creature might have done me when he found himself disturbed?"

"Then we will wake him, I give you my word. We will capture this vagabond. We will discover what there is about him diabolical."

The mayor's courage was applauded. There was Robert Perchon, his mother—in tears, at the thought of the peril which her son had only just escaped—a select assembly of the villagers, and the two gorgeous gendarmes from the St. Thégonnec gendarmerie. All these people perceived that the mayor was brave.

The assembly started, with the intention of making an example of the plunderer of the fields of honest men.

In front was the mayor, not looking particularly dignified, for he was white with flour, though void of fear.

In his hand he carried a mighty stick. Behind him came the gendarmes, as was befitting. They had forgotten to buckle on their swords, but in their case dignity was everything, and it was just possible that the stick of the mayor would render more deadly weapons needless. Behind—a pretty good distance behind—came the villagers. Some of them carried pitchforks, others spades. One gallant lady carried a kettle full of boiling water. It did not occur to her, perhaps, that the water would have time to cool before they reached their quarry. Madame Perchon brought up the rear, and behind her sneaked the gallant Robert.

It occurred to the mayor that this was not exactly as it ought to be. He suggested to M. Robert that as he alone knew exactly where the vagabond lay, it befitted him to lead the van. This, however, M. Robert did not see; he preferred to shout out his directions from the rear.

They entered the buck-wheat field. No persuasions would induce him to enter with the rest. He insisted on remaining outside, guiding them from a post of safety. His mother stayed to keep him company.

"By there! a little to the left! Keep straight on! If he has not gone, M. le Maire, which is always possible, you can touch him with your stick from where you are now standing!"

He had not gone.

The journey was almost done. The end was drawing near. Delirious, beside himself, fever-racked, hunger-stricken, not knowing what he was doing, the boy had sunk down in Madame Perchon's buck-wheat field to sleep. And he had slept—a mockery of sleep! A thousand hideous imaginations passed through his fevered mind. M. Robert Perchon, who had been contented with a single glance at the sleeping lad, had some warranty for his declaration that in his aspect there was something diabolical, for his limbs writhed and his countenance was distorted by the paroxysms of his fever.

Dreaming some horrible dream, the noise made by the advancing brave fell upon his fevered ear. Starting upright at M. Baudry's feet, with a shriek which horrified all who heard him, he rushed across the field, and flew as if all the powers of evil were treading on his heels. And, indeed, in a sense the powers of evil were, for he was delirious with fever.

The first impulse of the champions of the fields of honest men was to do, with one accord, what the boy had done, to turn and flee—the other way. Some, believing Bertie's delirious shriek to be the veritable voice of Satan, acted on this first impulse and fled. Notable among them were M. Robert and his mother. That gallant pair raced each other homewards, shrieking with so much vigour that it almost seemed that in that direction they had made up their minds to outdo the plunderer of the fields of honest men. But there were braver spirits abroad that day. Among them was the mayor. Besides, the public eye was upon him, and behind him were the two gendarmes. In France the representative of authority never runs—at least, he never runs away.

It is true that when Bertie sprang with such startling suddenness from right underneath his feet, and gave utterance to that ear-alarming shriek, M. Baudry thought of running. But he only thought; it went no further. He would certainly have denied that he had even allowed himself to think of such an ignominious contingency a moment afterwards.

The creature was running away. That was evident. It would be absurd for the champions of those fields to run away from him, when the rascal had been sensible enough to run away from them. M. Baudry perceived this fact at once.

"After him!" he cried. "I give you my word we shall catch him yet!"

Off went the assembly, helter-skelter, after the delirious boy.

"Forward! forward! We will teach this rogue a lesson! We will teach him to rob the fields of honest men! We will learn the stuff that he is made of—this vagabond!"

Courage revived. They all shouted, and they all ran.

If the mayor was in the habit of giving his word as lightly as he gave it then, it could not have been worth having. It was soon evident that they had about as much chance of catching the fugitive as they had of catching the clouds which wandered above their heads.

M. Baudry was not built for violent exercise. He had probably not run thirty yards in the last thirty years. He was in his sabots, and sabots are not good things for running. Fifty paces in Madame Perchon's buck-wheat field was quite enough for him. He perceived that it is not a proper thing for mayors to run; so he ran no more. Instead of running he sat down to think, and to encourage, of course, his friends.

The gendarmes kept on. It was evidently their duty to keep on. But they were not much fonder of running than the mayor, and a gendarme's boots, when it comes to running, are not much more satisfactory, regarded as aids to progress, than sabots. Especially are gendarmes not built to run across ploughed fields.

In fact the chase was prolonged for almost, if not quite, a hundred yards. Then it ceased. Most of the champions of the fields of honest men sat down upon the fields they championed; those who didn't gasped for breath upon their feet.

The affair was, perhaps, something of a fiasco, but they consoled themselves with the reflection that they would catch the vagabond next time, when they could run a little better and a little further, and he could run a little worse—or a good deal worse, in fact.

But for Bertie the chase was very far from done. He fled, not from things of flesh and blood, but from things of air—the wild imaginings of fever. On and on and on—over fields and hedges, dykes and ditches—on and on and on, until the day waned and the night had come.

And in the night his journey ended. Even delirium would no longer give strength unto his limbs. His style of going changed. Instead of running, like a maddened animal, straight forward, he went reeling, reeling, reeling, staggering from side to side.

Then he staggered down.

He rose no more. It was the end of the journey.

Chapter XXIII

THE LAND OF GOLDEN DREAMS

When he returned to life he was in his mother's arms. There were familiar faces round him, and, as out of a mist, familiar voices sounded in his ear.

He turned in his bed—for it was on a bed he was lying, and no longer on the stony ground—and opened his eyes, waking as from a delicious slumber.

Some one bent over him; some one laid a hand softly on his brow; some one's burning tears fell on his cheek. There was his mother standing by his side.

"My boy! my boy! Thank God for this, my darling boy!"

Then she kissed him; and she wept.

Out of the mist there came another familiar form. It was his father.

"Bertie! at last! Thank God for this, indeed, my son!"

And he, too, stooped and kissed the lad. And the mother rose to her feet, and became encircled in her husband's arms; and they two rejoiced together over the son who was lost and was found.

He had been ill six weeks. Six weeks delirious with fever; six weeks hovering between life and death; six weeks' sorrow; six weeks' pain. That was the end of his journey.

And it would have had another ending had it not been for the providence of God. He would have journeyed into that strange, unknown country, whose name is Death, but that he was found by the roadside, where he had fallen, and by a friend. It would be unwise to say that that friend was not sent to him direct from God.

Among his father's patients was a certain Mr. Yates. Mr. Yates was a county magistrate, a man of position and of wealth. Under God he owed his life to Dr. Bailey's skill. It was to him reference has been made as having given Bertie half a sovereign once upon a time—half a sovereign which, to Bertie's disgust, he had had to divide with his brothers and sisters.

Mr. Yates had known the youngster well. He was a bachelor, and had allowed the boy to run in and out almost as he pleased. On the eve of starting on a tour to Brittany he had heard that the young gentleman had disappeared from school, no one knew why, no one knew whither. There was a pretty to-do when it was known. It was almost the last straw for Mr. Fletcher, that last straw which, according to the proverb, breaks the camel's back.

In his bewilderment—in the general bewilderment, indeed—Dr. Bailey had not hesitated to lay his son's disappearance at Mr. Fletcher's door. He declared that he was alone to blame, that some act of remissness, some act of even positive cruelty must have goaded the lad into taking such a step.

The boy had left no trace behind. The distracted father advertised for him right and left, placed the matter in the hands of the police, seeking for him on every side without finding the slightest clue to tell him if his son were alive or dead.

Matters were in this state when Mr. Yates had left for Brittany. He had been there some days, when, wandering somewhat out of the beaten track, he had chartered a carriage at Morlaix to take him up among those wind-swept slopes which are grandiloquently termed the Montagnes d'Arree, and land him at the little town of Huelgoet. There are one or two things which people go to see at Huelgoet, but the place became memorable to Mr. Yates for what he saw upon the road.

He was about half-way to his destination when he observed, lying among the furze at the roadside, a lad. He might not have noticed him had not the boy been emitting cries of so peculiar a kind that they could scarcely have failed to catch a traveller's ear. Going to see what was the matter, he perceived at once that the lad was delirious with fever.

With some difficulty he persuaded the driver of the vehicle to convey so dubious a passenger. The same difficulty occurred at the Huelgoet hotel before they would let him in. It was only when he had undertaken to recoup them for any losses they might sustain, and had got the lad comfortably in bed, that he discovered that the waif who had found in him such a good Samaritan was none other than Bertie Bailey.

* * * * * *

So soon as they could move him they took him home. And, as he entered the old familiar home, he knew in his heart that this place which he was entering was in fact the Land of Golden Dreams. He had been in search of it afar off, and he had been a native of the country all the time. And there are many natives of that country who throw away the substance to grasp the shadow, not realizing their folly till the thing is done.

* * * * * *

They never found the "captain" nor "Mr. Rosenheim." In due time Bertie told his story, and the doctor thought it so strange an one that he felt in duty bound to communicate with the police. A detective came and heard all that Bertie had to say. He asked a hundred puzzling questions; but, although not always able to answer them to the detective's satisfaction, Bertie stuck to his tale. They took him to point out the house which had contained the "captain's room," but he had been a stranger in the great city, at night, hungry and worn. He had gone blindly where he had been taken, not noticing a single landmark by the way, and now when they asked him to retrace his steps, and lead them where Freddy had led him, he found it impossible to discover the house again.

So it came to pass that the police looked at his story with doubtful eyes. And for that cause—or some other—nothing has been heard of the Countess of Ferndale's jewels unto this day.

———